Books by Robin Maugham

THE WRONG PEOPLE

THE WRONG

PEOPLE

BY Robin Maugham

McGRAW-HILL BOOK COMPANY

New York   St. Louis   San Francisco   Düsseldorf
London   Mexico   Panama   Sydney   Toronto

For Honor

Antonio:

I am a tainted wether of the flock,
Meetest for death: the weakest kind of fruit
Drops earliest to the ground, and so let me:
You cannot better be employed, Bassanio,
Than to live still, and write mine epitaph.

The Merchant of Venice,
Act IV, Scene 1

. . . To where the Atlantic waves
Outside the Western Straits, and unbent sails
There, where down cloudy cliffs, through sheets of
    foam,
Shy traffickers, the dark Iberians come;
   And on the beach undid his corded bales.

The Scholar-Gipsy
by Matthew Arnold

PART

I

As he sat alone at his corner table drinking a gin and Dubonnet, Ewing watched the stranger sitting on the barstool and examined his appearance for a while because there was no one else interesting or attractive to watch in Wayne's bar that evening.

The stranger was a slender man of about thirty-five with a pink face and silky fair hair receding from his smooth forehead. His eyes were pale blue and slightly protuberant. With his uptilted nose and delicate skin he must have been quite attractive when he was a boy, Ewing decided. His tight-fitting tweed jacket and worn grey-flannel trousers were obviously ready-made, and so were his polished brown shoes. His eyes were peering surreptitiously round the room while he sipped a glass of beer. The man was certainly English, and probably a bank clerk, and perhaps a bore.

At that moment the stranger glanced up at the looking glass behind the bar. He saw Ewing staring at him

[3]

and blushed violently. Wave after wave of crimson rushed over the delicate pink of his face and neck. And a flicker of interest stirred Ewing, for he believed that blushing implied guilt.

Ewing beckoned to the tall emaciated American behind the bar.

"Wayne," he called out, "do you see any reason why I shouldn't have another drink?"

"No reason. No reason at all," Wayne replied in an exaggerated Southern accent. "It would be a pleasure to get you one, Master Ewing."

Wayne swayed quickly across the room and picked up Ewing's glass.

"You're not very full tonight," Ewing said.

Wayne bent his head and blinked his eyelids apologetically as if he had been accused of an unpleasant offense.

"It's always quiet in Tangier just after Christmas. You know *that,* Ewing."

Wayne's manner was friendly but deferential. Ewing looked away from the bar and lowered his voice so that the stranger could not hear what he said.

"Who's the new customer?" he asked.

"That one drinking beer with a face like an aging chorister?"

"That's him. Who is he?"

"The usual Christmas-holiday tourist who's saved up his pennies to visit this wicked city of vice."

"He looks rather sad," Ewing said.

"Perhaps our dear Tangier isn't living up to her

[4]

reputation. Perhaps he can't find any vice. You're not interested in him, are you?"

"Good heavens, no! He must be at least thirty-five. Look at that receding hair."

"Don't go too much by his hair," Wayne said. "Those slender blond types lose their hair quite young. They age terribly quickly, poor things. I know them by heart. Milk-and-roses complexion, pale blue eyes, snub nose, delicate features, a blush like a schoolgirl, wonderfully soft and silky fair locks—my dear, they're all as bald as coots by the time they're forty."

"What does this one do?"

"He works as a schoolmaster near London, the poor dear."

Ewing took a cigarette out of his gold case. Wayne obediently produced a lighter and flicked it into flame.

"One can just see him trying to look stern as he lectures the head prefect," Ewing said.

Wayne giggled. "He's not out of that kind of drawer *at all,*" he whispered. "In fact he's a master in an approved school. You know—the government schools in England where they send naughty boys to be trained into respectable citizens like you and me."

Ewing spread out his hands on the table and gazed at them in silence. Then he raised his eyes toward Wayne. "Ask him over to my table for a drink," he said.

"Now why should approved schools interest you?" Wayne asked, smiling coyly. "Going in for chickens at your age? Naughty! Naughty!"

[5]

Ewing laughed. "Will you never believe in altruism?" he asked.

"Not in Tangier, I won't," Wayne giggled.

Ewing looked up at Wayne's raddled face.

"You go and fetch me that schoolmaster," Ewing said impatiently.

PART

2

ARNOLD was alarmed when he saw the tall barman sidling toward him, for he knew that the squat man in the corner had been talking about him, and he now regretted his abrupt decision to enter Wayne's notorious bar.

The place was far more expensive and far less exciting than he had expected. A bottle of beer cost the equivalent of seven shillings, and there was not one single young person to be seen—nor one single Moroccan, apart from the cloak attendant with a harelip and restless eyes. Then Arnold had glanced up at the expanse of looking glass between two rows of bottles behind the bar and had seen the squat man staring at him intently.

The man was dressed in a grey cashmere jacket with dark-flannel trousers. He wore a white silk shirt and blue silk tie. He was perhaps fifty, and his rather coarse black hair was streaked with grey. His heavy build and thick shoulders gave an impression of solidity, yet his hands were small and plump, and his fleshy square-shaped face looked almost delicate. Deep lines ran from his wide nostrils to the corners of his narrow mouth. His cheeks and broad jowls looked as if they had been freshly shaved and powdered. His bleached face and muscular neck reminded Arnold of some marble bust of a Roman Emperor. The man looked firm yet dissolute, powerful yet effeminate. And when he called out to Wayne, the barman, his voice was loaded with authority yet curiously soft.

And now Wayne was mincing toward Arnold and fluttering his eyelashes at him. Arnold blushed and took a sip of beer.

"Do tell me your name," Wayne said to him. "You *did* tell me ten minutes ago. But like the silly old number I am I forget. What is it now?"

"Arnold Turner."

"Of course it is. What a dope I am. Please excuse me. Now I want to introduce you to a friend of mine who wants to meet you. Finish your beer, and I'll take you right over to him."

Arnold gulped down his beer nervously. He suspected a dangerous plot. But Wayne seemed a harmless pansy, and the other man was expensively dressed. Perhaps . . .

"Come along now," Wayne said. "Don't dawdle. We haven't got all night. At least I don't think so."

Wayne took Arnold's arm and led him across to Ewing's table.

"Ewing, this is Arnold Turner," he announced. "Arnold, this is my very old friend, Ewing Baird."

[1 0]

"Not all *that* old," Ewing said as they shook hands. "What will you drink?"

"Beer, please."

"Oh, you must have something more exciting than beer," Wayne exclaimed. "Dear Ewing's stinking rich, so he can afford it. Have a champagne cocktail."

"Perhaps he doesn't *want* a champagne cocktail," Ewing said. "Don't be such a bully, Wayne. Let him choose for himself."

Arnold decided that there was nothing unpleasant about Ewing's voice. It was quiet but resonant, with a faint accent that might have been Canadian.

"I'd like a Scotch," Arnold said.

"Hell! I could have charged him twice as much for a champagne cocktail," Wayne said as he swung away to the bar.

Ewing shrugged his shoulders. Then he looked at Arnold and smiled as if they were both conspirators in their attitude toward Wayne. He took out his gold case and slid it across the table.

"Smoke?"

"No, thanks. I gave it up last year."

"How long have you been in Tangier?"

"Three days."

"How did you spend Christmas?"

Arnold blushed. "Alone," he answered.

"Do you mean you were in Tangier all day and never met anyone?"

"Yes."

"But you must have picked up *someone* during the course of the day—some beautiful girl—or some boy."

Ewing was watching him carefully.

"No," Arnold said, trying to control his blushing. "Everywhere I went people seemed to be all set in their own groups. And I didn't like to butt in."

"You can't have gone to the right places. I could have taken you to bars where you wouldn't have been left alone for an instant. How much longer are you staying here?"

"Five more days."

"Where are you dining tonight?"

The question was put so quickly that Arnold was confused.

"I haven't decided yet," he muttered.

"Then I'd be delighted if you'd dine with me. I know a place with a view over the harbor, where the food's quite excellent."

"Thanks."

"You two *are* getting on fine," Wayne tittered as he handed Arnold his whisky. "I reckoned you'd hit it off together."

"Push off," Ewing said.

Wayne blinked at the ceiling.

"What language!" he said. "Who would have thought he'd been educated at Oxford!"

Ewing winked at Arnold. "Shall we sink down our drinks and go?" he asked. "The car's outside."

☙ ☙ ☙ ☙ ☙ ☙

WHILE he listened to Ewing's calm and precise voice and drank his champagne rosé, Arnold gazed through the window at the lights on the ships in the harbor below. He was happy, and he was beginning to get drunk.

When they had sat down in the French restaurant, which was on the top floor of a large block of flats in the Rue Rembrandt, Arnold had been afraid that Ewing would embarrass him with awkward questions. But since they had left Wayne's bar, Ewing had made casual though expert conversation about cooking. After their meal had been ordered—and this had taken some time, for his host evidently took great care over his food and drink—Ewing had begun to talk about England and his life there as a child.

Ewing's father, Arnold learned, had been a rich young American industrialist from Chicago who had visited London in 1910 and fallen in love with a girl he met at a dance in Belgrave Square and had married her a year later. Ewing was the only child of the marriage.

"My mother only visited the States once," Ewing said. "That was the year after I was born. I can remember asking her shortly before she died why she'd so firmly refused ever to go there again. 'Father always said you'd enjoyed your visit,' I told her. 'I did enjoy parts of it,' my mother answered. 'It was like a constant party in the servants' hall. But servants' halls do get awfully boring after a fortnight.' And that was it. One visit was enough. My mother refused to let me be educated in America. I could spend my holidays there, she said, but I must be taught how to think and how to behave in England. My father argued in vain. My mother got her own way as usual. And I stopped going over for my holidays when I was sixteen, because my mother divorced him."

Ewing paused to watch the waiter preparing the crêpes suzette, then he turned back to Arnold.

"I presume you're not married," Ewing said.

Arnold looked up at him, startled. "No," he replied, after a pause.

Ewing laughed.

"You don't seem very sure."

As Ewing spoke, a sallow pianist, followed by a thin woman in a plain black dress, got onto the platform.

"Who is she?" Arnold asked to conceal his confusion.

"Françoise Roussin. She sings old French folk tunes. She's rather good. Why should you blush when I said I presumed you weren't married?"

Arnold glared down at the tablecloth in vexation. The pianist played a few introductory bars.

"Why?" Ewing insisted softly.

"Because I *was* married," Arnold said angrily.

"Your wife died?"

"No. We got divorced."

"How wise of you," Ewing murmured.

Arnold was saved from having to make any response to Ewing's deliberately ambiguous comment because at that moment the woman began to sing, and Ewing leaned back comfortably in his chair to listen to her. The woman sang in a small quiet voice as if she were singing to herself. The little songs of shepherd girls floated across the restaurant as if they had been wafted across hillocks and warm shadowy fields.

Arnold listened intently and tried not to think of his

marriage. But while he gazed along the rows of small tables with their crimson-shaded lamps, and while the sad tunes lilted in his ears, he could not help seeing his wife's face swollen with rage; he could not shut out the screech of her voice. "You should never have married," she had screamed at him. "And you know why. You know why."

And he had known, by then, only too well. Lying beside Susan through the long nights of two years he had worked out the answer. He knew it by heart. He should not have married because of mere resemblance. Susan had the same oval-shaped head as her brother. She had the same grey eyes and short nose and wide mouth, the same freckles on her forehead as Jack had, even the same little cleft in her chin and the same smile. She was as slender as Jack and as full of life. And he had thought . . . no, he had persuaded himself into believing that it was Susan he was in love with— because he wanted so desperately to fall in love with a girl, because he wanted to be the same as the other men at the club, because his mother prayed every night that he would get married before she died, because he despised queers, because he wanted children, because—the last reason was the most painful— because he was a coward who was dishonest with himself. But he had tried to make the marriage a success. God, if there were a God, knew that he had tried. But his prayers had not been answered. He had been unable to turn away from his inclinations. He had been a failure.

"You know why," the high-pitched, almost unrecognizable voice went on screaming in his mind. "You know why. If you don't, then ask Jack. That day when you stripped off by the pond in Copley's Wood and went bathing together naked, Jack says you just couldn't keep your eyes off him. When you started larking about afterwards and wrestling he was dead certain of it. But he didn't tell me until last night because he thought it better I shouldn't know. But it doesn't matter now because I'm leaving you. I've found someone who can really love me and appreciate me. And do you know *why* he can give me proper affection? Because he's normal. Because he's a man, a real man."

So Jack had guessed, and Jack had been disgusted, Jack with his freckled face and slippery, white body. That was why Jack had seemed to avoid him ever since and had made excuses when Arnold had invited him to go for a walk or come to the local cinema. Jack had never gone out alone with him since that day in Copley's Wood when the air had been so close that it seemed to press down on them, fastening their drenched shirts to their skin. They had found the pond surrounded by thick undergrowth. Jack had grinned at him, and without a word they had peeled off their clothes and dived in. Later, as he lay drying on the bank, Jack had crept up behind him and cut at him with a switch of fern, and he had chased Jack and caught him. Then, for one instant, while they were wrestling—for one instant he had held Jack clasped firmly in his arms. And at that moment all his self-deceit had been burnt away in a searing agony of passion. Then, while he was still panting in bewildered fear and pain, he had felt Jack's body yield in his grasp,

[1 6]

and for perhaps two or three seconds he had reached an ecstasy close to oblivion, believing that at last he had found the person who could make him whole.

But suddenly Jack had laughed and broken away from him and dived quickly into the pool . . .

Yet for those two or three seconds . . .

"You've gone very far away." Ewing's voice ripped like a knife across the surface of his reflections. Arnold looked up with a start. The woman had stopped singing. Ewing was smiling across the table at him. There was now a small glass of brandy beside his glass of champagne.

"You were saying that you'd been married but had got divorced," Ewing prompted.

"Yes. It just didn't work out."

"I've made many mistakes in my life," Ewing said. "But not that one. Finish your champagne and try the brandy. It's old and quite gentle. I think you'll like it."

"Thanks."

Ewing spread out his plump, hairy hands above the table, then looked at them and folded them hurriedly across his stomach, as if he were ashamed of the movement they had made.

"After the failure of your marriage," Ewing said in his calm, even voice, "I suppose you began to branch out in other directions?"

"If you mean what I think you mean, the answer is 'no.' "

Ewing stared at him without blinking. "How old are you?" His voice sounded dispassionate, almost bored.

"Thirty-five."

Suddenly with a shudder of disgust Arnold wondered if the champagne and the brandy had been produced in order to seduce him.

Ewing leaned forward as if he had read his thoughts. "Fifteen years ago you must have been quite a dish," he said. "What a pity I didn't meet you then." He smiled. "But from what you've just said, perhaps it's just as well," he added.

Arnold was impressed by this candor. He felt that some reply was expected of him.

"So far as I'm concerned," Arnold said, "I don't mind which way people are or what they do—so long as they keep it to themselves."

Ewing snapped his fingers to attract the attention of the waiter and called for the bill.

"I agree with you," Ewing said. "I hate people who scream their sins from the housetops. There's a passage in *The Scarlet Letter* which sums it all up. 'Show freely to the world, if not your worst'—says Hawthorne—'yet some trait whereby the worst may be inferred!' "

Ewing's small round eyes were fixed on Arnold so steadily as he spoke that Arnold was afraid that he had guessed his secret. But he was pleasantly mellow with drink, and he no longer cared.

"Now where would you like to go?" Ewing asked.

"You know the town. You decide."

"Then I'll take you to Conchita's place. It's not exactly cheerful. But you'll get a good whiff of the real Tangier atmosphere there. It's so thick at that joint you can almost feel it."

Ewing waved his small plump hand toward the window.

"You see, Tangier isn't just a harbor with boats in it," he explained. "It's not the collection of bars and apartment houses and villas you see straggling up the hillside. Tangier is an atmosphere. The externals change. The atmosphere doesn't. When I first came here a dozen years ago, for instance, the town was far cruder and tougher than it is today. I've seen an American gangster draw a gun on a smuggler in Wayne's bar. You saw what Wayne's bar was like tonight—a few old queens and smart women just waiting to get back to their tatting and their gossip. Down in that harbor we're looking at there used to be twenty smuggling boats. Now, we can only see the lights of two or three and they're pretty decayed. Ground was increasing in value week by week. Blocks of flats sprang up around the town like mushrooms. But as soon as the international status of the town was abolished, fewer people wanted to live here. Businesses went broke all over the place. Tradesmen moved elsewhere. Tourists got nervous. There was a general move to clean up Tangier. Down by the Zocco Chico, there used to be a hundred open brothels. They've all been closed by the new Moroccan government. Brothels are now illegal. But gradually it's all drifting back to the same old scene."

Ewing took out some Moroccan dirham notes from his gold-edged wallet. He placed them tenderly on top of the bill and folded it over them. Then he raised his head.

"The externals change," he said, swirling the brandy round in his glass. "But the atmosphere remains unaltered. It's a strange atmosphere, hard to define. And it pervades everything. It drifts everywhere. There's even a faint tang of it in this restaurant—which as you can see is completely European. The atmosphere's not just cooped up in the white walls of the Kasbah or confined to the tortuous narrow streets that run down to the waterfront. It invades not only the markets and the mosques. You find traces of it in every shop and bank, in every flat and bar, in every cinema and villa."

Ewing seemed no longer conscious of Arnold's presence; he had withdrawn into his thoughts.

"Sometimes I believe I can smell it," he said. "I've even tried to analyze the smell. Burning charcoal and dung—I'm sure they're mixed in it. Then perhaps there's incense, and I know there's sweat. And there's the pungent sweet smell of kif—which I suppose you'd call 'pot.' But there's something more besides—I'll find out one day. And this atmosphere drifts into everything. It pervades all the Moors, of course. It even seeps into Europeans if they live out here long enough. That's why, however much we may loathe the place, however glad we may be to get away, we always come back in the end. The atmosphere's got inside our very bones, and we can't do without it in the air we breathe. Europe and America stifle us. We feel suffocated. So we grind our teeth and take the next plane back to our old Tangier. Knowing the unpleasant pangs and gnawing boredom that await us, knowing that we shall yearn for the friends and music and theatres we've left behind the instant we begin to tread these well-worn, blatant streets once again, knowing the remorse we shall suffer almost incessantly. But our plane lands. We take a taxi into town. And long before we've reached Wayne's bar, the atmosphere's swept over us once again. Our hearts beat firmer and quicker. Our heads feel lighter. We blink at the sunshine as if we'd come out of prison. We can breathe and live again."

Ewing finished his brandy and pushed back his chair. "I'm getting tipsy," he said. "Let's go and see Conchita."

* * * * * *

WHEN they walked out into the Rue Rembrandt they found Ewing's Moroccan chauffeur polishing the hood of the large convertible.

"Whatever time of day or night I appear, Mustapha's always rubbing away at that car," Ewing remarked. "I believe it gives him some kind of sexual thrill."

As they drove along the Boulevard Pasteur, flanked by banks and stores, Arnold wondered why Ewing had chosen Mustapha as his chauffeur, for the man was past middle age with a gaunt, pock-marked face.

"He's quite hideous, isn't he?" Ewing said, following the direction of Arnold's glance. Then, seeing Arnold's embarrassment, he added, "Don't worry. The man can't speak a word of English—which is just as well since there's no partition. I chose him because he's a good driver and his wife is a wonderful cook. And they know I pay them more than twice as much as they'd get elsewhere, so they behave themselves. He won't gossip about our visiting Conchita, for instance."

The car had turned down a side-street beyond the cafés around the Place de France and was passing one of the many half-built blocks of flats. In the faint light of the crescent moon the abandoned site looked as if it had been bombed.

"Conchita used to have a bar close to the Zocco Grande," Ewing explained. "But too many people could see her clients. This place is far more satisfactory."

The car was now bumping along an unfinished road. At the end of it was a two-storied house.

"Here we are. I hope you won't be shocked," Ewing said as they got out.

Arnold mumbled some reply. During the last three hours his whole world seemed to have changed. Mountains had sunk down into hummocks, craggy peaks had softened into easy slopes. In his fantasy, the heavy grey clouds on the horizon had drifted away, the sun was now blazing down from an azure sky, an endless plain glistened for miles around him and birds sang in the crisp air. Arnold was drunk.

Ewing walked along a narrow path and rang the bell on the right of the front door. Immediately a panel opened and a face peered out.

"*Msalkhair*," Ewing said. "Good evening."

The door was opened by a stoutly built Moroccan

with a scarred face and the bulge of some deformity on his back.

"*Msalkhair*. Welcome, Señor Ewing," he said. "Please to come in."

As they walked through a garishly tiled hall, Arnold could hear the jukebox playing. The Moroccan opened a door in the passage beyond and they walked into a smoke-filled bar. Arnold was immediately and almost unbearably disappointed. Thick clouds swept across the sun of his landscape.

The bar was almost empty. Half a dozen Europeans and three middle-aged Moroccans in tattered *djellabas* sat at little green tables at the far end of the room. A young man was sitting at the bar with his head in his hands. A couple were dancing. The room was drab and rather dirty. The walls were lined with dusty sticks of bamboo, wired roughly together. The bar itself was tiled like a lavatory. An attempt had been made to enliven the place for Christmas by fastening branches of fir trees to the ceiling and looping tinseled streamers over them. The photograph of the king which hung over the jukebox had been draped with paper flowers; the spotted looking glass had been festooned with tiny Moroccan flags. But Arnold's impression was of gloom and decay, which was certainly matched by the appearance of the old woman behind the bar. She was dressed in a greasy black dress. A large nose sprouted from her raddled face like a turnip in a ploughed field. She gazed round the room with suspicion and distaste through red-rimmed, watery eyes.

"Who's the old hag?" Arnold whispered.

"That's Conchita," Ewing said. "What will you drink? I advise you to stick to beer. It's safer in this place."

Ewing moved away quickly and walked behind the bar to greet Conchita. Her sour expression never changed when he took her hand, but Arnold noticed that she seemed to have a great deal to say to Ewing.

Arnold sat down at one of the green tables with tubular legs and looked around once again. As he watched the couple dancing, he noticed with a twinge of excitement that both of them were male. They were two Moroccan boys, chinless and effeminate, but at least they were young and obviously enjoying themselves. At that moment the other Moroccan boy sitting at the bar lifted his head from his hands and turned toward Arnold questioningly. Immediately the sun arose once again over Arnold's horizon.

The boy was about sixteen, with a slim oval face, a straight nose and large dark eyes, heavily fringed with lashes—like reeds around a pool, Arnold thought in his dazed happiness. The boy wore black jeans and a frayed white silk shirt which was open to the navel so that it displayed a large V-shaped expanse of light brown skin.

And as Arnold gazed shyly at the smooth skin stretched tight over the pectoral muscles, he was filled with the same mixture of pain and delight he had known when he had seen Jack beside the pond, the same restless yearning he had felt ever since when he looked at young boys. And while his eyes were fixed on the rippling tawny skin, his mind swung back with a drunken lurch to the approved school he had left for his ten days' holiday. He was enclosed again by the red-brick walls of Melton Hall. He could smell the damp heat of the washrooms and the damp clothes from the playground. He saw the water pouring over the gleaming white tiles; he saw the line of naked boys waiting their turn under the showers; he saw them twist and wriggle under the spray; he heard the voice of Joe Stobart, the housemaster, shouting, "Next three." He watched three boys dive for their towels and dry themselves vigorously. He saw them line up and move toward Stobart, who sat in a large wooden chair with a ruler in his hand.

"When I'm on holiday, you'll have to take over showers," Stobart had said the first time Arnold witnessed the ritual. "So you'd better see how it's done."

Each boy came up to Stobart with his towel in his hand.

"You have to make sure the little devils have dried themselves properly," Stobart explained cheerfully.

As the boy approached him, Stobart would shout out, "Hup," and the boy would raise his hands above his head.

"Turn," Stobart ordered, and the boy would turn round with his arms still raised so that Stobart could examine his back.

"Next." The boy would make a smart left turn, and as he moved away Stobart would flick him playfully with his ruler.

"Jolly Joe," the staff called Stobart, because of his raucous laugh and his spate of dirty stories—mostly about the girls he had seduced. "Captain Stobart," the boys called him respectfully, because he insisted on "being given his proper wartime rank," as he put it. In fact, he had been a lieutenant in the Catering Corps. Stobart was the most popular master in the school. And Arnold envied and loathed him. He envied him for his easy familiarity with the boys combined with strict discipline; he loathed him because Stobart was a bully. If a boy annoyed Stobart he would ridicule him in front of the rest of his house until the boy's self-control was broken and his humiliation complete.

But Stobart's bullying was usually done vicariously. Once, when a boy had run away from Melton Hall ("absconded" was the term used) and had been picked up by the police in his home town, Stobart had stopped weekend passes for all the boys in his house as a collective punishment. On Saturday afternoon he sent the boys to the gymnasium. Ten minutes later Stobart arrived, followed by the boy who had run away. While the boy stood in silence beside him, Stobart reminded his sullen, restive audience of the reason for which they had been confined to the school grounds for the weekend. He told them that he left the punishment of the "absconder" in their hands. He then walked out of the room. When Arnold heard shrieks he ran across to the building. Then he saw Joe Stobart peering through a window by the door.

"Leave them to it," Stobart said. "Let them have their fun."

Arnold would never forget the look on Stobart's face.

The boy was in the sick bay for a fortnight afterwards. Arnold went to see Blair, the headmaster. But, as he had feared, his protests were politely dismissed.

"Joe Stobart's the best housemaster we've ever had at Melton Hall," Blair had said, smiling at him apologetically. "And you know how difficult it is to find good men to be housemasters with the wretched pay they get."

"But the boy might have been maimed for life."

Blair scratched the side of his head absent-mindedly with a pencil. His face was almost as grey as his hair.

"I've done my best under the circumstances," Blair said wearily. "I've suggested to Joe that he deals with any absconder differently next time. I can do no more. As you know, a housemaster bears a heavy responsibility. You teachers have an easy time of it in comparison. A housemaster must be allowed to use his own judgement or the whole system breaks down."

The idiocy of it was, Arnold thought, that though he had little influence in the school, he was paid almost twice as much as Stobart. A teacher at an approved school needed proper qualifications and was paid a graduated salary with various "increments." A housemaster needed no educational qualifications whatsoever.

"There is only one qualification a housemaster *has* to have," Blair had once admitted sadly. "And that's vaccination—in case of an epidemic."

Blair was weak and getting old for the job. He would retire in a year's time. Perhaps his successor would keep Stobart under control. In the meantime Arnold went to visit the victim in the sick bay.

The boy's name was Dan Gedge, and he was thir-

teen years old. Arnold felt no constraint in talking to
him, for the boy, with his thin, delicate face and pale,
flat hair, did not attract him. If a boy appealed to him
—a young, tough little thug like Charlie Mason, for
instance—Arnold was so afraid his emotion would be
noticed that he found it difficult to make conversation.
But Dan Gedge was too small and too pale to be attractive. Even though Arnold felt no embarrassment with
him, conversation was not easy. The boy was very nervous. In moments of tension he had a slight twitch at
the right corner of his mouth, which repelled Arnold
and made him feel sick for some reason. And what was
there to talk about? The school? The boy hated it so
much that he had run away. His home? Dan's father
was dead. His mother was a drunk who had married
for the second time a man far younger than herself.
Dan's stepfather resented his presence in the house.
Both of them were glad when he was committed to an
approved school. The only person Dan loved in the
world was his aunt who was dying of leukemia. It was
to visit her in hospital that Dan had run away to Guildford.

Arnold had found it hard to make Dan forget his
worries—even for a few minutes. But he visited him
when he could spare the time, and after the boy got
well and rejoined the herd he still tried to encourage
him whenever he had the chance.

Arnold shook himself violently, as if the memories

of Melton Hall could be shaken off like drops of water. His eyes remained fixed on the handsome young Moroccan boy at the bar who was now smiling at him and making blatant gestures of invitation. Arnold wished he could control the fierce beats of his heart. He was finding it difficult to breathe.

"Moroccan chickens are wonderfully attractive, aren't they?"

Arnold's nerves jerked in alarm, as if he had been caught in a crime. He looked up. Ewing was standing beside him with two glasses of beer in his hand.

"That one's called Saïd," Ewing said. "He's one of the most hard-working little tarts in town. Saïd will go to bed with you for ten dirhams—which is less than a pound."

The taut string of Arnold's desire slackened.

"Now what's worrying you?" Ewing asked.

"Even if I were a fat old man with warts, would he still go to bed with me?" Arnold asked.

"He'd be still keener then."

"Why?"

"Because you'd probably expect less and give more."

"Doesn't it shock you to think that he's ready to give his body to anyone who'll pay a quid for it?"

"Doesn't it shock you to think that over ten thousand children in England are flogged savagely or beaten about till their screams for mercy can't be ignored any longer by the neighbors—ten thousand children in English homes every year? Doesn't it shock you to think of the millions of refugees all over the world?

[29]

Doesn't it shock you to think that America and Russia have got thousands of hydrogen bombs, each capable of destroying a whole city? The entire world may be destroyed at any moment in a nuclear war. Doesn't that shock you?"

Ewing's eyes were glittering with passion. "Can't you see that there's no point in being shocked—it's just a selfish emotion like any other—unless you're prepared to do something effective to stop it? And so far as Saïd is concerned I may tell you that if he didn't make his money out of us Europeans he'd go with the Moors, who'd be far rougher and give him far less."

"What's to stop him getting an ordinary, decent job of work?"

"I can see you don't know Saïd," Ewing said with a laugh. "Drink up your beer and let's go up to my villa for a nightcap. Or would you rather stay with Saïd? Conchita's got a room upstairs if you don't want to take him back to your hotel."

Suddenly through his haze of excitement, at the mention of the word "hotel," Arnold saw the end of the evening looming darkly ahead like rusty buffers at the end of a shining railway line. When the evening came to a stop, he would get out on to a cold empty platform and walk alone through the station, his footsteps echoing beneath the grimy vaults. Later, after some more drinks with Ewing, the prospect of the evening finishing would need to be contemplated. For the time being it was easier to move on to the branch line Ewing offered.

"Let's go back to your villa for a nightcap," Arnold said.

❧ ❧ ❧ ❧ ❧ ❧

As he moved his tall glass, the cubes of ice in his drink made a pleasant sound—like cowbells, Arnold thought, leaning back drowsily against a mound of silk cushions and gazing round the ornate room with its tiled walls and mosaic floor and fretted pillars. He wondered vaguely why Ewing had not chosen to stay in the light grey drawing room with the gilt French furniture. It was a cheerful room with comfortable sofas, whereas the low divan which ran along one end of this Moorish room was hard and uncomfortable be- cause the cushions kept slipping out of place, and the *décor* was rather oppressive. However, the evening was running smoothly once again; and the rails shone brightly for miles ahead; and while Ewing talked to him about the villa, Arnold allowed his mind to ram- ble over the confusing impression of the last half-hour.

On the outskirts of town the road had plunged ab- ruptly down a steep hill flanked with small houses. Ahead he could see a field of white sticks gleaming in the moonlight. This, Ewing told him, as the car swung left, was the Moslem cemetery. The road now began to climb and curl up the hillside, past narrow lanes with signposts pointing to darkened villas, past the long white façade of the governor's palace, until suddenly the car reached the eucalyptus forest, and the headlights shone on dappled trunks of trees with pointed leaves, and swept across broken billboards that advertised building lots and lit up a signpost leading to Cape Spartel. Then the headlights had picked out a long grey wall about ten feet high with smooth sides and a jagged top.

"Here we are," Ewing said.

The car stopped outside a heavy wrought-iron gate. Mustapha sounded the horn. Three large mongrel dogs rushed up to the grille and began barking fiercely. A light went on in a window of the lodge. A few seconds later a bearded gatekeeper muffled up in an old army greatcoat shuffled out of the porch and unlocked the gate, blinking in the glare of the headlights. Slowly the old man pulled aside the two massive sections of wrought iron. The car drove up a rutted drive of eucalyptus trees and stopped in front of one of the oddest villas Arnold had seen in Tangier. It was built in the shape of the letter T, with small turrets at each of the three extremities and a tall tower in the center.

"It's quite hideous," Ewing said as they walked through a square hall lined with tiles into the octagonal high-ceilinged drawing room. "It was designed by Reggie Gault—I don't suppose you've heard of him. He was an English eccentric who left London hurriedly at the time of the Oscar Wilde trial and settled down in Tangier. Most people hate the place—which is why I got it cheap. I find it has a distinct Edwardian charm, and I've done my best to make it comfortable."

"I think it's very romantic," Arnold said.

"It is in its way," Ewing replied, splashing out whisky into two glasses and dropping in cubes of ice. "I like to think of old Reggie Gault living here all alone for the last ten years of his life."

Ewing glanced at Arnold. "When one says 'all alone,' one means without any of his English cronies," Ewing explained. "In fact, gossip relates that the old man was surrounded by a seraglio of boys of all shapes and sizes. I wonder if he missed London society? Sometimes I think of him limping along the terrace outside, staring down in distaste at the wonderful garden he'd carved out of ledges on the cliffside, his eyes half-closed against the glare of the African noon, yearning for the fog of London and the dark leather chairs of his club. At other times I like to think of him stretched out in a deck chair, watching the sun setting behind the golden sweep of Cape Spartel, thanking his lucky stars that he didn't have to put on a stiff shirt and go out to a smart dinner party and make witty remarks, reveling in the thought that he could dine quietly alone with a novel propped against the decanter before retiring to bed and the soft embraces of his latest acquisition."

Ewing crossed the room and pressed a bell beside the marble chimney piece.

"We won't stay here," he said. "We'll take our drinks into the Moorish room. It's got more atmosphere. I've given you a whisky without thinking. I hope it's what you want?"

"Exactly what I want," Arnold replied. "Exactly."

The far door opened. A plump, smooth-faced Moor

of about thirty came in and bowed to Ewing. Then he bowed to Arnold and smiled at him—rather too knowingly, Arnold decided. The man was dressed in a dark blue, embroidered waistcoat with gold buttons and dark blue pantaloons. His eyes were very heavily made up with antimony; his gestures were slack and effeminate. Ewing spoke to him quickly in Arabic. Arnold could only catch the word "chocolata" which occurred frequently. The man bowed again and walked out with his hands swinging loosely.

"That's Bashir," Ewing explained. "I found him in an Arab café my second night in Tangier—twelve years ago. He was sixteen then and rather attractive in a farouche kind of way and surprisingly virile. So I took him on as a houseboy. He's been with me ever since. He now runs the entire ménage. So *there's* a moral story for you."

Ewing picked up his glass.

"Let's go into the Moorish room," he said. "That was where Reggiè Gault had all his orgies."

So Arnold thus found himself propped against the cushions on the divan, clinking the ice in his glass, wondering what was going to happen next. Now that he was convinced that Ewing had no designs on him, Arnold had given up worrying about his motives for entertaining a stranger throughout the evening. He no longer cared. His sun was shining again, and far away in the distant haze of the blue mountains the cowbells tinkled merrily. Somewhere in a tiled room with Moorish arches a man was speaking to him—asking him a question, in fact. Arnold wrenched himself away from the contemplation of his sunlit plain.

"I'm sorry," Arnold blurted out. "What did you say?"

"I was asking how much longer you were staying in Tangier," Ewing said patiently.

"Only five more days."

"Can't we persuade you to stay longer?"

"I have to be back in the school where I teach by January the third."

"At least you must let me show you what Tangier has got to offer before you go. Have you seen any of the dancing?"

"None."

"Well, you'll be seeing some tonight."

"Tonight?" Arnold asked in surprise, as Ewing stretched out to press the bell in the wall beside him.

"Tonight," Ewing said. "I've laid it on in your honor. Unfortunately the boys haven't got their traditional clothes with them. But I think you'll find this particular dance is not without charm."

While he spoke, Bashir came in through the door at the far end of the room, closing it carefully behind him. Then he bowed to them, and sank down onto the floor as if his bones had suddenly melted. From out of his glittering waistcoat he produced a flute which he began to play softly. At first Arnold could discern no pattern of melody—only a series of notes rising and falling slowly up and down a scale of quarter-tones which jarred on his ears. But gradually he perceived

[3 5]

that there was a tune, tenuous yet discernible—a tune which was repeated over and over again with seemingly endless variations. The effect was hypnotic. Arnold felt that he was floating away into a trance in which the elaborate arches and the vivid green fields of his plain were mingled with the soft silk cushions he was leaning against. Vaguely he noticed the door at the end of the long, narrow room opening again. Suddenly he sat upright.

Two young, slightly built boys came into the room and bowed reverently. Then they raised their heads, listened carefully to the sound of the flute and began a slow, solemn dance. Their hands were clasped behind their heads, their feet moved carefully over the tiled floor, a step forward then sideways, then a pace sideways and a pace backwards, as if they were draughts being moved over a checkered board. They wore white shirts and dark blue jeans and sandals. They were both about fifteen years old, and Arnold thought they were both extremely handsome. The taller one had wide dark eyes. The deep chestnut-colored skin of his soft face glistened in the glow of the sconces set against the wall. Short wiry hair curled close to his head, and his thick lips were parted as if in surprise.

At first sight the dark boy was the more attractive, Arnold decided. But there was a mischievous look about the smaller, fair-skinned boy which was interesting. Heavy clusters of black curls fell over his forehead and down his neck. The boy needed a haircut, Arnold the schoolmaster noted automatically. But though his hair was dark, his skin was the color of cream and his eyes were violet. He had thick eyebrows, a short straight nose and a mouth which was far too large for his face. He was amazingly slender and delicately made. Yet there was something intensely animal about him, Arnold felt. He might have appeared suddenly in the glade of a wood. He moved gracefully: his steps seemed to be more assured than those of the dark boy. Yet all the time he danced there was an expression of amused detachment, as if—should the dance become irksome to him—he could change into a faun and leap away.

"The dark-skinned one opposite me is called Chocolata," Ewing said. "His real name is Abdelaziz. But Conchita christened him Chocolata because of his color. He's always down at her place. That's where he came from tonight."

"I never saw him there," Arnold said.

"He was in the room upstairs. I arranged for Conchita to send him here by taxi. He's an attractive boy and delightfully obedient. As you can see, he's got Negro blood. His ancestors were probably slaves from the river Niger. But I can see that he's not the one you're interested in. The pale-skinned one you're staring at is called Riffi."

Arnold mumbled some denial.

"Why bother to deny it?" Ewing asked. "What's wrong with staring at anything so pretty? Well, that one's real name is Salah but they call him Riffi because his family lives in the Rîf Mountains above Chauen. He's a Berber. That's why his skin is so light. The Berbers were the original inhabitants of Morocco before

[3 7]

the Roman and Arab invasions. They were blue-eyed and fair-skinned. The boy moves wonderfully gracefully, doesn't he?"

"Does Riffi come from Conchita's place?" Arnold asked, dreading the reply.

"No. He works here in this villa. He's very lazy and rather naughty. But I put up with it because he's so entrancingly graceful. It's like having a young gazelle wandering about the grounds, or a diminutive satyr. I thought you might be taken with him. But for some reason I'd decided that you'd prefer the Negro type, so I had Chocolata sent up specially for you."

Arnold was embarrassed. He could feel the hot blushes surging over him.

"They dance beautifully," he said, to change the drift of Ewing's remarks.

"Just you wait," Ewing said.

Arnold could not move his eyes away from Riffi. The boy had noticed that he was staring at him and was smiling back in amusement.

Suddenly Bashir changed the rhythm of his playing. The tune did not alter, but the music was now urgent and compelling. As if in answer to a command, the two boys stopped their pacing. They now stood motionless with their feet together. Then, without moving their feet, they slowly began to undulate their hips, circling the air with their loins while their heads remained perfectly still. Their movement was more sensuous than anything Arnold had imagined in his most erotic dreams. He could feel the blood throbbing through his veins while his heart beat heavily against his chest.

[3 8]

The music was growing faster, the gyrations wider and more violent. Then, without pausing, the two boys stripped off their shirts and threw them over their shoulders to the door. They moved forward a few short paces, remained motionless for a second, and then began to writhe again. But they were now standing only a few yards away from the divan. Arnold could smell the musky ferine odor of their bodies; he saw the sweat glistening on the tightly stretched skin of Riffi's chest; he watched the folding and unfolding of a little crease of flesh below the boy's navel.

The music became more urgent and more insistent. As if in response to a new command the two boys unclasped the belts round their narrow waists and threw them back to the door, And now as they writhed, carving invisible circles in the air, their arms clasped once again behind their heads, gradually, inch by inch, their jeans slipped slowly down their lean thighs until they were naked.

The music stopped. Arnold was only vaguely aware of Bashir bowing and leaving the room, closing the door behind him, for his eyes were fixed on the two boys who had stepped out of their jeans and flung them against the door. They were moving pace by pace closer to the divan. Chocolata was approaching Ewing. Riffi, smiling rather shyly now, was coming near to Arnold. The sweat was running in streaks down the ivory of the boy's thighs.

Arnold was trembling; his mouth was dry. He could neither speak nor move. Chocolata had now moved close to Ewing. His knees brushed the divan. Gently the boy thrust his dark body forward. The room seemed very quiet. The silence was shaken by Ewing's laugh. He slapped Chocolata lightly on the thigh and pushed him away, saying a few quick words in Arabic. Chocolata shrugged his shoulders. He slouched toward the door, swinging his arms loosely in imitation of Bashir's walk. Then he picked up his clothes and left the room.

Riffi was no longer smiling. He was standing in front of Arnold, taut and quivering. He looked anxious, almost afraid. He had moved so close to him that Arnold could feel the heat of his body. Slowly Riffi unclasped his fingers from behind his head. He stretched out his hands and put them on Arnold's shoulders and gazed questioningly into his eyes. The desire to clasp the boy in his arms was so intense that Arnold could feel the pain of it stabbing his chest. His whole being yearned to hold Riffi and feel the softness of his skin. His emotion beat so strongly he was certain that Ewing must be aware of it. He glanced quickly to his right. Ewing was staring fixedly at the last inch of drink in his glass. Arnold's hands moved unsteadily toward the boy facing him.

But even as Arnold raised his hands, the picture of a different naked body slid into his mind, and he saw Saïd, the boy at Conchita's bar, Saïd with his tawny skin, lying naked on stained sheets, making love to a withered old man for the sake of a one-pound note. And Arnold's desire slackened. Riffi's hands, he felt sure, were only rubbing his shoulders because he wanted to earn money. Those violet eyes only peered

[4 0]

at him anxiously because the boy was afraid that he would be turned away like his friend Chocolata. To hold this boy in his arms could never be the same as to clasp Jack against him beside the pond. He had not endured long years of frustration to betray the ideals of his love for a night in the arms of a little male tart, for obviously Riffi was just as much of a prostitute as Chocolata or Saïd. Riffi would still be standing there, rigid and eager, if Arnold were old and deformed and vile. Riffi's fingers would still brush across his neck and stroke his cheek—just as tenderly as they were stroking him now.

Arnold stood up abruptly. "I must be getting home," he said.

Ewing looked at him in silence for a moment, then spoke quickly to Riffi in Arabic. The boy winked at him, bowed to Arnold with a cheerful grin, ran three paces, turned cartwheels across the room, landed on his feet by the door, picked up his clothes and vanished.

"Let me get you a whisky," Ewing said.

"No, thanks," Arnold said, trying to smile. "I've drunk far too much as it is. But can I phone for a taxi?"

"Yes, by all means. But I don't think you'll persuade a taxi to come out here at this time of night, and I'm afraid Mustapha will have gone to bed. Why don't you stay the night? I've told Bashir to get the main guest room ready for you. You'll find a toothbrush and shaving kit and so on. There are even pajamas if you need them. Please do stay. Mustapha can drive you back to your hotel in the morning. It'll save so much trouble. I must confess I'm dropping with drink and fatigue."

"It's very kind of you," Arnold said cautiously.

After all, it would save him an expensive taxi fare, and Ewing had made it only too obvious that Arnold was not his type. In case Bashir or someone got the wrong idea he could always lock the door.

"Thank you," Arnold said. "I'd love to stay the night."

"I'll show you to your room before I fall sound asleep."

Ewing led him along a wide corridor and across a patio to the far wing of the house. He stopped outside a polished oak door.

"Here we are." Ewing said. "I hope you'll find all you want."

Ewing opened the door, flicked on the lights, walked quickly across a small sitting room furnished in conventional Regency style and flung open the far door revealing a large brightly lit bedroom dominated by a huge double bed with a white-and-gilt baroque headboard. An alcove led to a blue-tiled bathroom flanked with dark mirrors and fitted with a glittering display of gadgets. Bottles of lotions and face creams and bath salts stood in rows along glass shelves. Thick yellow bath towels of different sizes were draped over the chromium pipes set in the wall. A white dressing gown hung from the door.

"Bashir seems to have done you proud," Ewing said. "I'm never allowed half as many bottles. So now, if you'll excuse me, I really must go to bed."

"Thank you for a terrific evening."

"I enjoyed every moment of it."

"I can never be grateful enough," Arnold insisted. He could hear that his voice was still slurred.

"Don't try."

"You've given me a wonderful time."

"I'm glad. Don't hurry up in the morning. I generally have breakfast at about ten on the patio, if you care to join me. Otherwise they can bring you breakfast in bed. By the way, my bedroom's at the far end of the corridor, if you want me, which I don't suppose you will. Should you wake up in the night and feel hungry or should you need anything brought to you, ring the bell by your bed. And if you ring long enough Bashir will appear and fix you up. Good night."

"Good night and thanks once again."

Arnold locked the door of his bedroom. He undressed slowly, hanging up his clothes neatly in the painted cupboard which ran along the far wall of the room. Then he put on the trousers of the lilac pajamas Bashir had laid out on the bed and went into the gleaming bathroom. While he washed his face and hands and cleaned his teeth, Arnold examined himself drunkenly in the wall mirrors that reflected him from different angles. At least he was still slim. He weighed the same as he had when he was eighteen. Even though his hair was slightly receding, it was corn-colored and curled crisply over his head. His skin was smooth and clear, his teeth were good, his waist was small, he was well-built generally. Some people might still find him attractive. But where in heaven's name were such people? Beneath what roofs did they lurk? In what country did they dwell? And would he ever meet one single one of them?

Arnold sighed as he slipped between the pink silk sheets. He switched out the light by his bed, shut his eyes and tried to sleep. But the shape of Riffi's taut body glowed like a torch in the darkness of his mind. A disturbing uncertainty now slipped through the mist of his confused thoughts. Ewing had said he had arranged for Chocolata to be sent up to the villa for his guest's benefit. Yet almost from the very moment Riffi had come into the Moorish room he had kept his eyes fixed on Arnold. Was it possible that the boy was attracted to him? If so he must have been hurt by Arnold's abrupt move to break away from him. If Riffi worked in the villa he most probably slept there. Why had he grinned so cheerfully at Arnold before he turned to go? Perhaps Ewing had told him that Arnold might be staying the night. Perhaps Riffi was waiting for him. Perhaps . . .

Arnold got out of bed. He could cross to the door without switching on his bedside lamp, for moonlight filtered dimly into the room through a gap in the tall brocade curtains. Arnold unlocked the door. He got back into bed again and lay there aching with desire, cursing himself for the opportunity he had missed, wondering if perhaps Riffi might visit him in the morning, tortured by the memory of the skin stretched tightly over the boy's chest and the sweat running down his pale thighs.

He could hear the leaves of the eucalyptus trees rustling in the wind. Each time there was a distant creak of a door his heart began pounding. Perhaps Bashir had taken Riffi. Perhaps . . .

Suddenly he heard the outer door of the sitting room open quietly and then close again. He waited, struggling to control the quick hammer blows of his heart. But perhaps it was Ewing who had come to see if he were all right. Or perhaps it was Bashir or Chocolata. . . .

The door of his bedroom opened slowly. In the faint light he saw the gleam of a white shirt. He could not speak for terror. The door closed. A slight figure moved across to the armchair in the center of the room. The white shirt gleamed again as it was raised and then put down on the chair.

A second later the figure turned and stepped silently toward the bed. As he turned, the wind ruffled the curtains and for a moment a sliver of moonlight shone into the room. In that instant Arnold saw the small, pale, naked shape of Riffi moving toward him.

In silence Riffi slipped into the bed and put his arms round Arnold's neck and pressed against him.

❦ ❦ ❦ ❦ ❦ ❦

WHEN Arnold awoke, sunshine was sliding through the curtains. He was alone. For a moment he wondered if Riffi's arrival in his bedroom had been a dream. But a faint smell of the boy's body still lingered in the air, and there was a dent in the pillow where his head had been.

[4 5]

Arnold felt sick. His head ached fiercely. He turned over onto the pillow and tried to sleep again. He wanted to forget what had happened if only for the space of an hour's oblivion. Vaguely he hoped that sleep might wipe away the memory of the unexpected passions that Riffi had unleashed. But he could not sleep. The scent of the sheets reminded him of Riffi. Had the boy left him in fear or in disgust? Was he still in the villa? Traces of the ferine smell increased the pain of Arnold's remorse. He got out of bed and walked into the bathroom. The dark mirrors reflected a dozen aspects of his guilt.

Presently, as he lay in the bath into which he had poured verbena salts in order to overwhelm the persistent smell of Riffi's body, the pangs of his conscience grew less acute, as if they were being assuaged by the soft-scented water, and he found he could even bear to think about Riffi again.

Unless the boy had left the villa for good, he was probably at work in the house. Arnold wondered if he would meet him before Mustapha drove him back to his hotel? He dreaded seeing the boy again, yet he wanted to get a glimpse of him in the daylight so that he could fix him soberly in his memory. Would Ewing know that the boy had spent the night with him? Would he somehow take advantage of it if he had found out?

Arnold dressed and walked out to the patio. Ewing, wrapped in a heavy blue dressing gown, was sitting at a table laid for breakfast, drinking coffee and reading a newspaper. He was unshaven. His heavy blue jowls quivered as he lifted the cup to his lips.

[4 6]

"Good morning," Ewing called out cheerfully. "I hope you slept well."

There was not a trace of insinuation in his tone of voice or in his smile.

"Yes, thanks." Arnold said.

"You'll find scrambled eggs under that dish. I couldn't face them, but you're probably stronger than I am. If you want tea for breakfast you'll have to ring for it. The coffee's piping hot for once."

To his surprise Arnold found that he was hungry. He helped himself to the eggs and coffee and sat down.

"Though I trust I didn't show it," Ewing said, "I was, in fact, extremely drunk last night."

"So was I," Arnold said quickly.

"When I reached my bed I fell into a deep stupor from which I've only just emerged. But I've got a cracking headache, haven't you?"

"Terrible. I can hardly think."

"There's only one cure, and that's a dip in the sea. Shall we drive out to the Caves of Hercules for a swim and have a picnic lunch on the beach afterwards?"

"That would be fine."

"Shall we say in half an hour's time? Mustapha should be ready for us by then. I think we might have the top down, don't you?"

"Fresh air might do the trick," said Arnold.

The ferine smell still lingered inexplicably.

Half an hour later Arnold found the car waiting in front of the ornate stone porch. Mustapha was polishing the hood. Riffi was sitting in the front seat. He waved his hand excitedly when he saw Arnold.

[4 7]

"*Sbalkhair*. Gud morny," Riffi cried, smiling cheerfully and looking at Arnold with wide, untroubled eyes.

Arnold felt himself blushing.

"Good morning," Arnold said.

How could the boy's manner be so natural and assured? How could he appear so innocent? Each moment that Arnold watched him brought back another shaming memory.

"We go to Caves of Hercules," Riffi said. "Me swim very good."

"Don't you believe it," Ewing said as he joined them. "He flounders about like a lunatic. I'm always terrified he'll get drowned."

"Me swim very good," Riffi repeated obstinately.

"You'll get your bottom smacked if you're not careful," Ewing said laughingly as he got into the car.

Two hours later they were lying on the sand in a cleft of rock that protected them from the wind on the Atlantic beach. Mustapha had stayed behind with the car.

"He likes to brood over it," Ewing explained.

As they stepped down the stony path leading to the sunlit beach Arnold looked in wonder at the vast broad stretch of sand extending for miles into the distance without another human being in sight.

"Thank your stars it's a weekday," Ewing said. "There's no one about and we can sun-bathe stark naked."

The sight of Ewing sun-bathing made Arnold feel

[4 8]

sick again. Ewing's thick-set body was covered with hairs. He lay on his back, his oddly scarred stomach rising and falling as he breathed, his legs stretched open as if to draw attention to his gross virility.

Riffi was splashing in the surf of the slow-rolling Atlantic breakers. The sight of him no longer filled Arnold with guilt. Last night's experience was obviously an ordinary part of the boy's existence. It had left no mark on his mind or his body. As he watched the boy now, he felt an overwhelming tenderness toward him, which made him sad because he would have no chance of expressing it. Riffi ran out of the sea and began to turn somersaults on the sand. While Arnold gazed at his firm but delicate limbs he was shocked to find that desire was creeping back again.

Arnold turned away to find Ewing looking at him.

"He's an attractive little creature, isn't he?" Ewing said with a glance toward Riffi.

"Very," Arnold agreed briskly. "How long have you known him?"

"Six months. I first met him down in the town. He was unhappy in the place he was working in, so I took him back with me to the villa that night. He's been there ever since."

An unpleasant vision of Riffi yielding himself to Ewing flashed into Arnold's mind. As if he could read his thoughts, Ewing said, "The boy doesn't interest me particularly from the point of view of sex. But I find him entrancingly decorative."

"How old is he?"

"Fourteen, he thinks. They're never absolutely sure.

[4 9]

Most of the boys in this town are hardened little devils. But Riffi might be capable of affection. You never can tell. The boy's taken a fancy to you. Did you know that?"

"Nonsense," Arnold mumbled.

"He has, I promise you. What's more, I can see you're quite taken with him. I'm glad that last night was such a success. Since you've only got a few more days here it seems a pity that you shouldn't see something of each other. So why don't you move in? Why don't you come and stay at the villa for your last few days?"

So Ewing knew about last night and didn't care. The implications of his invitation made that plain. Arnold's heart pounded with joy. He felt ashamed of his uncharitable thoughts about Ewing's character and physique.

"It's awfully kind of you," he said. If you're sure I won't be a nuisance I'd love to move in. It would make all the difference."

"That's settled then," said Ewing. "We'll collect your luggage from your hotel this afternoon and drop in at Wayne's bar for a drink on the way home."

❧ ❧ ❧ ❧ ❧ ❧

THAT evening Arnold dined late and alone with Ewing up at the villa in the pale blue dining room with its Empire furniture. He was already a little drunk because when they had been about to leave Wayne, who had been ecstatic to learn that Arnold was staying up at the villa, a friend of Ewing's called Lavinia Morris had come in and joined their table and stayed for several rounds of drinks. Lavinia Morris was a gaunt-looking woman of about fifty with a handsome but wrinkled face. A few streaks of grey showed in her untidy thick black hair. She was extravagantly outspoken and self-opinionated. But she was obviously warmhearted in a confused way, and her manner became more confused as the evening progressed. She was evidently an alcoholic. Arnold had liked her. He had enjoyed the session with Wayne. But he was now worried because Riffi had disappeared as soon as they had got back to the villa, and he was too shy to ask where he could find him again. He could always ring for Bashir when he reached his bedroom and ask him to fetch the boy, but he did not like the sly way Bashir had glanced at him when he carried Arnold's suitcase into the villa. Arnold disliked Bashir and was afraid of him.

They were waited on at dinner by Ismail, a dark-skinned, wizened man of about fifty, dressed in dark-blue-and-gilt Moorish livery and wearing white gloves, which impressed Arnold even more than the silver plates. The food was delicious and the wines were excellent. Arnold only wished that Riffi could have eaten with them. But perhaps that would cause trouble with the staff.

"What did you think of Lavinia Morris?" Ewing asked.

"I thought she was great fun. She seemed a kind person."

"She's kind all right," Ewing said. "Kindness is her

main trouble apart from drink. She's giving away more than she can afford. I wish she'd take a cure."

"Who was the plump little American woman with platinum hair—the one that came up and kissed you just as we were leaving?"

"That was Milly Sprague. She owns a paper factory in Detroit. She's worth over a million, but she won't own up to it because she's afraid of being taken for a ride. How old would you say she was?"

"Fifty?"

"Sixty-five if she's a day. Everything that plastic surgeons and masseurs and cosmetics can do, they've done for dear Milly. She's had her face lifted so many times she can't close her mouth and eyes at the same time. The skin's stretched tight as a drum."

"She seemed very fond of Lavinia Morris."

"She is. They go hunting together."

"Hunting for what?"

"Twenty-year-old Moors mostly. But Spaniards or Greeks will do. Or American sailors at a pinch. At least Milly's got some self-control. But Lavinia's a menace. She picks up some Moorish lout and falls hopelessly in love with him. Before you know what's happening she's keeping the oafish bore and his whole family. And she can't afford it."

Ismail came in with a cheese soufflé. Arnold wished that Riffi was there to enjoy it. Perhaps he would be given some in the kitchen.

"I'm worried about Lavinia," Ewing said, gazing at the soufflé with approval. "I'd hate to see her flat broke. She and Milly are my two best friends over here. In fact, they're the whole of Tangier society as far as I'm concerned. I don't go out very much anyway."

"If I had this villa I'd never go out at all," Arnold said.

"There's a covey of smart old queens who live out here permanently and flit madly in and out of each other's overwrought houses. I can't abide them. Milo Branch, who's in Tenerife now with his new boy-friend, is the least poisonous of the bunch. If you can get him to stop talking about Chinese porcelain and Greek icons for two minutes he's almost pleasant. Then there's Cecil Mayhew who writes desperately un-successful historical novels full of buckles and bows. He's a mean old bitch, but at least he works—which is more than you can say for Luke West and Geoffrey Purcell, who've never done a stroke of work in their lives and never will."

Ewing finished his glass of champagne.

"Either you've got to work or you've at least got to try to learn something about art. You must either be industrious or cultivated. Few people are both."

Ewing pushed back his chair. "And with that ex-tremely smug and rather platitudinous remark I shall bid you good night," he said. "If you want coffee ring for it. Ismail will bring it to you in the living room. Forgive me for abandoning you, but my headache's come on again, so I simply must go to bed. Let's hope the weather keeps fine. We're asked to lunch at Lavi-nia's villa tomorrow, and it looks so grim when it's soaked. So does she, bless her heart. Good night."

Ewing walked rapidly out of the room. Arnold could hear his quick short steps crossing the patio.

Arnold finished his champagne and moved slowly to-

[53]

ward his bedroom, looking through each open door he passed in the hope of seeing Riffi. He paused outside the polished oak door leading to his apartment. The lights were switched on in the little sitting room. He walked in hurriedly. Perhaps Riffi was waiting for him. But the room was empty. He switched out the lights and pushed open his bedroom door which was ajar. Spread out neatly on the green leather armchair were a white shirt and a pair of blue jeans. Only the bedside lamp was alight, and Riffi was lying in his bed asleep.

Arnold stood in silence gazing down at him. The boy's left hand was under his head; the fingers of his right hand were touching his lips. He looked very small curled up beneath the massive baroque headboard. The light shone on the polished skin of his narrow shoulders. Arnold had only to bend down to touch the dry curls of his head. But he did not move. He could not bear to disturb the expression of innocence that Riffi had assumed in sleep. Patiently and sadly Arnold waited for the inevitable surge of reckless passion to sweep over him and overwhelm his immediate feeling of tenderness. Then, as he stood looking down at the boy, Riffi stirred and turned and stared up at him in alarm. When he recognized Arnold, he smiled at him drowsily and spread out his arms and lay back against the pillows. But Arnold still did not move, so Riffi raised himself, stretched out a hand and pulled him down onto the bed.

❧ ❧ ❧ ❧ ❧ ❧

THE lunch party the following day was not as alarming as Arnold had feared. The marble table in the garden was laid for six. Lavinia Morris, who had evidently been drinking all morning, sat at one end, with Milly Sprague upholstered in white silk like a bolster at the other. Arnold sat between Lavinia and Luke West, who was extremely tall, with a tiny head and a long neck set on narrow shoulders that expanded to a thick waist and bulging thighs. He reminded Arnold of a prehistoric animal he had seen in illustrations to a natural history schoolbook, nibbling at the leaves of a tree. Luke's friend Geoffrey Purcell sat opposite, eating with fierce concentration, pausing only to fill up his glass of wine from the nearest decanter on the table. He was a fat little man, about fifty years old, with glassy blue eyes and dyed yellow hair.

When Arnold had first arrived at the large ramshackle villa, led into the room by Ewing like a child by its nurse, Lavinia and her guests had all made a fuss of him, offering him drinks and plates of cocktail food, asking him polite questions and pretending to listen to the answers. Now they all ignored him and, after three strong daiquiris and two glasses of Sidi Larbi, Arnold did not mind. He could gaze at the flowers beyond the fierce green of the lawn and at the blue shadows on the lion-colored hills, stretching to the horizon, while he listened vaguely to their conversation.

"I like poor Milo," Luke West was saying, tilting up his head as if to reach some particularly juicy leaves on a high branch. "He's totally devoid of any taste whatsoever. His villa looks like an oriental bazaar collected by a Victorian spinster. But he's a pleasant enough creature."

"I like Milo, but he's a bloody snob," Lavinia announced, spilling wine into her glass and onto the table.

"He's such a snob that if he catches a common cold he has to call it bronchitis," Ewing said quietly.

Lavinia clapped her hands together in ecstasy. "Perfect!" she cried. "I must remember that one."

"I wish I had Ewing's wit," Milly Sprague said, stretching her mouth into a smile. She had not heard Ewing's remark, but she was a good-natured woman.

"I'd rather have Ewing's income," Luke West said, lowering his head for a moment from the foliage.

Geoffrey Purcell put down his knife and fork and turned to Milly Sprague. "Have you ever tried boiling a chicken in the juice of another one?" he asked.

Milly Sprague closed her eyes and opened her lips in a smile. Then she slid an arm heavy with jewelry across the table, laid her plump fingers trustingly on his wrist, closed her mouth and opened her eyes and looked up at Purcell rapturously.

"Tell me, dear," she said. "Tell me *just* what it's like. Is it really and truly marvelous?"

"Fabulous," Purcell said, looking round for a decanter. "Terrific."

"We all eat far too much," Lavinia proclaimed loudly. Her hair now fell in wisps over her glazed eyes, and she swayed from side to side like a priestess of the Siwan oracle. "Food will be the death of us," she prophesied.

"I wouldn't have said that you need worry over

dying of too much *food,*" Purcell said, looking sadly at the half-empty cheese tray that was being handed round.

"Poor Milo certainly eats too much," Luke West said. "He's getting quite bloated. I bet his new Spanish boyfriend leaves him within a month."

"Dear Milo," Milly Sprague murmured. "Such a lonely boy."

"We're all lonely," Lavinia said, looking over her shoulder toward her twenty-year-old Moroccan servant who was wheeling a trolley of liqueur bottles toward them. "Who isn't lonely? Tell me *that.* We come into this bloody world alone and we leave it alone."

"Not necessarily," Ewing said.

"What do you mean 'not necessarily?' "

"Well, one might be born a twin and die in an earthquake."

"Ha, ha. Very funny," said Lavinia, scowling at her young servant who had wheeled the drink trolley straight to Milly Sprague.

"Before I die," Luke West said, raising his eyes as if to contemplate celestial arbors, thickly leaved, "I'd like to think I'd left my name behind me. I'd like to be known for somthing."

"Like Onan, for instance," said Ewing. "Or the Marquis de Sade."

"You're just showing off in front of your new friend," Lavinia said. "Let's take our drinks and move into the garden so that Hassan can clear away."

Arnold was staring at the branches of a tall mimosa tree pouring like the streams of a yellow fountain onto the lawn when Lavinia joined him. She put an arm round his shoulder.

"I like you," she announced. "You must come here more often. I like your face. You must be queer, of course, or you wouldn't be staying with Ewing. But I like you all the same. Will you have some more brandy?"

"No, thanks very much. I've drunk too much as it is."

"So have I. But I couldn't care less. What do you make of Ewing?"

"He's been wonderfully kind to me."

"He always seems kind enough. I don't understand Ewing. I can't make him out. I can't find the flaw."

"The flaw?"

"There must be a flaw somewhere, mustn't there? I mean, he's rolling with money. He's strong and healthy. He's quite intelligent and amusing at times. He's well-read and cultivated. As you say, he's fairly kind and generous. And at heart he's surprisingly sentimental. So where's the flaw? I know he goes in for boys. But I don't call that a flaw—not a proper one. He's brave too. He had a terrific war record."

Though she was drunk, Lavinia noticed the look of surprise on Arnold's face.

"You don't believe it, do you?" she said, leaning heavily on his shoulder. "But it's true. I knew someone who was in the same outfit with him. Ewing started off in motor-torpedo boats. Quite a tough lad, he was. Commando raids and the lot. My friend said that Ewing was positively bloodthirsty, the way he'd get himself on raids and operations with the partisans and suchlike. You'd almost think he enjoyed all the massacre. He finished up in Yugoslavia, covered with blood and glory. He was horribly badly wounded. You must have seen the scars on his body. Our friend Ewing was a big hero."

"You wouldn't think it to look at him now," Arnold said.

"It's over twenty years ago, remember. But I'm not so sure that he's changed all that much. Now and then when he's annoyed there's a glint in his eyes that makes me shudder. He was quite savage with a Moroccan taxi driver who tried to get money out of him by blackmail some years ago. There'd have been a scandal if Ewing hadn't paid off the family and hushed it up. He's a strange character is our friend Ewing Baird. But I suppose he's no stranger than the rest of us out here. Now let's go and have one more glass of brandy before I send you all packing."

Ewing said little at first on the drive back. His nerves seemed on edge. He shouted angrily at Mustapha for driving too close to a herd of goats that were being driven back from the rough pastures around Cape Spartel.

"Lavinia's lunch parties always exhaust me," he said presently, as if in explanation. "There's always too much to drink and too little to eat. Lavinia could hardly wait to get rid of us so that she could pop into bed with Hassan."

"Surely she doesn't . . ."

"Surely she does. He won't be her butler for long, mark my words. He'll have moved into her spare room as an honored guest before the week's out. And he'll suddenly be discovered to possess a distinguished ancestry. Lavinia will give out that he's a grandson of the Glaoui and that his mother was a Turkish princess. I've seen it all happen before. Why she has to ennoble all her lovers, heaven only knows. Perhaps she finds it more exciting to think of blue blood coursing through their dusky bodies. Talking of bodies, I'm going to have a siesta as soon as we get in. Would you like me to ask Bashir to send Riffi to your room?"

"Yes, I'd like to see him."

Ewing's hands cut the air with an impatient gesture.

" 'Yes, I'd like to see him,' " he repeated in Arnold's cautious, almost prim, tone of voice. "Come off it! Riffi slept with you last night and the night before that. Even this morning when he was watering the flowers in the patio, you could hardly keep your eyes off him. So why bother to pretend to *me* of all people? I'm not a fool, and I don't care two hoots if you've got a lech on him or not."

Arnold was stung by the contempt in Ewing's voice. "If you want to know, I love him," he said.

"Call it what you like," Ewing replied. "I call it having a lech. But do you want Bashir to send you the boy or not?"

"Yes, I do."

"Right. I can now tell you this. Today is Riffi's afternoon off. He's stayed in for your sake. So you might just as well take advantage of it. And if you don't mind

[6 0]

a word of advice, I suggest you should give him a small present."

That afternoon Riffi came openly to Arnold's room, and Arnold gave him fifty dirhams—which he could afford to do because he had no hotel bill to pay. And Riffi was even more affectionate than before.

        🎗 🎗 🎗 🎗 🎗 🎗

THE next morning as Arnold was eating breakfast on the patio—he had left Riffi in the bath playing with the chromium sprays—Bashir appeared with a note from Ewing.

"I hope you slept well," Ewing wrote. "I had a vile night because I've got a tummy upset—probably due to Lavinia's food. So I'm staying in bed. But I've asked Bashir to put up a picnic lunch for you, and I've ordered the car to take you and Riffi out to the Caves. Under the circumstances I don't suppose you'll miss me. See you drink-time. Your stricken host, Ewing."

Once again the beach was empty. Miles of untrodden sand gleamed in the sunlight. Riffi splashed in the waves, turned somersaults and cartwheels, and taught Arnold a Moorish version of hopscotch in the sand. He was never still for a moment. His energy seemed inexhaustible. And after a lunch of lobsters and Chablis, Arnold was relieved to see Riffi lie down between the rocks and close his eyes.

Arnold found a patch of shade, turned over onto his

stomach and tried to doze. But he was disturbed by a fly that seemed to settle persistently on his back. He tried ineffectively to swat at it with his hand. A second later it was back again. Then he heard snorts and gasps from behind an outcrop of rock, and Riffi appeared with a reed fastened to the end of a cane of bamboo. He was rolling from side to side with laughter. When Arnold waved him away and relaxed once again into a comfortable position, Riffi flung the cane at Arnold like a javelin and rushed away shouting with pleasure. Arnold leaped to his feet and pursued him. Riffi ran fast, but Arnold was lithe and his stride was longer. He caught up with him and brought him down tumbling on the sand. Riffi writhed and wriggled in his grip, but Arnold held him fast. Suddenly Riffi stopped struggling and yielded to his grasp, pressing hard against him as Jack had done by the pond. But this time there was no breaking apart. The boy slid his arms round him and lay without moving. This time it was Arnold who let go his grasp and edged away, for he was afraid of the violent waves of passion that rose high with the Atlantic breakers and crashed down on him mercilessly, and he was acutely aware of the harsh lights of the sun and of the flat stretch of sand spread out around them. A dozen eyes might be watching them from behind the far dunes or from the headland.

When Arnold moved, Riffi raised his head and looked up at him with solemn eyes, staring at him almost mournfully—as if Arnold had told him sad news. Then an idea must have flashed into Riffi's mind, for his face brightened. He stood up and grasped Arnold's hands.

"Come," he said. "Come wid me."

Arnold allowed himself to be pulled to his feet and led across the beach to a stony track that led up the side of the cliff.

"Where are you taking me to?"

"Come," Riffi said. "I show."

They climbed along the side of a narrow ledge of rock. As Riffi stepped delicately from stone to stone, the ledge grew narrower and the ascent steeper.

"You've gone mad," Arnold shouted. "Come back."

"Come," Riffi cried, pointing to a corner of the cliff-side. "One minute, you see."

Trying not to look down at the drop beneath, Arnold followed Riffi round the corner and found him standing triumphantly in front of a cave in the side of the rock.

"You see," Riffi said. He took Arnold's hand and drew him out of the dangerous glare of daylight, into the protecting dusk of the recking, damp cave, guiding him along a narrow passage toward a black enclosure. There, Riffi knelt down and cleared a space between the foul-smelling stones.

But Arnold was scarcely aware of the unpleasant smell and the stony ground. He knew only that he and Riffi were alone in the security of the dark womb of the cave.

Later, as they walked back along the beach and he looked down at Riffi's head of curls all dusty from the cave, Arnold realized with a violent shock of dismay that the words he had said to Ewing in his temper were true. He did love the boy. He loved him not only with the craving passion that Jack had aroused in him but with tenderness and an overwhelming desire to protect him from all harm. But the boy probably believed that Arnold only wanted him for sex. Perhaps that was the reason for the solemn look in his eyes when Arnold had edged away from him on the beach. The boy had been sad to think that Arnold only wanted him for a brief session. Even if he were never to see Riffi again in his life, Arnold was determined to make the boy understand that he was genuinely fond of him.

Slowly, using short simple words, Arnold tried to explain. But it was hopeless. Riffi did not even try to understand.

"Me your freng," Riffi kept saying as he patted Arnold's arm. "You my freng."

"But it's more than that," Arnold insisted.

"Yis. More than that. I know. Me your freng. You my freng."

And that, it seemed, was all he needed to know.

"If only you could speak English," Arnold sighed.

Riffi looked up at him, his wide eyes full of reproach.

"Me speak gud Engliss," he protested. "Me can say many tings in Engliss."

Then Riffi clasped his hands together primly and began to recite a set speech slowly and painfully, enunciating each word with such an effort that at first Arnold could not understand what he was saying.

"Mai husbend end I," Riffi said, "are verree pleeced tu declare yar bazaar open."

[6 4]

Arnold was bewildered until he suddenly understood the grotesque parody.

"Who taught you that?" he asked sharply. "Ewing?"

"No. A freng."

"What friend?"

"An Engliss freng."

"Is he in Tangier now?"

"No. He go back to London."

"How old was he?"

"I not know."

"Older than me or younger than me?"

"He have grey hair—older than you."

"What was his name?"

"Why-for you wan know his name?"

"Tell me his name."

"His name Paul. Why-for you angry? He my freng."

Riffi held up his right hand and pointed to the silver ring on his middle finger.

"He give me dis ring," Riffi said. "But now you my freng. I give you ring."

Riffi pulled off the ring and handed it to Arnold, nodding his head solemnly.

"But if the man gave it to you," Arnold began doubtfully.

"You now my freng," Riffi interrupted. "I give you ring. Give your hand."

Arnold stretched out his right hand, and Riffi slipped the ring on his little finger.

"You have dis ring. You are my freng."

Suddenly Riffi bent down and kissed the back of his hand. "You keep ring," he said. "You keep Riffi. You in London. You take ring. You take Riffi like in cave."

"I love you," Arnold said quietly for his own benefit —because he wanted to hear himself speak the words in the boy's presence.

"I love you," Riffi replied. "You my freng."

The sun had set in a red glow behind Cape Spartel by the time they reached the villa. Riffi disappeared with Bashir. Arnold wandered into the light-grey drawing room where he found Ewing, lying on a sofa.

"Help yourself to a drink," Ewing said. "My inside is still torture, so I'm drinking Fernet Branca and hoping for the best. Dr. Valdez is coming up to see me at any moment. Did you enjoy your day?"

"Very much indeed."

"Did the boy behave himself?"

"He was a wonderful companion."

"I bet he was,". Ewing said dryly. "Do help yourself to a drink."

Arnold walked over to the drink table and poured himself a strong whisky and soda.

"Who was Paul?" he asked.

"Paul?"

"Riffi said he had an English friend called Paul."

"Oh that one!" Ewing said. "Paul Ashton. He's one of those madly cautious English 'county' queers. They lead lives of monumental respectability and boredom for eleven months out of twelve. But once a year they unleash themselves from their horsey wives in the shires and beetle to some louch spot like Tangier to make up for lost time. Paul Ashton escaped from his grossly rich and wholly repellent wife in Nottingham-

[66]

shire and came out here last October. He made up for his very lost time with Riffi."

"I see," Arnold said after a pause.

"Don't look so depressed. Surely you didn't imagine you were exploring virgin soil?"

"No, I didn't."

"Then why so gloomy?"

"I was just thinking . . . I expect Riffi must think of me as another Paul Ashton in his life."

"I expect he does. Is there any reason why he shouldn't?"

"No, I suppose not. Though it's not the same."

"Why not?"

Arnold glanced up from his glass in surprise. Ewing's voice was unexpectedly soft and sympathetic.

"Why not?" Ewing repeated gently.

"I told you. Because I love the boy. I really do. I only wish I could prove it to him."

"Why shouldn't you prove it?"

"There's so little time. Tomorrow's my last night."

"Why not stay another fortnight?"

"Because I have to be back at Melton Hall by January the third."

"Can't you cable asking for your holiday to be extended?"

Arnold thought of the expression on Blair's face as he opened the cable and read it.

"Not possibly," Arnold said.

"What if you were ill?"

"That would be different. I couldn't fly back then, could I ?"

"Then you can be ill."

"But I'm not."

Ewing spread out his hands impatiently and let them drop on the table.

"How are they ever going to know that you're not ill?" he asked. "You cable them that you've got severe bronchitis and you airmail them a medical certificate."

"Where do I get the medical certificate?"

"From my good and extremely useful friend Dr. Valdez when he comes here this evening to give me something which I only hope will settle my stomach. Dr. Valdez has looked after me ever since I first arrived in Tangier and was convinced I'd caught some ghastly disease. He's very keen on the natives. He was down at Conchita's bar the other night, but you probably didn't notice him."

"You mean he'll write me out a medical certificate, just like that?"

"It's the least he can do, when you think how much I pay him each year. Mustapha can take the cable down to the post office first thing in the morning. Forget about it. You're here for another fortnight. It's all fixed. Besides, you can't leave just yet. There are all kinds of things to settle. Riffi's future, for instance."

"Riffi's future?" Arnold asked slowly. He felt dazed by the speed with which Ewing made plans for him.

"Well, you've said you're devoted to him. I see that he's given you his ring. And I really do think he's fond of you. So obviously you want to organize your joint futures somehow."

"But how can I? Thanks to your kindness and Dr. Valdez I may be able to stay out here another fortnight. But then I'll have to go back. I shan't get another holiday for six months."

"You don't intend to work in an approved school for the rest of your life, do you?"

"What else can I do?"

"Lots of things, I should say. Supposing some dreary old aunt you'd never heard of suddenly died and left you enough to live on, would you go on working at Melton Hall?"

Arnold shook his head and laughed.

"I don't belong to the class that has rich aunts," he said. "That's not my background at all. My father taught in a day school, and my mother worked in a teashop. I've got no rich aunts lying about anywhere."

Ewing got up and leaned against the chimney piece. For the first time Arnold noticed that he had a slight tremor in his left eye. The lid was gently quivering.

"I believe that if you want something sufficiently strongly you can always get it in the end," Ewing said.

"If you've got the money to start with."

"You *may* have money one day. Money isn't impossible to get—even if you've got none. But first you have to want the money badly enough. You want Riffi and you want to help him. That's a start. And I'd say you were very lucky."

"Why?"

"Let me ask you this. Supposing that tomorrow you woke up to find yourself rich, what would you do?"

"Give up Melton Hall and live with Riffi."

"Where?"

"Somewhere out here, I suppose."

"Right, let's suppose that you're living in a little villa with Riffi. How would you spend your days?"

"Well, we'd go for picnics to the caves, but not every day. Then I wouldn't want any servants in the villa because I'd want to be alone with Riffi. Besides I'm not used to servants, so Riffi would have to do the cooking and clean the place. That would give him something to do. While he was doing the housework, I'd learn Arabic so I could talk to him. And I'd try to learn something about music."

"You don't see yourself having long conversations with him about Greek drama?"

"No, I don't," Arnold said laughing. "Not for one moment."

But Ewing did not even smile. He was staring down at the pattern in the faded pink carpet.

"That's why you're lucky," he said. "Because if I'm interested in a boy, I do want to be able to discuss art and literature with him. I want to impart to him the little fraction of it all that I know—so that he can look down at this carpet and tell me that it's Aubusson and appreciate that it's quite good of its kind. For me that's the main point of the whole business. I'm not interested any more in attractive bodies and pretty faces. I've known enough of them in my time. My trouble is that I want more than that. Essentially I'm only interested in what I can achieve for the person I love. I like teaching him to enjoy music and books and painting. I like watching the petals of his mind unfold into a flower I can cherish. That's what education should really be—drawing out the person from the tight-closed buds of ignorance and prejudice."

[70]

Ewing crossed to the drink table and poured himself a neat brandy. His hands were trembling.

"But I'm convinced that you can only succeed in a relationship of the kind I want with someone of your own race," he continued. "He must even be of your own nationality. And once he's that, all kinds of social complications of class and income and accent enter in. That's why *you're* so lucky to want Riffi. You don't need to get inside his mind and mold his thoughts. You're content to love the wonderfully attractive little animal that he is."

Arnold was about to protest that Riffi was more than an attractive animal, when there was a ring at the front door.

"That will be Dr. Valdez," Ewing said. "I'll take him to my room. When I see you next—which will be for a cocktail before dinner—I'll have got your medical certificate. I only hope that he'll have given me some dope to help my wretched stomach."

❧ ❧ ❧ ❧ ❧ ❧ ❧

THE certificate, written on headed note paper, looked impressively official. Arnold had composed a cable with Ewing's help and had written a covering letter for the certificate. He had then found Riffi and told him that he would be staying in Tangier for another fortnight; he had been touched by Riffi's almost hysterical excitement. The food and the wine at dinner had been as excellent as usual. Riffi was now safely tucked up in his bed. Arnold sat contentedly on the sofa sipping Benedictine, beaming gratitude at Ewing. He felt far more at ease with Ewing since their talk before dinner. He now even had the courage to begin a conversation.

"What made you come out to Tangier in the first place?" Arnold asked.

Ewing glanced down at the brandy in his glass and smiled.

"I could give you so many romantic reasons why I first came here," he said. "I hate to disappoint you by telling the true one. Even now I find it faintly shaming. You see, the truth is that before the war I was one of those desperately cautious queers we were talking about just now. That's why I know the type so well. My mother died and left me a large house near Newmarket when I was twenty. As an Anglo-American I led a respectable 'county' existence. Staying away for weekends with other people with equally large houses and equally large incomes and equally narrow outlooks. I was so determined to be normal that I almost got engaged to be married. Of course, I had a flat in London. Occasionally I'd unleash myself with someone I'd picked up in a pub. But I was careful, and I was deeply conventional. At heart I despised myself for not being capable of falling in love with a girl."

Ewing paused and lit a cigarette.

"The war changed all that," he said quietly. "When I was faced with the prospect of being killed I realized the importance of living and living fully—not leading a pale imitation of the business. Secondly, I discovered that in the Services there were simply hundreds of men from every walk of civilian life—but mainly, I must tell you, from the working, not the middle classes

[7 2]

—who had exactly the same emotions as I did. Gradually I came to realize that I wasn't an almost unique,
rather odd product of an effete society. Ordinary com-
mon-or-garden men who before the war had been min-
ers or bus drivers, factory workers or mechanics, had
pretty well the same sexual desires as I did. Up till
then I'd always thought of queers as being unfortu-
nate, and handicapped—people born on the wrong
side of the tracks as it were. I now realized that we
might be on the wrong side. But there were an awful
lot of us. I can tell you it was a great discovery. It
changed the whole of my life. When the war was over
I went back to England and sold the big house and let
my flat. You see, I knew that I couldn't lead the kind
of life I wanted to in England. I found the conventional atmosphere stifling. So I packed my bags and
left. For a few years I wandered through France and
Spain. Then one morning I took the ferry from Algeciras and crossed over to Tangier—just to look at the
place. And here I am."

Arnold envied not only the wealth but the ruthless-
ness that enabled Ewing to make such drastic decisions
and abide by them.

"Did you find this villa right away?" he asked.

"No," Ewing said. "I lived up on the Marshan until
Tim left the place."

Ewing's thin lips were pressed tightly together. He
put down his liqueur glass and examined Arnold's face
thoughtfully.

"I haven't told you about Tim, have I?" he said. "I
think I should tell you about him, because Tim proves

a point that it's most important that you above all people should understand."

As Ewing's eyes focused on his face, it occurred to Arnold that perhaps the dope that Dr. Valdez had brought to ease the pain in Ewing's stomach was having an unexpected effect on him. He was certainly not drunk, but there was an odd, almost vacant look in his eyes.

"Where shall I begin?" Ewing asked with a twirl of his right hand.

"I suppose I'd best start at the beginning . . .

"Well, I'd taken a villa up on the Marshan—I'll show it to you tomorrow. And I'd been up there for a year, with Mustapha and his wife to look after me, and sixteen-year-old Bashir to entertain me. And I must admit that I was getting rather bored. The affair with Bashir was over. It never really started. We had only one thing in common. But Bashir was a wonderful servant. I liked having him around the place. All the same I was finding the villa a bit dull, so I'd gone down to dine in town . . .

"I sat late over dinner at the *Pavillon* cursing myself for not appreciating the advantages I had in life. A man of forty in good health with plenty of money and no responsibilities has no right to be bored, I told myself. I drank a Kümmel. Then I went round to Wayne's bar for a nightcap.

"I was listening to Wayne's stock of gossip when a young man of about nineteen walked in. As soon as I set eyes on him I felt I had really met my destiny. I tried to control my ridiculous imagination. I decided I must be drunk. I looked at him again. With his tousled fair hair and check shirt and shabby grey-flannel trousers he was obviously English. My first thought was that he was off one of the smuggling boats. I heard later that he'd tried to get a job on one of them only that morning, so I wasn't far wrong. The young man sat down at the table next to mine and ordered a beer. I found it hard to keep my eyes off him . . .

"How shall I describe him? He was about six feet tall and obviously wonderfully made, with heavy broad shoulders, a small waist and narrow hips. He was as fair-skinned as you are, but his eyes were deep brown—which made a disturbing contrast. He was lean and tough, but he seemed shy and awkward. He had big red hands which he kept putting under the table, as if he were ashamed of them. His features were too large and fleshy to be classically perfect, but his radiant health and the odd, rather wistful, expression of his eyes made him wildly attractive. Perhaps the best way I can describe him is to say that with his quite astonishing good looks he reminded one of every illustration one's ever seen in magazines of the ideal schoolboy hero. His firm jaw, straight nose, clear eyes and curly hair—they were almost laughably typical of the junior prefect who was kind to the smaller boys, but a demon on the rugger field. They were typical, I repeat, until one looked closer. Then one saw that the jaw was a shade too heavy, the lips too full, the nostrils too wide, the eyebrows too thick, and the hair far too long. But I was fascinated. I signaled to Wayne to go and talk to him. Presently Wayne introduced us, and over a drink the young man told me that his name was Tim Deakin—which was true—and that he was a steward on a cargo boat in the harbor—which was not. However, I was too elated to distinguish truth from falsehood, because some instinct told me that Tim Deakin was what I had been searching for—ever since the war ended.

"When Wayne said—on cue—that he must close the bar, I asked Tim up to the villa for a drink. He accepted cautiously. He said that he'd got to be back on board his ship by two a.m. I told him that he would be. I drove him up to the Marshan.

"But when he arrived at the villa, the young man was shy and rather embarrassed. I began to be afraid that the evening was going to turn out a failure . . ."

Tim, it seemed, had felt ill at ease in the brightly lit living room with its shining walls paneled with Japanese paintings. He had been afraid that his shoes would dirty the thick white carpet or that he would knock over one of the jade figures on the black lacquer table beside him. He had been conscious of his rough voice and coarse, red hands.

"What will you drink?" Ewing had asked.

"Scotch—if there is any."

"There's a couple of bottles at least."

Tim tried to laugh. "One will do," he said.

Ewing smiled back at him.

"You're too modest," Ewing murmured.

After he had poured out two large drinks, Ewing

crossed the room and switched on the record player. Earlier that evening he had been listening to a new recording of *Figaro* and the sound of Cherubino's aria wafted across the room. Ewing had supposed that Tim would prefer jazz. But at least there was now background music to fill the gaps in their conversation.

"What part of England do you come from?" Ewing asked.

For a moment Tim did not reply. His mind seemed far away. Then he looked up at Ewing.

"I'm sorry," Tim muttered. "I didn't hear what you said."

"Where do you come from in England?"

"My parents come from York. I was born in London. In the war I was evacuated to Dorset. My parents were killed in the blitz."

Ewing could think of no suitable words of sympathy.

"I'm sorry," he said after a pause.

But Tim did not hear what he said. His head was tilted back, and he was listening intently to the music.

"Mozart, isn't it?" he asked. "Isn't it *Figaro?*"

"It is indeed. How did you know that?

"I saw it once at Glyndebourne."

Ewing could not conceal a gesture of surprise.

"I did. Really, I did," Tim said. "There was a friend I used to stay with for weekends when I was on leave. He'd got this little cottage near Mayfield that he went down to in the summer. Well, he'd taken two tickets for *Figaro,* and he asked me if I'd like to go with him.

[7 7]

So I thought I would—just for the lark. We made a real evening of it. He hired me a dinner jacket and all. I'm glad I did go. It was great."

"How old was your friend?" Ewing asked.

Tim laughed. He looked down at the glass in his hand.

"I thought you'd ask that," he said.

"How old was he?"

Tim raised his head and stared at Ewing steadily with his deep brown eyes.

"About your age," he said slowly.

At that moment Ewing realized that Tim had known from the beginning why he had been invited to the villa. Ewing had only to make the first move. But he wanted a permanent relationship with Tim—not a brief adventure. Already he had begun to doubt Tim's story of being a steward on a cargo boat. And even if the story were true, in time Ewing could persuade Tim to leave the job. The essential thing was not to start the relationship on the wrong basis. Ewing therefore suppressed the questions he longed to ask about Tim's friend in Mayfield. He began to discuss opera in particular and music in general. To his delight he found that Tim derived intense pleasure from music. His brown eyes shone as he spoke of the concerts he had heard.

Toward two o'clock Ewing looked at his watch and got up.

"You ought to be going," he announced.

"Don't let's move," Tim said. "Can't I bed here somewhere for the night?"

"I thought you said you had to be back on board by two?"

Tim smiled up at him happily. "That was before I got to know you," he said. "I wanted an excuse to get away if we didn't get on."

Ewing picked up their glasses and poured out two strong drinks.

"Now then," he said, handing Tim back his glass, "what's the true story?"

Tim shuffled his feet awkwardly.

"The truth is that I'm here with a friend," he said. "He's a boy called Don. He's eighteen. You can meet him tomorrow if you like. We hitchhiked here through France and Spain. We were fed up with the factory we worked at in Croydon. So we thought we'd come out here and try to get a job on one of the smuggling boats. We're still trying."

Ewing resisted an impulse to put his hand on Tim's shoulder.

"I can find you a better job than that," he said.

"What about Don?"

"And Don too."

Tim stared up at him, radiant with gratitude.

"It would be great if you could," he said.

Ewing sat down in the armchair opposite Tim and settled back to play the game carefully. He held good cards. But he knew that one single mistake would finish him.

"What kind of work do you think Don would like?"

"Anything," Tim said. "He was a waiter before . . . before he came into the factory."

Ewing pretended not to notice the hesitation.

"Do you think he'd be happy working up at the villa of a friend of mine?"

"Is your friend a man?"

"No. A woman," Ewing said. He was thinking that if Don were half as handsome as Tim he would suit Lavinia.

"That would be fine," Tim said quickly. "So that's got Don fixed up. Now what about me?"

Slowly Ewing prepared to play his ace card.

"Do you know anything about diesel engines?" he asked.

"A bit. Why?"

"I've got a yacht down in the harbor. How would you like to train to be the mechanic on it?"

Tim rushed across the room and clutched his shoulder.

"Do you really mean that?" he asked. "You'd really have me trained to be the mechanic?"

"Of course I would."

"But isn't there a mechanic already?"

"Not at present," Ewing said. "The yacht's laid up."

"How big is she?"

"Fifty tons. You can see her tomorrow if you like. But I honestly think that right now we ought to be going to bed. It's madly late. I think the bed's made up in the spare room on this floor. Let's go and see."

"Doesn't matter if it isn't made up," Tim said as he followed Ewing to the door. "I can just bed anywhere."

Ewing could feel the tremor in his left eye that only

[8 0]

occurred when his nerves were tense. Now, if ever, was the moment to strike. But he resisted the temptation. He was determined that it should be Tim who made the first move. He opened the door of the spare room and pulled back the bed cover.

"Yes. The bed's made up all right," he said briskly. "And the bathroom's through those curtains. If you want anything, my bedroom's across the corridor, bang opposite. Good night."

Tim gazed at him uncertainly.

"Thanks for the evening. It was great," he said, after a pause.

Ewing turned and left the room, closing the door behind him. Perhaps he had been too abrupt, he thought as he undressed. Never mind. There was always tomorrow.

Ewing was lying in bed reading *Le Grand Meaulne* when there was a knock at the door and Tim came in. He was naked except for a towel round his waist.

"Hello," Ewing said quietly.

Tim closed the door behind him and stood with his weight on one foot, staring at him in silence. With his tousled hair and finely shaped shoulders he reminded Ewing of a statue of Antinous in Athens.

"You know, I guessed right away why you asked me up here," Tim said.

"I expect you did," Ewing replied in his calm, even voice.

"But then . . . when you started talking about music, I thought I must be wrong."

"You most probably were in a way."

[8 1]

Tim took three steps toward him and then stopped.

"Only in a way?" Tim asked.

"Yes. It's hard to explain."

"I suppose it is."

"Don't worry about it."

"But I do. You see, I'm grateful."

"I expect it'll sort itself out."

Tim unwrapped the towel round his waist and threw it into the corner.

"Yes. It will," he muttered.

Then he crossed the room quickly and got into Ewing's bed.

"I'd feel as if I were staying here under false pretenses otherwise," Tim said with a nervous laugh.

❧ ❧ ❧ ❧ ❧ ❧ ❧

EWING spread out his fingers, palms outward, glanced at them, and then let his hands fall to his side and turned back to Arnold.

"Of course, I still wasn't certain," Ewing said. "I could see trouble on the horizon. The main problem was Tim's friend—the eighteen-year-old Don . . .

"Well, we met Don before lunch at Wayne's bar the next day.

"Don was a pert little Cockney, with curly black hair, a snub nose and an impudent grin. As soon as I set eyes on him I realized that he'd never do for Lavinia. Unfortunately that idiot Wayne decided he'd do for *him*. Wayne behaved outrageously. He fluttered his eyelids, made the boy drunk on champagne cock-

[8 2]

tails, bought him cigarettes, hung on every word he uttered, and generally behaved like a camp old queen.

"The four of us went off to lunch at the *Pavillon*. Before we'd even ordered food, Wayne had suggested that Don should come and work for him as an assistant barman. Of course, the whole idea was ridiculous. Wayne didn't need an assistant barman. It was just a transparent excuse to get hold of Don. But it worked. The boy was thrilled with the idea. He started work that evening. But Tim wasn't at all pleased.

" 'Don's my friend,' he said. 'I'm the only one that's allowed with Don. So don't let anyone start getting ideas about him.'

"But what could I do about it? I didn't know Wayne as well as I do now. I'd got no influence over him to speak of. How could I interfere? It was all very well for Tim to say that he was the only one allowed with Don. The trouble was that Don didn't subscribe to that view at all. I knew he was going back to Wayne's flat every night, and I knew what went on there. Tim was almost obsessively devoted to little Don. For him it was a David and Jonathan affair. Don was fond of Tim as a friend. And that was all. Don was definitely and unashamedly on the game. So I thought Wayne was making a mistake—but not for the same reason as Tim did. With his snub nose and perky little cherubic face, Don was provocatively attractive. If Wayne paraded him nightly behind his bar, he was bound to lose him in time to someone who had more to offer.

"Meanwhile Tim was settling down in my villa on the Marshan. The villa's built on two floors—I'll show it to you tomorrow. I'd installed Tim on the top floor, which formed a self-contained flat, and apart from worrying about Don he seemed very happy. He was thrilled with the yacht. I'd found a Spanish engineer, who spoke English, to put him through a course on diesel engines. I'd got hold of a retired drunken old Danish skipper called—originally enough—Knud Christiansen to teach him about navigation. All was going well.

"Then the crash came. Tim had been asked out to dine by the old skipper Christiansen and his wife in their little flat in the Rue Goya. They'd asked me as well but I'd made an excuse and got out of it, because I wanted Tim to get asked out on his own, independently of me. So Tim went alone, and I dined up at the villa, with Bashir waiting on me. I'd told Tim all about Bashir, of course. And he didn't mind. Nor did Bashir—once he'd realized that I'd no intention of getting rid of him. In fact, they got on quite well together, so that was *one* complication out of the way.

"After dinner that night I felt restless, so even though it was late, I drove down to Wayne's bar. To my surprise I found it shut. But there was a light on inside so I battered on the door. Presently the door opened a crack and Wayne peered out.

" 'Oh, it's you,' he said dismally. 'Come in.'

"I went in. Wayne shut the door quickly behind me and locked it. Tears were streaming down his painted cheeks.

" 'What on earth's wrong?' I asked.

[8 4]

" 'He's left me. Without even a word, the ungrateful

" 'Who's gone?'

" 'He's left me. Without even a word, the ungrateful little brute. Don's left me. He's gone off on a cruise to Mexico with that horrible Belgian man. He never even said good-bye or thank-you. And I shall never see him again. He's gone for good.'

"The Belgian man was Louis Dubois—a retired banker of about sixty with a castle on the Loire and a villa in Acapulco. Exactly what I had foreseen had now occurred.

" 'Does Tim know?' I asked.

"Wayne nodded his head wearily.

" 'Tim was here half an hour ago,' Wayne said.

" 'Where did he go?'

" 'Back to your villa, I suppose. Where else could he go? Don left by plane with that cretin two hours ago. They've flown off to Marseilles to pick up the yacht.'

"Well, I asked Wayne to lunch with me the next day, and I did my best to console him. Then I drove quickly back to the villa. But Tim had not returned. I waited up for him for an hour. Then I went to bed.

"Three hours later Tim came back. He was very drunk. He staggered into my room and threw himself down on the bed.

" 'I've lost him,' he said. 'I've lost the only thing I'd got in the whole bloody world.'

"Then he broke down completely. I'd heard of people being rent by grief, but I'd never seen it before. His whole body was shaken by his sobs. I tried to com-

[8 5]

fort him—without much effect. But gradually he got calmer. And then the real truth came out at last. In fact I'd almost guessed it.

"Tim and Don were on the run. They were deserters from the Army. They'd got into trouble once already for overstaying their leave, and they'd been sent to the prison. They saw trouble looming ahead again. Their sergeant had got it in for them, Tim said, and they couldn't face another stretch in a military prison. Then their unit was posted to Cyprus. The troopship stopped in Gibraltar. They decided to take their chance. They were close friends—they would face the world together. So—with the kind of quixotic lunacy that only those who've had experience of the breed can credit—they deserted in Gib and crossed over to Tangier, their idea being that they'd get a job together on one of the smuggling boats. But it hadn't worked out that way. And now the mainstay of Tim's life had been taken away. He was shattered and inconsolable."

❧ ❧ ❧ ❧ ❧ ❧

"I COULD bear anything so long as Don was around," Tim had said. "I could bear having no parents and no home to go back to, and not a penny. I could put up with the thought that one day they were bound to catch up on me and I'd be sent back to the prison. I could put up with living from hand to mouth, selling what I'd got to offer in exchange for cash to get food and drink. Somehow it didn't seem to matter. I'd share the money with Don anyhow. And I'd rather it was me that picked up a geezer and went back with him than Don did. I'd learned to look after myself. I didn't care all that much. I'd got Don, and so long as I'd got him nothing else counted."

Tim raised his head with a long sigh.

"But now I've lost him," Tim said. "I've lost him for keeps, I know that. And I've got nothing left in the world. Nothing."

Tim lay back and stared up at the ceiling, his face twisted with grief. And as Ewing gazed at him in the stillness of the night he made his plan.

The next morning he took Tim for a walk round the Marshan and told him the plan in outline.

Essentially, Ewing's scheme was simple and logical. Tim must give himself up. He could not live out his life with the shadow of a prison sentence spreading over him. Eventually, the authorities were almost certain to catch him. Tim must surrender of his own accord. Ewing would provide the best solicitor he could find to appear on Tim's behalf at the court martial. Tim would plead guilty. In extenuation he would say that he had been driven to desert from his unit by the intensity of his inclination toward his own sex. This would make certain of his discharge from the Service. Even if his sentence were as much as six months he would serve it in a civilian prison. Ewing would give him a testimonial as his employer, and he would write a letter to the authorities guaranteeing to employ Tim as a mechanic on his discharge.

As Ewing had expected, Tim rejected the plan violently.

"I'm not giving myself up," he said. "Not after all I've been through to get away from them. Do you think I'm soft in the head? Give myself up—just for them to do what they like with me? I'm not a complete fool."

But Ewing was both patient and persuasive. By the following evening Tim had agreed. Ewing immediately telephoned his solicitor in London. The plan was put into operation, and it worked. Tim was discharged from the Service. He was given a sentence of three months which he served in Winchester jail.

Ewing redecorated the top flat in the villa. He counted the days before Tim should rejoin him permanently.

"I shall never forget those days of waiting for him," Ewing said, smiling at Arnold ruefully.

"It was agony to be parted from him. Yet I'd got so much to look forward to. Each day I'd make fresh plans for our future together or I'd think of some new present I could give him. Then there was all the excitement of getting a letter from him. He hated prison, he said. But he was well and, like me, he was counting the days until he was released.

"I'd worked out every detail of his first night back in Tangier. I'd rehearsed our meeting at the airport and our drive back to the villa in the new convertible I'd had shipped out. I knew what cocktail I'd make him, where we'd sit, what we'd talk about. I knew every

[88]

course I'd order for him at the *Pavillon,* the vintage of each wine.

"I suppose I'd looked forward to his return so much that the reality was bound to be an anticlimax. And it was.

"Tim arrived back tired and nervous. He'd been drinking on the plane on the way out. By dinnertime he was tight. Our meal at the *Pavillon* was a disaster. I was partly to blame. You see, I'd expected him to be grateful for what I'd done for him. I should have known better. So far as Tim was concerned, I and I alone had been responsible for sending him to prison.

"What's more, I should have known better than to imagine that Tim had spent his time in prison thinking about me. He'd scarcely given me a thought. During the long dark nights in his cell he'd worried about one person, and one person only—Don. For some perverse reason—probably from wishful thinking—he'd got it into his head that Don now bitterly regretted leaving with Louis Dubois, the Belgian banker. Tim was convinced that Don was unhappy and needed him. So during the dragging hours of his sentence Tim had formed the lunatic plan of setting out in search for Don and bringing him back to Tangier.

"Naturally, I refused to take this plan seriously, and our first evening ended in a row. When we got back to the villa, Tim rushed to his room and locked the door. I spent a lonely sleepless night, wondering if I hadn't made a ghastly mistake. But the next morning Tim was very penitent, and I must say delightfully affectionate. He never mentioned Don's name once all day.

"I reckoned I had won the first round.

"The next two months were the happiest I'd ever known. It was spring. The weather was perfect. The countryside was very green and dappled with wild flowers. We drove out to the caves for picnics. We spent a weekend in the Rîf mountains. We went for a trip on the yacht. I bought Tim a wardrobe of clothes and a gold wristwatch. We went out to dine with Lavinia and Milly, who adored him, and with Milo Branch and the rest of the gang, who didn't.

"Though Tim still refused to go to Wayne's bar because he thought that poor Wayne was responsible for Don meeting the Belgian—which was true in its way —he now mentioned Don's name so seldom that I began to believe that he was forgetting about him. I only had two small worries toward the end of those wonderful sun-blessed days. I worried because I seemed to be making little headway in the gradual process of extending the horizon of Tim's knowledge of things. He was still narrow-minded and surprisingly bigoted. His mind was so firmly set in the grooves of his old likes and dislikes that it was difficult to dislodge him from the prejudices of his previous background. For instance, he refused to believe that Proust was a great writer, because someone had told him that Proust was an old queen. Tim went in for what he called 'masculine writers.' He admired Kipling— which was a good start. He also admired the works of Peter Cheyney—which was not quite the same thing. And I always found it difficult to reason with him. Tim had got the persistent obstinacy of a really stupid person who clings to his argument as fiercely as a dog to a favorite bone. But Tim wasn't stupid by any means, and I was determined to develop his natural intelligence.

"My second mild worry was that he was drinking too much. I tried to stop him. But I had to do it gently. I was afraid of sounding like a governess.

"In spite of my two worries. I was still wildly happy as the third month began. But I knew that my state of almost euphoric bliss couldn't last. I knew there'd be a row sooner or later. And there was—all because I was fool enough to accept the invitation when Milo Branch suggested giving a dinner party for my birthday. There'd be nine guests, Milo said. We'd change into evening dress for the occasion. It was the evening dress part of it that made me accept. Tim had just had a dinner jacket made, and I wanted an excuse for him to wear it. So I welcomed Milo's dinner party—idiot that I was. I ought to have known that Milo was gunning for Tim in his jealous way.

"The evening began badly because Tim came back late from the yacht and had to dress in a hurry. He was nervous. He'd already drunk too much. Then he couldn't tie his bow tie and he was irritated when I had to do it for him. He was in a vile temper even before we arrived at Milo's overfurnished and overheated villa. And of course the whole gang was there— including Joanna Keating and Rosemary Burke, whom you've never met, and never will meet, if you're lucky.

"For some reason dinner was delayed, so we stood

around Milo's stuffy drawing room, gazing at Ming bowls on top of red lacquer cabinets, as we drank round after round of tepid Martinis. By the time we got into dinner Tim was drunk. I saw Luke West wink at that podgy boor Geoffrey Purcell when Tim tripped on the step leading down to the dining room. I was furious with myself for having accepted the invitation in the first place, and I was yet more furious with Tim for being drunk. You've got to appreciate how angry I was with Tim to understand what happened.

"All went well until the meat course, when Milo began telling a long and completely pointless story about an Italian princess who went to stay with Louis Dubois in his castle on the Loire. Inasmuch as Milo's stories generally have *some* point, I'm convinced to this day that he did it on purpose. But at first his game didn't work because Tim didn't connect Louis Dubois with the Belgian banker who'd whisked away young Don.

"It was Luke West who did the trick . . ."

Luke West had raised his bony head from his plate and put the fatal question.

"Do you think the princess will follow our dear Louis out to Mexico?" he asked.

At the word "Mexico" Tim sat up and began to listen.

"If she *does* follow him to Mexico, whatever will she make of the new boyfriend he's taken out with him?" Milo said, patting the side of his smooth grey hair. "Quite a pert little number I thought. But a shameless little gold digger if there ever was one."

Tim put down his knife and fork.

"Are you talking about Don?" he asked, scowling.

Milo turned slowly toward Tim and examined him as if he were surprised to see him sitting there.

"I honestly can't remember the boy's name," he said. "It was some piece of trade he picked up in Wayne's bar."

Conversation had stopped. Every person at the table was now listening.

"Just say that again," Tim said threateningly.

"I don't see why I should say it again," Milo replied shrilly. "I should have thought it was perfectly clear the first time."

Ewing decided that it was time he intervened.

"Don was a great friend of Tim's," he explained.

"Then I can only say I'm sorry for him," Milo answered.

"*You'll* be sorry in a moment," Tim said.

Milo swung round and faced Ewing.

"Are you going to allow your friend to threaten me at my own table?" he asked.

"Forget it, Tim," Ewing said appeasingly. "Milo didn't know Don was a close friend of yours."

"I don't care if he did or not," Tim blurted out. "He still hasn't said he's sorry."

"And I have no intention whatsoever of doing so," Milo said, trembling with annoyance. "I'm sorry, Ewing, but I simply refuse to be shouted at and menaced in my own house."

"Don't let's spoil the evening," Ewing said quickly, before Tim had time to speak. "Let's talk about something else. Shall I confess to you all how old I am today?"

"That would be interesting to know," Luke West murmured.

Tim pushed back his chair and got up.

"You talk about something else then," he said angrily. "I'm off."

In silence Tim walked out of the room.

With an effort Ewing raised his head from his brandy glass and looked into Arnold's eyes.

"I suppose you think I should have left Milo's dinner party when Tim did," Ewing said. "You're right. I should have done. But after all, the dinner party had been given in my honor. Though Milo had provoked the row, Tim had been tiresomely drunk, and I was livid with him. So for one fatal second I hesitated; and by the time I'd decided to leave, it was too late. Milo was apologizing, Lavinia was consoling me, and Milly was saying that her whole evening would be wrecked if I didn't stay and that she'd put on her new dress from Dior especially for my benefit. Lavinia then announced with mistaken loyalty that if I left the party she would feel obliged to leave too. What could I do but stay and try to make the best of it?

"After dinner, when someone suggested going on to a nightclub, I applauded the idea enthusiastically. I was dreading going back to the villa.

"I got back home at three in the morning. I climbed up the spiral staircase that leads from my living room to the top flat. The door was unlocked. I went in. Tim hadn't come back yet. His pullover and jeans were lying on the bed where he had thrown them when he changed for the dinner party. How long ago that seemed! I looked vaguely round the room. On the dressing table was a small leather photograph frame, with its two panels hinged together so that it stood upright. In the left panel was the photo of a young newly wed couple, sprinkled with confetti, smiling resolutely in the grimy church porch. They were Tim's parents. The father had the same build, the same tousled hair, the same handsome, rather fleshy face. It gave me a shock to think how young his parents must have been when they had married. No more than Tim's age. In the right-hand panel was a photo of Don in a bathing slip on the beach of some seaside town. There was a blurred pier in the background. Don stood with his hands on his hips and his head thrown back, grinning almost contemptuously at the camera. He was an attractive creature—but there was more to it than that. There was something beguiling in his impudent little face. I could understand Tim's obsession for him.

"Suddenly I saw the whole evening from Tim's point of view. He had put on a dinner jacket and gone to Milo's villa to please me. But he had got drunk, so he had failed. Then the one person alive he really loved had been insulted, so he had lost his temper. Who could blame him? I couldn't. I blamed myself—and bitterly—for my lack of loyalty to him. As I stood looking down at the photographs, I heard a taxi draw up outside the garden gates. I went downstairs to the living room.

[9 5]

"Tim was very drunk. He staggered in and closed the door behind him and stood there swaying as he peered at me through bloodshot eyes.

" 'I'm leaving in the morning,' he said. 'I'm fed up with you, and I'm fed up with your friends. I've had it in a big way. I'm sick and tired of being told to do this and do that, read this and read that. I might be at school the way you carry on. Anyway, you're just a bunch of bloody snobs, the lot of you. Ask old Christiansen and his wife what *they* think. They just despise the lot of you—the whole fucking bunch. I've had it, I tell you. I'm off!'

"Then Tim said a great deal more that I can't even bear to remember because it was so wounding. But I kept my temper through it all. I made myself remember that it was I who had first been disloyal . . .

"At last Tim had exhausted all he'd got to say, and I managed to persuade him to go to bed. He slept till noon. He appeared before lunch looking pale and tired.

" 'I was drunk last night,' Tim said. 'I made a fool of myself. I'm sorry. Can we forget about it?'

" 'Let's forget the whole evening,' I said. 'I promise you it was all my fault.'

" 'Can we have a cocktail to celebrate our forgetting it?' Tim asked.

" 'What shall we have then?'

" 'Bacardis,' Tim said. 'They're my favorite.' "

"So the third stage of our relationship began over a cocktail shaker. Perhaps that was symbolic of it—

because from that day on Tim began to drink pretty constantly. When drunk he was nervous and surly. I knew it was only a question of time before he turned on me again. But what could I do? That evening at Milo's villa Tim had been humiliated, and he never forgot it. From that day onward he was on the defensive. The slightest interference by me was apt to send him into a sullen rage. The infuriating part of it was that I knew the precise reason for his rage—though I could do nothing to prevent it. I knew the reason because I'd listened to his drunken outpourings that fatal night. It was quite simple. Tim now resented me because—in his mind—I represented authority. I was the foster parents who cared for him after his parents had been killed in the blitz. I was the headmaster who'd beaten him at his approved school. Yes. Tim was sent to an approved school when he was fifteen, and he had loathed it. One of his reasons for joining the Army was to get away from the place. To him, I was the officer in charge of his troop. In his mind, I stood in the position of the sergeants in the prison who'd systematically bullied him and tried to break down his resistance. More recently, I was the prison warder for his cell.

"I knew the position I was in. How could I escape from it except by giving him complete freedom? But if I let him come and go as he pleased, he'd drink his way round the bars all night and limp back to the villa, sick and exhausted, at breakfast time. It was an impossible position. Each evening that he went out on his own I was terrified of what might happen . . .

"I realized that sooner or later I'd have to exert my authority. I'd have to tell him to behave himself or get out. But I dreaded the moment. I couldn't face the possibility of losing him for good. Tim was the incarnation of everything that I'd hoped to find in life. I'd backed him with all my dreams of happiness. How could I face losing him? Day after day I delayed the final showdown—though I was near the breaking point. It was Tim who put an end to the period of uncertainty.

"It was a dismal evening. Rain had been falling steadily all day. But I was delighted, because for once Tim had promised to stay in. I'd bought a new recording of *Der Rosenkavalier,* and I suggested that we should play it after dinner. But when we'd finished the extremely carefully planned meal I'd laid on for the occasion, I could see that Tim was restless. He walked nervously about the room, chain-smoking. He poured himself a large brandy and gulped it down neat. He was obviously in no mood for music. I sat down on the sofa and pretended to read a book. When I looked up Tim was standing over me.

" 'Do we have to stay here fooling around all evening?' he asked. 'Can't we go down to some bar with some life in it? Why don't we look in at the Parade Bar or Dean's? The Mar Chica might even be open. Or Paul's place. For heaven's sake let's go somewhere—and not sit about in this dull room all night.'

"I was tired, and I'd got a headache. Even so, I might have gone with him if he hadn't said the room was dull. If I'd gone with him, everything might have been different. Might have been. Though I expect it would have ended much the same in the end."

"I'm tired," Ewing said. "Why not go on your own?"

"I can't," Tim muttered sulkily. "It's raining. I'll never get a taxi. You know that as well as I do."

"Take the car then," Ewing said, throwing the keys across to him, as he had done several times before.

"Thanks," Tim said.

As before, Ewing stopped himself from warning Tim to drive carefully. He was now morbidly afraid of sounding like the voice of authority.

"Enjoy yourself," Ewing said.

"Don't worry. I will. I don't expect I'll be long. But if I'm back late, I won't disturb you."

Ewing knew what that meant. With an effort he forced himself to smile while gusts of rage and frustration swept over him.

"Have a good time," Ewing said.

"Good night," Tim cried out cheerfully as he closed the door behind him.

At three o'clock in the morning the telephone extension rang beside Ewing's bed. His heart was thudding as he picked up the receiver.

"Mr. Baird?" It was a man's voice with a foreign accent.

"Ewing Baird speaking."

"Here is Captain Martinez," the man said. "I am speaking from the police station on the old mountain road."

Ewing's mouth was dry.

"Yes," he said. "What's happened?"

"Half an hour ago your car was found wrecked in a ditch near the Moslem cemetery," the police officer said. "The driver of the car is in the hospital."

For a moment, while pictures of Tim's mangled body flashed across his mind, Ewing could not speak.

"Do you hear me?" the man asked.

"Is he badly hurt?"

Ewing was surprised to notice how calm his voice sounded.

"Do not worry yourself too much, Mr. Baird," the police officer said. "He is very much cut about and his leg is broken. But he will live."

❧ ❧ ❧ ❧ ❧ ❧

EWING walked across to the chimney piece and stood looking down at the logs smoldering in the grate.

"By the time I could move Tim out of hospital," Ewing continued, "the summer had gone—which made a cruise on the yacht out of the question. So I drove him up to Marrakesh in the car I'd bought to replace the one he'd wrecked.

"The period of Tim's convalescence was wonderfully serene on the whole. He could limp on his crutches round the garden of our hotel, past the orange trees and flower beds to the little olive grove beyond, where we'd spend the morning in the sunshine, reading the English papers, which were sometimes only a day old, gossiping about the other guests, learn-

[1 0 0]

ing Arabic from a grammar I'd bought, and gazing up at fleecy clouds fringing the vast chain of the Atlas mountains.

"Tim seemed quite happy. As soon as his nerves had been strong enough to stand it, I had a showdown with him. I told him he must reform or get out. And I was delighted how well he took the ultimatum. He seemed genuinely penitent. He promised to lay off hard liquor for good and take only a little beer or wine. He promised to stay in more.

" 'I owe you a big debt of gratitude for the way you've treated me since the accident,' Tim said. 'Just give me time, and I'll do my best to make it up to you.'

"From that moment I could see that he was making an effort to please me. I was thrilled. I prayed to the gods it would last, I racked my brains to think of new ways of keeping him amused in Marrakesh . . .

"On the whole Tim was contented. He was certainly interested by the other guests in the hotel—particularly by a loud-voiced, flashy Frenchwoman of about fifty, who was always at the bar standing huge rounds of drinks. Her name was Yvonne Blanchard. She was the widow of a button manufacturer in Lyons. She was embarrassingly buxom but she always wore low-cut tight-fitting dresses. She reeked of scent and positively dripped with costume jewelry. And she fell hook, line and sinker for Tim.

"I must confess that Tim was looking superb. Giving up spirits had restored all his radiance. The scars on his neck and forehead somehow made him all the more attractive. Poor Yvonne made a play for him. It was pathetic to watch her, pointing her breasts at him as if they were loaded pistols that could penetrate him with the bullets of her charm, ogling her bulbous eyes at him, waggling her hips, making coy gestures with her bejeweled hands, crooning at him in what she imagined to be a seductive, broken accent. It was pathetic—but at the same time faintly revolting.

"Tim was fascinated and rather impressed. She flattered him monstrously, of course. But I didn't mind. I was even glad that she took him off my hands occasionally, because—to be completely honest—though I was as devoted to Tim as ever—if not more so—I found his company twelve hours a day slightly wearing. I was only too pleased to be able to retire to my bedroom with a book.

"One evening after dinner, I'd left her drooling over him at the bar and I'd gone to bed. Shortly after I'd put out my lights I heard Tim come into his room, and begin undressing. Presently he opened the communicating door and walked into my room. I switched on the light. Immediately I saw that he was a little bit tight. He stood with his weight on his sound leg, swaying slightly and smiling down at me. He was stark naked. He looked more like Antinous than ever . . ."

"Did I wake you?" Tim asked.

"No," Ewing said. "I'd only just stopped reading. Come and sit down."

"Thanks," Tim said, obeying him.

"Had a good evening?"

"Fabulous. Yvonne was in cracking form. She ordered a whole magnum of champagne."

"And you drank it?"

"Only some of it," Tim said with a laugh. "There were others to help."

"What others?"

"Yvonne and the barman, for instance."

"Jolly little party."

"You know, Yvonne must be terrifically rich. Did you see the diamond bracelet she was wearing tonight?"

"One could hardly miss it."

"Do you know how much it's worth?"

"No, but I can guess."

"Ten thousand pounds."

"Yvonne told you that?"

"Yes. She told me herself."

"Then she's a vulgar and stupid woman."

Tim jerked back his head as if Ewing had hit him.

"Why?" Tim asked.

"She's a vulgar woman because it's vulgar to tell people how much your jewelry is worth."

"And why is she stupid?"

"She's stupid because she ought to have guessed that you'd tell me."

"Perhaps she did guess. I don't see why that was stupid."

"She's perfectly aware that I'm not a country bumpkin. I've been around quite a bit. So I was bound to know."

"Know what?"

"Know that her bracelet is paste. It's worth a hundred pounds at the most."

"I don't believe you."

"Would you like to watch her face when I ask her?"

Slowly Tim lowered his head.

"I suppose you're right," he said.

"I'm certain I'm right."

"Then she was telling me a lie."

"She wanted to impress you."

"So she's not only vulgar and stupid. She's dishonest as well."

"That's correct."

Tim gazed down at the scars that were healing on his large, red hands.

"I don't understand you a scrap," Tim said. "You get livid because poor Yvonne is vulgar and stupid, as you call it. But you don't give a hoot that she's dishonest."

"That's probably because I'm more disturbed by sins against aesthetic values than I am by sins against morality."

Tim got up from the bed where he had been sitting.

"Or is it because you're a cracking snob?" he asked, and walked back into his own room.

"But that evening was the only time we came near to a quarrel," Ewing said. "The rest of our stay in Marrakesh was entrancingly peaceful, and Tim seemed cheerful enough—though I noticed that he spent less time with Yvonne at the bar.

"Three weeks later we drove back to Tangier. I

think both of us felt the old familiar excitement of being home again. Tim could hardly wait to visit the yacht. Even though we couldn't go for long cruises, we could always cross over to Algeciras for a weekend at the Reina Christina. Now that he'd learned to navigate and supervise the engines, I'd made Tim the skipper of the yacht, and I was paying him a regular skipper's salary. Tim was taking the job extremely seriously. I could hardly tear him away from the harbor. I began to believe that at last he was settling down.

"There was only one slightly disturbing element during that period. Down in the harbor Tim had made friends with a couple of engineers off one of the larger smuggling ships. George and Harry their names were. They were tough young louts from Liverpool. Their one idea of having a good time was to get drunk and find a woman to sleep with. For some reason Tim thought they were both wonderful. He enjoyed nothing better than to go drinking and wenching with them around the town.

" 'I like going about with ordinary folk for a change,' Tim said. 'I'm tired of witty old queens.'

"So long as I didn't have to meet George and Harry and so long as Tim kept off the spirits and didn't catch any ghastly disease, I didn't mind too much. But I do admit I was delighted when the two of them left on their ship for their usual smuggling run to Naples, Marseilles and Barcelona. It was glorious to have Tim all to myself once more.

"Six weeks later George and Harry were back in Tangier. With them was a little Spanish tart called

Inez whom they'd picked up in a brothel in Barcelona. She was sixteen years old, quite tiny, with sleek black hair and a snub nose. Her pert, rather *gamine* expression reminded me faintly of Don. Perhaps that was why poor Tim fell for her so badly.

"Tim went mad about her. 'It's the normal coming out in me at last,' he said.

"The very first night he met her he managed to get her away from George and Harry—I expect she was fed up with their clumsy love-making by that time. I don't blame her. They were both quite hideous.

"One of my few firm rules was that Tim wasn't allowed to bring any of the pieces of trade he picked up back to the villa. So he took Inez to a house off the Zocco Chico in the Calle Los Arcos, one of the dark narrow alleys in the Moorish quarter. And there they spent their first strenuous night together.

"During his time in the army before he met Don, Tim had slept with several prostitutes—because it was the accepted thing to do. But he had never enjoyed the experience. Inez was different. I gather from what Tim told me that she was extremely passionate and skillful. Tim made an assignation with her for the following night. The next afternoon George and Harry attacked him as he walked along the quay. Tim got the better of the fight, so they never troubled him again. But I realized that in their frustrated rage they would certainly have told Inez about Tim's relationship with me. However, Inez turned up in the house in Calle Los Arcos that very night. And Tim was pleasantly surprised by the variety of her technique. There seemed nothing she didn't go in for. Almost instinctively she seemed to know how to touch the nerve that thrilled him most. By the end of the week he was besotted by her. The strange thing about it was that the more besotted he became, the more generous he was in his displays of affection toward me. So I had nothing to complain about.

"One afternoon after our siesta—when Tim had shown himself unusually affectionate—he asked me if he could possibly bring Inez to supper at the villa some evening. I'd been waiting for that question for some time.

"My answer came pat. 'Why not bring her up to dine tonight?' I said.

"You see, I wanted to meet the girl. I wanted to discover what the charms were that so beguiled my friend.

"Tim's face brightened. 'Thanks,' he said, pressing my hand. 'I was afraid you'd be cross with me for asking. But I do so want you to meet her. After all, you're the two best friends I've got in the world.'

"It was hardly flattering to be put on the same level as a little prostitute from a Barcelona brothel. But I didn't say anything. I smiled as I listened to Tim splashing in the bath. I smiled and bided my time."

That evening, punctually at a quarter past eight, Tim brought Inez to the villa.

Inez was nervous and unsure of her reception. On

the way she had stopped at several bars to give herself courage; her breath reeked of *pastis*. She was wearing a brightly colored dress that obviously came from one of the Indian shops off the Zocco Grande, and she had put on too much make-up. But Ewing found her extremely attractive. His first thought was that he would like to sleep with her. He imagined himself stripping her naked, stretching her out on his bed, then slowly wiping the make-up from her pert urchin-like face before lying down beside her. He wondered how much he would have to pay her. He then dismissed the idea as wild fantasy, for nothing could be more certain to wound Tim deeply.

Tim was standing awkwardly beside her chair, looking toward Ewing with anxious eyes. Ewing smiled at him reassuringly while he mixed a strong cocktail. When they sat down to dinner, Inez made her first mistake. She held out her right arm and rattled the gold bracelet on it in Ewing's face.

"Is it not pretty?" she asked.

"Very pretty," Ewing answered politely.

"Do you know who give it me? Tim here give it me this evening."

Before their siesta that day, Tim had asked Ewing if he could borrow half of his next month's wages. Partly for the joy of seeing the gratitude on his face, partly to maintain his influence over him, Ewing had given him the money as a present. Tim had promptly spent the money on Inez . . .

Ewing struggled to control the irritation that was spreading over him. He still had got to find out about

Inez. He had worked out his plan with fastidious care. He began talking rapidly about Tangier, using deliberately long and unusual English words. Inez could not follow what he was saying and looked blank. This was Ewing's excuse to break into fluent Spanish, for he knew that Tim only understood a few words of the language. In quick colloquial jargon, Ewing told Inez that she was smashing, a winner, a complete knockout, and that already he was hopelessly in love with her. Because he was genuinely attracted to her his words were all the more convincing. Inez smiled and sat back more comfortably in her chair. Ewing began to talk about Barcelona. From Barcelona it was easy to switch to her meeting with George and Harry, and then to the brothel where she had worked. Meanwhile, Bashir was filling up the wineglasses unobtrusively and as yet Tim suspected nothing.

"Did they treat you well at the house you worked in?" Ewing asked.

"Fairly well."

"How long have you been at the job?"

"Four years."

"Do you mean you started when you were twelve?"

"Yes. Or rather they started me."

"Then you must have known a good few men already."

"That's true enough."

"Met anyone like our friend here before?"

"Never."

"Oh, come now," Ewing said, "he's not all that terrific."

"*Sí,*" Inez said. "*Una polla enorma.*"

Tim looked up at one of the few words of Spanish that he knew. Ewing was afraid he would interrupt.

"Does he pay you well?" he asked Inez hurriedly, in Spanish.

"He pays me nothing. I would not take money from him."

"What about your bracelet?"

"That was a present."

"How long do you think the affair will last?"

"As long as he wants it to. I will never leave him."

"Is he as valiant in bed as that?"

"He is very valiant with me. But I do not stay with him for his *polla.* I stay with him because I love him."

"Nonsense," said Ewing. "You love him because he's good in bed."

"I love him because he's honest and true."

"You've been reading too many magazine stories."

"He is the only man I have ever loved. He is all man, through and through. I love him, I tell you."

Inez turned excitedly to Tim. "I have tell him how very much I love you," she said.

"Yes. And she's been saying how good you were in bed," Ewing added. "She says you're the best she's ever known."

"I do not speak of bed. He is lying to you," Inez cried.

"You heard her use the word *polla,*" Ewing laughed. "What do you suppose she used that word in connection with? Cricket?"

"Stop it, both of you," Tim shouted suddenly. "Stop it."

"I not stop it," Inez said. "Your friend is no good friend to you, Tim. He does not want you to love me because he is a *maricón*. How you say it in English? He is one of the wrong people."

Ewing laughed. "I've never heard it called *that* before," he murmured.

His calm poise enraged Inez. Her narrow eyes glared at him. "You think Tim stay with you because he love you," she cried. "I tell you Tim stay with you because you have money."

"Shut up, Inez," Tim said.

"I tell you Tim will never love you as he love me, because Tim is not a *maricón*."

"Who are you trying to convince?" Ewing asked her.

"Tim is valiant. He is a man. A real man."

"Not one of 'the wrong people,'" Ewing prompted with a laugh.

Inez glowered at him. "You can laugh. You make me sick. You are no man. You are a *maricón*," she said, quivering in fury. Then she gathered the saliva into her mouth and spat across the table.

In silence Ewing examined the yellow gob of spittle that was lying on his lace table mat. Then he turned round to Tim.

"And now," he said, "I suggest that you should take your common little tart away from my villa."

"Don't worry. We're going all right," Tim muttered.

"Yes. We go," Inez cried. "And I not come here again."

"One moment," Ewing said sharply, as Tim flung open the door. "One moment . . . Tim, I want to see you later this evening."

"I shan't be coming back tonight."

"I'm asking you to come back. I want to talk to you."

"You can talk tomorrow morning on the yacht."

"I'm asking you to come back this evening."

"I've already told you that I'm staying out."

"I'm asking you, Tim."

"You know the answer, don't you?"

"Please."

"Do not listen to him, Tim," Inez said. "He want to take you away from me."

"Are you coming back?"

"For the last time—no. Good night, and thanks for sweet nothing," Tim shouted angrily as he followed Inez out of the room.

Ewing stooped down and put a log on the fire.

"For quite a while that night I'd made up my mind to get rid of him," Ewing continued. "I rehearsed the very words I'd use when I sent him packing. But by midnight I'd realized the truth. Even after all that had happened, I still couldn't face the prospect of life without him—without hearing his footstep, seeing his smile of welcome, listening to his rather hoarse laugh, watching the flecks of light in his strange brown eyes. I needed the brightness of his presence, the warmth of his affection. I couldn't imagine living a single week without him—let alone a month or a year. He'd got under my skin. He was part of me. I couldn't exist without him.

"So I'd got to put up with Inez. I'd got to endure it

until his infatuation with her was over. But my immediate problem was to smooth over that night's flaming row. Tim would probably go down to the yacht in the morning. But I wanted him to have plenty of time to cool down, so I stayed up at the villa . . ."

The following day Tim had appeared an hour before lunch, looking as if he had spent a sleepless night. The scent Inez used still lingered about him—her scent and the reek of *pastis*. Tim had not gone to the yacht; he had been drinking all morning.

"I'm sorry about the scene at dinner," Ewing said quickly.

"So am I," Tim replied.

Tim's sullenness annoyed Ewing. After all, Ewing thought, *he* hadn't shouted about queers or spat on the table.

"I'm afraid little Inez got overexcited," Ewing said.

"She wasn't the only one."

Ewing tried to smile. "Then let's say that Inez was the *first* to get excited."

"Hadn't she every reason to?"

"No. Quite frankly I don't think she had."

"Not when you asked her to go to bed with you, and then insulted her because she refused to?"

Ewing stared at Tim in real astonishment. "Is that what she told you?" he asked.

"It's the truth, isn't it?"

Ewing crossed over to Tim. "Can you see me being such a fool as to ask her to go to bed with me?" he asked.

Tim was silent. Ewing put an arm round his shoulder.

"Come on, Tim," he said. "Let's forget about it all, shall we?"

Suddenly Tim broke away from him.

"Don't touch me," Tim said. "I'm sick of being mauled about by you."

"Then you're a better actor than I supposed— because you've never given me that impression. Quite the contrary."

"I feel unclean afterwards."

"That's a very dramatic expression. Who put *that* idea into your head? Inez or George and Harry?"

"Can't I have an idea of my own?"

"You can. But you very seldom do."

"Thanks for the compliment."

"I'm afraid sarcasm doesn't suit you."

"What about you? You always seem to be so calm and condescending. But I know better. Look at your hands. Why, you're trembling with rage—and all because I said you made me feel unclean. Well, you *do*."

"Be careful, Tim. I must warn you that I'm getting rather tired of our unending quarrels."

" 'Be careful, Tim!' Why should I have to be careful? Why not you? I'm not frightened of you. I'm just telling you that you revolt me. Why do you think I always take a bath afterwards? Because it makes me feel clean and a man again."

Ewing turned his heavy, sad face toward Arnold.

"Then I lost my temper completely," Ewing said. "I

[1 1 4]

went quite mad. I can't even remember half the things I said. But I suppose they were the usual kind of cheap insults one uses on such occasions. I can remember telling him that I didn't intend allowing my life to be inconvenienced by a common little slut like Inez. I pointed out to him that the money he spent on her was mine. Then I went back into the past. I reminded him that when I first met him he was a deserter. I reminded him that while he'd been on the run he'd gone with any man who'd give him money—bath or no bath. I rehearsed all I'd done for him—including my forgiveness for the smashed car. I reviled him for his crass ingratitude and his gross stupidity. I'd never lost my temper completely with him before.

"Tim never said a word. He just stared at me in a dazed kind of way. I could see that his face had gone very white. I wanted to stop now. But I'd lost all control. It was horribly frightening. I could hear my voice grinding on and on. And I couldn't stop it.

"Suddenly—as if he couldn't bear the sight of my face an instant longer—Tim turned away from me and stared down at the floor. The sight of his bowed head calmed me. I stopped my tirade. For an instant there was dead silence. Then—with a kind of wild cry of anguish—Tim rushed across the room and ran up the spiral staircase leading to his flat. He left the communicating door open, so I could hear him moving about upstairs. I could hear the sound of drawers being pulled out and cupboards opened. Tim was packing.

"Even then I believe I could have stopped him. But

[1 1 5]

something held me back—pure pride, I suppose. I rang for Bashir and told him I'd be alone for lunch and dinner. The calm tone of my voice as I spoke helped to restore my confidence. I poured myself out a drink. I could hear that Tim was still packing. Part of me longed to rush upstairs and explain that it was all a mistake—some ghastly nightmare we must both forget. I wanted to tell him I loved him. But I stayed downstairs, sipping my brandy and ginger ale, forcing myself to make an inventory of all of Tim's misdeeds.

"Half an hour later, I heard a taxi pull up outside the garden gate. This was my last chance. But I didn't move. I stayed crouched in my chair staring at my glass. Then I heard the back door of the top flat open and close. I went to the window. I saw Tim walk down the drive to the garden gate, carrying the two suitcases I'd bought him to take to Marrakesh. I saw him drive away in the taxi. The time was one o'clock.

"Throughout that afternoon I tried to persuade myself that I was doing the right thing in letting him go, that it would be showing fatal weakness to take him back, that even if we had a reconciliation the same kind of scene would occur all over again. By seven o'clock I'd failed dismally to convince myself that I'd done anything except behave like an hysterical idiot. And I started phoning the bars . . . I didn't track him down, but I discovered that Tim was still in Tangier. At each bar I left a message asking him to call me urgently. I didn't say why.

"Then I got on to Lavinia and to Milly. I confessed

that Tim and I had had a blazing row. I asked them to be kind enough to try and contact Tim in town and tell him I was sorry and wanted him back. They were both sweet. They said they'd do all they could. I then wrote a long letter of apology to Tim, begging him to forgive me and come back. I rang Bashir. I asked him to take the letter to the house in Calle Los Arcos where I expected Tim and Inez would be staying the night. After Bashir had left I thought of going down into town to find Tim myself. But I was afraid he might ring while I was out. Besides, I couldn't abide the thought of meeting him with other people around —especially Inez. I couldn't face another scene. So I stayed up on the Marshan, waiting, waiting for the phone to ring. Just waiting.

"I tried to read a book. I could only think of Tim's white face staring at me in horror. The silence seemed to press down over the room like a grey cloak.

"Shortly after midnight the phone rang. I leaped up and rushed across the room. I snatched up the receiver. It was Lavinia speaking from some nightclub. I could hear dance music in the background. She'd been drinking. Her voice was slurred.

" 'I've seen Tim,' she said.

" 'Where?'

" 'In the Mar Chica.'

" 'Did you give him my message?'

" 'Of course I did.'

" 'What did he say?'

" 'He just said thank you.'

" 'Nothing else?'

"'Well, that little Spanish girl of his was with him. I don't suppose he *could* say much more.'

"'But you're sure he understood?' I asked.

"'Of course he understood. I'm not paralytic or anything.'

"'How long ago was that?'

"'Less than half an hour. I paid my bill and came straight here to phone you—loyal friend that I am.'

"'Bless you, Lavinia. Thank you very much,' I said.

"I then rang up the Mar Chica. As I dialed the number I could see the bar—a long slab of marble with a looking glass on the wall behind it. I could see the sawdust on the floor, the green walls and fluorescent lighting. But Tim and Inez had just left. They had probably gone back to Calle Los Arcos—which meant that Tim would get my letter.

"I didn't sleep that night. I kept hoping Tim would come back—though common sense told me that he was bound to spend the night with Inez. I waited in the living room. The night was very still. I could hear cars approaching from miles away. Each time I heard the sound of a car climbing up the hill to the Marshan I hoped it might be Tim.

"At three o'clock in the morning I heard a taxi stop outside. I rushed out into the garden. But the taxi had stopped in front of a villa farther down the lane, and I saw two Moors get out. I could see the gleam of their white *djellabas* in the moonlight.

"My last hope was that Tim would return in the morning—after he'd spent the night with Inez.

"It was a perfect day. The sun was shining from a

cloudless sky, and there was a pleasantly crisp breeze. I made a vow that if Tim came back I'd take him down to town and buy him a secondhand sports car I'd seen in the garage where my convertible was serviced. He'd never had a car of his own.

"At eleven the phone rang. Once again I rushed across the room. I grabbed the receiver. It was Wayne. He'd been down to the harbor to see off some American friends of his. Tim and Inez had left by the early morning ferry.

"I knew then that I'd lost him for good."

* * * * * * *

EWING stared down at the ashes in the grate.

"And all that took place over ten years ago," he told Arnold. "Over ten years."

Ewing glanced at Arnold's empty liqueur glass. "I'm afraid I've been a very bad host," he said. "I've talked far too much, and I've given you nothing to drink. What can I get you now? Shall I fix you a whisky and soda?"

"Thanks," Arnold replied. "I'd love one."

Ewing crossed to the drink tray.

"I've never told anyone that story before," he said. "And I've always wanted to—because I felt that telling it all, living through it all over again, might possibly have some kind of cathartic effect. I wonder if it has. Perhaps it's too early to tell."

While Ewing was getting the drinks, Arnold tried to sort out his thoughts. He had listened to the story in bemused horror. But what had surprised him most was that Ewing, who had appeared to be cold and ruthless, should reveal a side to his character that was sensitive and unashamedly sentimental. Arnold still could not make up his mind about Tim. Was the boy purely an opportunist? Had he lived with Ewing simply for what he could get out of him? Or had there been a genuine streak of affection? Probably he would never know, for it was difficult to perceive the boy's nature through the veil of Ewing's personality. Only one thing shone out clear beyond doubt. Tim had been devoted to Don, and Don had abandoned him.

Ewing handed him a glass.

"Did you ever hear of Tim again?" Arnold asked.

Ewing took three long gulps of whisky. "Yes," he said. "I heard of him. Less than a year later."

"Was Inez still with him?"

"Heavens no! That little affair only lasted three months. I gather they quarreled continually. Tim left Inez in Barcelona. I suppose she went back to the brothel where she belonged. When I heard of Tim he was working in a queer club in Soho. I was told he was unhappy. I still missed him terribly. So I cabled him, and I wrote to him. But I got no reply. Then Wayne announced he wanted to go on holiday to London. I rather suspect he was still hoping to pick up some news of little Don. In fact, we did eventually hear that Don had left Louis Dubois for a rich Canadian magazine proprietor. Don was happily established in Toronto. I believe he's still there.

"Anyhow Wayne wanted to go to London, so I paid

his return fare on the understanding that he'd do his best to persuade Tim to come back to me. I knew that Tim disliked Wayne, but I thought that he'd listen to him—particularly if he was unhappy. I'd even bought an open-date plane ticket from London to Tangier made out in Tim's name.

"His very first night in London, Wayne went round to the queer club. It was a dingy, smoke-filled room in a basement off Berwick Street. Serving behind the bar was Tim—much the same as ever, Wayne told me, except that he looked a bit pale and rather worn.

"Wayne went up to the bar and ordered a drink. Tim recognized him, but he didn't smile or say a word. Wayne waited for a suitable moment when the bar wasn't too full, then he gave Tim my message. He showed him the air ticket back to Tangier. Tim listened in silence to all that Wayne said about making a fresh start and leaving the squalid club with its avid-eyed clients. Then Tim spoke.

" 'Will you give Ewing a message from me?' he asked.

" 'You bet I will,' Wayne replied.

" 'Just tell him I don't want to know.'

" 'Nothing else?'

" 'Nothing. So do me a favor, will you, and push off.' "

Ewing sighed. He finished his drink and walked quickly to the drink tray to pour himself another.

"I can see him so clearly," Ewing said. "Standing with his weight on one leg, looking wonderfully like

Antinous. I can hear him saying it. 'Just tell him I don't want to know.' Anyhow that settled it. Wayne realized it was hopeless to try further. He finished his drink and left. That was ten years ago."

Ewing lit a cigarette.

"And you never saw Tim again?" Arnold asked.

To his surprise Ewing smiled. "Yes," Ewing said. "Yes, I did see Tim again. Only this last June, as a matter of fact. My tenants' lease of my London flat had come to an end, so I'd taken the opportunity of going over to England for a month, while the agents found me new tenants. I was drinking in a gay pub in Chelsea one evening at about seven o'clock. I was sitting at the bar and across the room, with his back turned to me, I happened to notice a burly, hefty-looking man, swilling down a pint of bitter. At that moment the man turned round, and I saw it was Tim. At first I could hardly recognize him, he'd put on so much weight. He looked a stout, middle-aged gentleman. I'd never have believed anyone could change so much. But there was no doubt of it. The thickset moon-faced man advancing toward me was Tim. He'd become gross past belief. However, I was delighted to see him again. All was forgiven if not forgotten. I took him out to dinner, and afterwards we did a round of the bars and clubs.

"I was interested to hear Tim's news. He'd got fed up with London after a while, it seemed. He'd drifted with a 'geezer' to Sheffield. But that hadn't worked out, so he'd come back to London where he'd met an out-of-work actor who'd persuaded him to start up a coffee-bar. So they'd opened their coffee-bar, in Folkestone of all places. Surprisingly enough, it was doing quite well. The actor had now found himself a job in television, so Tim was running the bar on his own with a paid staff. He'd just come up to London that night for a jaunt. Incidentally, he'd never heard a word from his friend Don since the day that Don left Tangier. He hadn't even got his address. Tim had long since given up worrying about him."

"He's not married?"

"Who? Tim? No. And to judge from his interests that evening I don't think he ever will be. Inez was his only deviation in that direction, and he got over his infatuation for *her* pretty soon, as I told you. After the first week he discovered she was going with other men on the sly. After a month she gave up pretending that she wasn't working as a prostitute. While they were in Barcelona she even tried to persuade him to act as her pimp. Tim soon left her."

"Did he ever tell you why he'd left you?"

"Because of the girl. That was obvious."

"Did he tell you so himself?"

"He may not have done, because during the first part of the evening he seemed oddly reluctant to discuss the past. He kept nattering on about his coffee-bar and his gay friends in Folkestone. I must now admit something terrible to you. I must confess to you that his conversation bored me stiff. As he droned on about his little flat near the harbor and the potato plant he'd persuaded to coil round the room and the new television set that he'd bought on hire purchase, suddenly I

[1 2 3]

realized with a shock how little we'd ever had in common. He was just an ill-educated lout. He was pleasant enough, but he was devastatingly dull. And as I looked at the little rolls of fat sliding over his collar and his heavy jowls, I wondered how soon I could escape from him without hurting his feelings. But there was still one question I had to ask—a question that had haunted me for ten years . . ."

Ewing waited until they were sitting in a quiet corner of the Bellingham with their drinks. Then he forced himself to ask Tim the one question that still tortured him.

"Tell me this," Ewing said. "If I'd driven down into Tangier that last fatal night, if I'd come into the Mar Chica while you were still there with Inez, would you have come back to me? Would you?"

"It depends," Tim answered.

"Depends on what?"

"It depends on how you'd been."

"How I'd been? I don't get it."

"If you'd ordered me back to the villa, I'd have told you to clear off."

"If I'd apologized . . ."

"That's different. If you'd said you were sorry, then even if you'd asked me to leave Inez right away and come back with you to the villa on the spot, I'd have gone with you willingly, I promise you."

Ewing stared into Tim's watery brown eyes. It still seemed incredible to him that up to that very last moment, Tim had been prepared to return to the fold.

That an action on his own part could have saved him such intense suffering was too painful a thought for Ewing to bear.

"Then why didn't you answer my letter or my cable? When I sent Wayne to you, why did you say that you 'didn't want to know'?"

Tim smiled at him sadly. "You weren't the only one that was proud," Tim said.

"How does pride come into it?"

"In this way. I'd been hurt, and I didn't want to be hurt again. I wasn't sure what you really felt about me. If I'd thought you'd *really* wanted me, I'd have come back."

"But you must have *known* I wanted you back desperately. Didn't my letter say so? Didn't Wayne tell you?"

Tim looked steadily into Ewing's eyes.

"If you'd really wanted me back, you wouldn't have cabled or written or sent Wayne," Tim said slowly. "You'd have come to me yourself."

At that moment Ewing knew that he could no longer avoid the truth. He had been responsible for his own misery. His suffering had been as unnecessary as it was pointless.

Tim pulled back his cuff and glanced at his watch. With a twinge of remorse Ewing saw that it was the gold wristwatch he had bought him after Tim had returned to Tangier from serving his prison sentence.

"My last train leaves at eleven-thirty," Tim said. "I don't suppose you came out on the town this evening to take a fat old thing like me back to your flat."

Ewing laughed to conceal his embarrassment. "Let's have one more drink," Ewing said.

"All right."

Ewing saw that there was a crush round the bar. He felt worn and tired. The evening had made him feel that his way of life was futile. He had learned nothing. He had taught Tim nothing. He dreaded meeting someone he knew, for he felt incapable of making an effort. Ewing took out a pound note and handed it to Tim.

"Be kind and you order them," Ewing muttered.

Tim laughed. "How that takes me back!" he said. "You never could abide getting drinks for yourself at a bar, could you?"

As Ewing watched Tim's burly figure pushing through the cluster of men round the bar, he thought, with another twinge of anguish, that if Tim had stayed with him he might still be lean and handsome. Tim was fat because he ate and drank the wrong things. Fried fish and chips, bread and cheese, pints of bitter —it was the cheapest food and drink that was the most fattening. But Tim would have had steaks and salads and fruit on the yacht. The work would have kept him lean.

Tim came back with the drinks. Streaks of sweat were running down his swollen face. He raised his glass of beer. "Cheers! It's great to be with you again."

"It was tremendous luck meeting you," Ewing said steadily. "But you're a brute not to have dropped me one single line over all these years."

"You'll never know how often I nearly did," Tim replied. "At least twice I wrote you a long letter. But each time I tore it up."

"Why did you?"

"I didn't want you to think I'd come crawling back to you just because I was broke and things were going bad for me. I was plain proud, I suppose. But I've been through some pretty foul times, I don't mind telling you. When they know you're really down and out, some geezers take advantage of it. They can be real bastards. I've been through it, I really have."

"If only I'd known."

"If only I hadn't been such a mug. You'll never understand just how much I regretted leaving you. I only wish I could be a young chicken again. Do you know I'd give my right arm to live each one of our days together all over again. God, what a little fool I was! I just didn't know when I was lucky. I didn't appreciate it when I was well off. I just hadn't a clue. Even nine months after I'd left you I still hadn't learned my lesson. So I told Wayne I didn't want to know. I chucked away my last chance of making something worthwhile out of my life. It was my last chance, and all I said was I didn't want to know."

Ewing looked toward Arnold and nodded his head wearily.

"Something in Tim's voice stirred memories I thought I'd killed," Ewing said. "Visions of our life together came rushing back. I turned away from him because my eyes were full of tears.

"I thought of the lean young soldier I'd known with

his shining eyes and clear skin and slender waist. I looked back at him across the table. Just for one moment the rolls of flesh seemed to melt away, and I saw the young man that I'd known and loved. So I asked Tim to my flat for the night. But it was a disaster— utter and complete . . . You see, it was quite hopeless . . . I couldn't go through with it. And when Tim realized that I couldn't even summon up a tremor of passion for him, he turned away from me. Presently I saw that his shoulders were heaving, and he began to cry like a child . . .

"He was crying because his vanity had been hurt. He was crying for his lost youth and beauty. But it wasn't only that. The real bitterness of his grief sprang from the fact that he knew, now, that he had come back to me too late. You see, while we were going round the bars together earlier that evening he'd realized I was no longer attracted to him as a person. He'd noticed I no longer listened spellbound to every word he uttered. I no longer gazed rapturously into his eyes. He'd seen the form. But he still hoped—almost in some mystic way—that bed would do the trick and bring us together again. But it didn't. And he was now sobbing because he knew that he'd lost me forever.

"And I lay staring up at the ceiling of my bedroom in the flat, looking back on it all, wondering where it first went wrong. Why couldn't I be content with his companionship *now* as I had been ten or eleven years ago? After all, sex had only been one part of our relationship.

"I think it was then I realized finally that although I had touched him *emotionally* at times, I'd never really reached his mind. And I'd never got through to him and never could have done because I'd arrived too late on the scene. By the time he was nineteen, all Tim's prejudices and ways of thought had been formed. His reactions had already been conditioned. His responses were as set as those of Pavlov's dogs. For instance, Tim would always prefer to spend an evening roving round the pubs with people like George and Harry than to dine well and go to a concert with me. From the moment I met Tim and took him on, I had been fighting a losing battle. The most important formative years of his life had been the six years before I met him. He had accepted the values of the boys in the street where he lived in London and the boys he'd made friends with at the approved school where they sent him. Later, he'd accepted the code of behavior he learned in the ranks. By the time I met him—when he was nineteen—Tim Deakin and I belonged to two different worlds. We could make contact emotionally and physically. But our minds could never meet."

Ewing took three paces toward Arnold and raised his forefinger as if to give a warning.

"But if I could have met Tim Deakin when he was thirteen or fourteen," Ewing said, accentuating each word with his finger, "I am convinced that he would still be with me, and I'm convinced that we'd both be happy. You see, he would have been such a wonderful companion . . . Do you know that in a curious way I'm still fond of him—even after that last dreadful meeting. I don't suppose you'll be all that surprised when I tell you that we now correspond regularly. Occasionally I send him a little present to buy himself a new suit or go to Paris for a gay weekend. After all, it wasn't Tim's fault that I met him five or six years too late. I shall never forget the months of happiness we had together . . .

"But I must come back to the point that may affect you . . . When Wayne told me that morning in Tangier that Tim had left with Inez on the early ferry, and I knew that I'd lost him, I made up my mind that I wasn't going to be weak and escape from it all. I determined to stick it out in the villa . . . But it was anguish. Each room, each piece of furniture, every record, every dish, every sound held memories. The *muezzin* calling the faithful to prayer from the minaret of the mosque on the Marshan, the liquid notes of Bashir's flute, the hoarse shout of the water carrier, the birds in the garden toward dawn—all reminded me of episodes in my life with Tim. It was the same on the yacht—the binnacle in the wheelhouse, the fixed mahogany table in the saloon, the broad-based heavy ship's decanters in the tantalus, the double bunk in my cabin, the looking glass over the washbasin in the lavatory, the Hogarth prints between the portholes . . . I couldn't bear to stay in Tangier an instant longer. I knew that I must get right away from everything that reminded me of Tim. So I went to a travel agency in the Boulevard Pasteur and booked a passage on a ship calling in at Gibraltar on its way to India. I was away eight months.

"When I left on that ship I'd made up my mind to sell the villa and leave Tangier for good. But as the months went by and I felt less unhappy, I changed my mind. After all, Tangier had got very definite advantages—no income tax and almost unlimited license to indulge one's own particular tastes. But I still couldn't face living alone in my villa on the Marshan —particularly after the failure of Wayne's mission to London. However, at about the time I got back to Tangier, the Villa Gault where I'm now living was up for sale and reasonably cheap. So I bought it, and here we are. I didn't sell the villa on the Marshan because I couldn't get the price I wanted. So I kept it on as an investment. It's generally empty during the winter months. It's empty now, for instance. But I let it at an exorbitant price during the other seven or eight months of the year. I'll take you to see the villa tomorrow after lunch—if you can bear to forsake the lures of Riffi and the Caves of Hercules. And after I've shown you the villa, I'll explain why I've told you about Tim in such detail. You see, there's a reason— quite apart from the dope that Dr. Valdez gave me for my stomach, which seems to have had the most peculiar effect on me, and quite apart from my hope of achieving catharsis. There's a reason. And I promise I'll tell it to you tomorrow. Meanwhile I'm sure you're longing to get to bed, but help yourself to a nightcap if you feel like one. I've talked so much I've worn myself to a frazzle. Thank you for putting up with me. I'm off to sleep. Good night."

Ewing hurried out of the room with his quick, short steps.

Arnold sat staring at the dead ashes, wondering at the infinite capacity of men to inflict pain unwillingly on each other and on themselves, wondering if he could have managed Tim any better, wondering what had really caused Ewing to tell him the whole story from beginning to end.

But Arnold soon gave up his search for any answers. He could always continue his speculations when he had returned to the grim routine of Melton Hall. Meanwhile he must savor each moment of the present. He must store up the memory of each experience. During his few remaining days in the villa he must try to amass a hoard of memories, for he realized now that he might have to exist on that hoard for the rest of his life.

Arnold picked up a cold cinder that had fallen on the carpet. Then he walked along the corridor to his room where Riffi was curled up in bed, asleep.

Arnold was awakened by a faint tinkling sound. Riffi, wearing jeans and Arnold's slippers, was wheeling a breakfast trolley into the bedroom.

"We eat here," Riffi said. "Far better. I have lock door so no one come in. Why-for last night you no wake me when you come to bed?"

"Because you were fast asleep."

[1 3 2]

"I sleep. Later I can wake."

"You were sleeping so soundly I didn't want to wake you."

Arnold could not explain to Riffi the pleasure it had given him to gaze down at the sleeping boy and to lie down very quietly beside him so as not to disturb the unguarded expression on his face.

"I tink you no like me any more."

"I've told you, Riffi. I love you."

"I love you," Riffi repeated. "You my freng."

The heavy brocade curtains were still drawn. Arnold got out of bed and drew them aside. Rain was falling steadily from a leaden sky.

"No," Riffi said.

"Now what's wrong?"

"Not good. People look in."

Riffi carefully closed the curtains.

"Last night you tired and me sleep," Riffi explained. "After we now eat, you no tired and me no sleep."

Ewing appeared in the drawing room in time to mix a daiquiri before lunch.

"Thanks to the almost overeffective dope provided by Dr. Valdez, my inside has completely recovered," Ewing said. "Please forgive me for keeping you up so late. But once I'd started telling the story I found I just couldn't stop. Did you sleep well?"

"Yes, thanks."

"And is that wayward child you seem almost to have adopted behaving himself?"

"Perfectly."

"Shall we take our cocktails with us in to lunch? I'm simply starving. I rather think that we're starting with *oeufs en cocotte,* which don't like to be kept waiting. You lead the way."

While Ismail, his large hands encased as usual in white cotton gloves, poured out the wine into the long-stemmed glasses, Arnold glanced out of the window. The rain had stopped. Small patches of blue were beginning to show through the grey clouds.

"Now it's your turn," Ewing said as he finished eating his eggs.

"My turn for what?"

"Your turn to talk about yourself. Do you realize I know practically nothing about you? For instance, what made you decide to be a schoolmaster?"

"I didn't decide," Arnold said grinning. "Events decided it for me. I think I told you that my father was a schoolmaster. He was terribly keen for me to get a scholarship. He wanted me to have the university education he'd missed. Well, I failed to get the scholarship. So then it was decided I should study to be a chartered accountant."

"That was quite a bright idea," Ewing said. "We all seem to need chartered accountants nowadays."

"I'm afraid you'll never use my services. The exams were too steep for me. I gave up the struggle after three years. I drifted around for a while until I'd spent the money my father left me. Then there was nothing for it but to get a job of some kind. Well, I'd got the qualifications to teach, so I got a job at an elementary school. Then for various reasons I moved to an approved school."

"What were the 'various reasons'?"

"Pay, for a start. At an approved school teachers get two increases above their salary for their special work —and because we only get eight weeks a year holiday instead of twelve. We also get a small cottage at a reasonably cheap rent on the estate if we live out. I don't suppose that sounds of any consequence to you. But I can assure you that it makes a lot of difference when one has got a small salary."

"What other reasons made you go to an approved school?"

"I suppose it sounds rather smug, but the work there really does provide far more opportunity for doing something to help the kids. At an elementary school they've got their parents to go back to every night. At an approved school they've got no one."

Ewing glanced down at his hands, then gazed steadily across the table at Arnold. "I expect your school provides far more opportunity for other activities," Ewing said.

"I don't get you."

"The boys sleep in the school at night, don't they?"

Arnold felt himself blushing.

"I'm not a housemaster so I live out. But I should say that very little of that kind of thing went on."

"But haven't you been tempted now and then to have a little dally with one of the boys?"

"If you want to know, yes, I have. I've been tempted. That's true. But I've never touched one of them, and I never will."

"Is that virtue or cowardice?"

"Perhaps it's both."

"How old are the boys at your school?"

"Melton Hall's an intermediate school. We take boys who are thirteen or fourteen on admission. The maximum period they can be sent to us for is three years."

"So there are boys of Riffi's age?"

"I expected you to say that."

Ewing smiled at him blandly. "Now don't get cross," Ewing said. "I'm not asking you these questions to irritate you. I really do want to find out about your school. And I've a particular reason for doing so. Tell me this. How do boys get sent to your school?"

"They're sent by a juvenile court."

"For doing what?"

"All kinds of things—stealing a bicycle, pinching milk bottles, shop-breaking, smashing open the money-box in a phone booth with a crowbar, pawning their fathers' boots, breaking open the gas meter, pilfering off stalls. And if a juvenile court wants to, it can make an Approved School Order in the case of a child found by the court to be 'in need of care or protection, or beyond control.' "

"What do you think causes juvenile delinquency?"

Arnold smiled at Ewing's calm assumption that he could answer in a few words across a lunch table the question that experts had spent their lives working on.

"You'll hear all kinds of reasons given," Arnold said. "You'll be told it's the influence of the cinema and television—or bad schoolteachers or overcrowded classes or the result of the Welfare State. But, in fact, I believe that most children who are brought before the juvenile courts come from broken homes or unkind parents. Their delinquent conduct begins as a kind of escape from their basic need for affection. It's a kind of compensation for their deprivation of tenderness and love—you might almost call it emotional malnutrition."

"But how can an approved school provide tenderness and love?"

"That's just it. That's the whole trouble. It can't. At best it can only satisfy two other human needs—the need for companionship and the desire for expression. But what a deprived child really wants—if the parents are divorced or dead or simply brutal or callous—is to be put with affectionate foster parents. The difficulty is to find them."

"I'd imagined that the boys in your school were criminally vicious little thugs," Ewing said. "You're giving me a very different picture from what I expected."

"Some of them are thugs," Arnold said, thinking of Charlie Mason, with his slanting green eyes and bristling red hair. "But I'd say that few of them were criminal."

"How many boys are there at your school?"

"Nearly a hundred."

"And you believe that most of them are there because they come from homes that have been split up or from homes where they've been ill-treated?"

"Yes."

"Then why do boys run away? One sometimes sees little paragraphs in the English papers about boys running away from approved schools."

Arnold laughed. "The term we use for it is 'absconding,' " he said. "You must remember that an approved school isn't a prison. The gates aren't locked. And boys escape for various reasons. They may want to go back to a parent they really love or to see their friends in their home town. They may want to be free of all restrictions and go on the bash. Or they may abscond because they just can't bear the school a moment longer."

"What happens when a boy absconds?"

"Why are you so interested in all this?"

Ewing pressed the bell by his right hand for Ismail to clear the table.

"I'll tell you when we get to the Marshan," he said. "But first you tell me what happens when a boy has absconded. What's the drill?"

"First we ring up the local police. We give them the boy's name and a description of him which they circulate to all police cars. As often as not the boy is soon picked up at a bus stop round the corner or from the railway station and brought back to us. At the same time we notify the police at the boy's home town. If at the end of forty-eight hours we've heard nothing, then we ring Scotland Yard, and a description of the boy is printed in the *Police Gazette*."

"But after a boy has escaped, don't the press buzz round you?"

"Heavens no! While I've been at Melton Hall we've had seven boys abscond at different times. But there's never even been a paragraph in the local paper. It's only when a boy on the run breaks into a shop or gets into trouble of some kind that the press get interested."

"Good," Ewing said. "That's just what I wanted to find out. Let's finish our coffee and go straight up to the villa, shall we?"

The car bumped slowly along a narrow cobbled lane of single-storied decrepit houses with the plaster peeling round the Moorish windows, skirted a trim white mosque, clattered yet more slowly up a rutted drive of dripping trees, and stopped in a sudden clearing where a compact villa with whitewashed walls and green shutters glistened in the afternoon sunshine. The villa stood on a projecting tongue of land with a view of the sea on three sides. It was built on a slope so that both floors could be entered from the garden. As Ewing and Arnold got out of the car, a grimy-looking Moor with a torn *djellaba* and a gnarled face came up to Ewing with a bunch of keys and began a long conversation in Arabic.

"That's Abdessalam," Ewing explained, as the old man shuffled away toward the villa. "He's really the gardener. But he keeps an eye on the house when there's no one here. He's now gone to open up the place. Let's go into the top half first."

They walked into a long, pale-green room with light

rosewood furniture and a wide divan covered with cushions of different shapes and colors. Three french windows opened onto a veranda. Below the veranda was a terraced garden and below that the sea.

"This is the flat where Tim lived," Ewing said. "It's got a large bedroom with a huge double bed. It's got a kitchen with a refrigerator. There's a bathroom and lavatory and a spare room. In fact, as you can see, there's really everything one could want."

The rooms were light and cheerful. Whatever window Arnold looked out of seemed to have a view of the sea sparkling in the sunshine.

"This villa's on the Mediterranean side of Tangier," Ewing said. "The Mediterranean's far warmer than the Atlantic, but alas the beaches are more crowded. Now come and inspect the downstair flat."

The living room downstairs looked smaller because it was darker and more elaborately furnished. The walls were paneled with Japanese paintings of gardens and landscapes. Arnold stared with distaste at vermilion-painted pagodas beside lotus pools, groves of pink and white blossoms along river banks, billowing hummocks of moss beneath golden pavilions, waterfalls tumbling down ravines above temples, white peacocks and willow trees. The black lacquered tables in the room, the porcelain jars and pottery bowls depressed him. Arnold preferred the spaciousness and simplicity of the flat above.

"This downstair flat is far the larger," Ewing explained. "It's got three spare rooms."

"Did you live here all the time Tim was with you?"

"In this very room. I'm devoted to it."

"I like the top flat best. The views are fantastic. Wouldn't it be wonderful if we could move here for my last week. I could live in the top flat, and you could live down here."

Ewing carved the air with his plump hands in an expansive gesture.

"If only you played your cards right," Ewing said, "you could stay here for the rest of your life."

Arnold laughed. "You always manage to make my life sound so easy," he said.

"I suppose you realize that if you had this villa you could live all the year round in the top half from what you'd get from renting the lower half. The top flat would be perfect for you and Riffi."

"But I haven't got the villa, and I never shall have. So stop teasing me."

"I'm not teasing you."

Ewing crossed to the window. He stood in silence gazing out at the banks of wild iris and narcissus and the blue sea beyond.

"It's a wonderful view, isn't it?"

"I've never known a better," Arnold replied truthfully.

"It's odd when you come to think of it," Ewing said after another pause. "I've got this villa which I suppose could bring you as much happiness as anything else in the world—because you could live here all the year round with little Riffi. And you've got—or rather, you could provide if you wanted to—the very thing that I most want in the world."

"And what is that?"

Ewing stretched out the fingers of his raised hands and then let his arms down to his side.

"Shall I tell you the reason I gave you such a detailed account of my relationship with Tim?" Ewing asked. "It was because I wanted you to appreciate the *moral* of the story. I hope you've understood it. You see, the moral is this. It's quite hopeless to take on a boy as old as Tim was. By nineteen he's already formed. His character and tastes and prejudices are already set. There's nothing you can do to change him. At best you can only hope to modify him. Tim had been molded by his environment long before I met him."

Ewing turned away from the window and faced Arnold.

"But supposing Tim had been five or six years younger when we met," Ewing said slowly. "Supposing Tim had been thirteen or fourteen, *then* what a very different story it would have been. I could have taught him to understand painting and sculpture. I could have taken him to see the works of El Greco and Praxiteles. I could have encouraged him to appreciate Bach and Beethoven. I could have taught him to prefer Proust to Peter Cheyney. I could have taken the unhardened clay of his mind and molded it into a shape of beauty. Perhaps I could have achieved the greatest work of art that any artist can ever hope to create—a perfect human being."

Ewing was staring at Arnold with glittering eyes. He was breathing heavily.

[1 4 2]

"A Moroccan of thirteen or fourteen is no good to me," Ewing said. "I explained that to you last night. You're all right. You can be happy with Riffi because you love him as he is. You don't *want* to mold him. But I must find a boy who's English. That's my only hope. And he mustn't be more than fourteen. The clay must still be soft. But where can I find him?"

Ewing took three quick paces toward Arnold and then stopped, his feet placed neatly together, his arms outstretched as if he had just concluded an intricate dance.

"Where can I find an English boy of thirteen or fourteen?" he asked, gazing intently into Arnold's eyes. "I can't. I don't know any. And I'm in no position to get to know any. How can I find a boy who's going to be prepared to leave England for good—which means that he must have no emotional ties there? How can I find a boy who's not anchored to his background, a boy who won't suddenly be reclaimed? I can't."

Slowly Ewing extended his forefinger and pointed it at Arnold.

"I can't," Ewing repeated. "But you can. You're in the perfect position to do so. The boys at your school are there for the very reason that their family background is rotten. You said so yourself. If they had pleasant home environments they wouldn't be at Melton Hall. Probably over half the boys at your school detest their parents or guardians. Over half of them have got no emotional tie to anchor them to England. And you see them every day. You're ideally situated."

"Ideally situated to do what?" Arnold asked coldly.

Ewing tried to smile. He stretched the corners of his mouth and parted his thin lips. Though the lid of his left eye was quivering, his mouth was steady.

"You're ideally situated to find a boy of thirteen or fourteen who's intelligent and sensitive and malleable —a boy who wants to get away from England to begin a new life."

Arnold controlled a gesture of revulsion. "And if I find a boy like that, what do I do?"

"You arrange for him to join me in Tangier."

"You're not serious?"

"So serious that I promise I'll make over this villa to you on the day the boy arrives. You can let out the lower flat and live in the top flat with Riffi. You'll have enough money to keep you both in food and drink."

"I'm sure you must be joking."

"I'll put it in writing if you like."

Arnold took a deep breath. "You're not seriously asking me to kidnap one of the boys at Melton Hall and ship him out to Tangier?"

"I'm not asking you to kidnap anyone. I'm suggesting that you find a boy who's only too anxious to get away from the place. Once we've found the boy and you've told him the form, your part in the operation will be finished. I shall be responsible for getting the boy out to Tangier. You'll just sit pretty at your school till the scandal's blown over and it's safe for you to come out here and move into this villa."

"You can't really believe I'd do it?"

"Why not?"

"But the boys are in my charge. I'm responsible for them."

"So what?"

"I'm not going to be responsible for shipping one of them abroad to be seduced."

"Who said anything about seduction?"

"Isn't that what it amounts to? Why are you so keen that the kid should hate his parents and have no ties of affection? Isn't it because you want him to fall for you? Isn't it because you want to make certain he's got nowhere else to go? No other choice?"

Suddenly Ewing clapped his hands together enthusiastically as if he were applauding a brilliant aria.

"You must forgive me," Ewing said laughing. "I really am sorry. But, my dear man, I simply can't resist teasing you. I adore the expression on your face when you get all flushed and indignant. It's enchanting. You're so wonderfully easy to take in. Of course I wasn't being serious. Now the sun's gone in and it's getting chilly. I suppose we ought to go back to our log fire at the villa."

When they returned to the villa on the mountain Ewing announced that he was afraid of catching a chill and intended to take a hot bath. Arnold wandered along the corridor to his bedroom and was disappointed not to find Riffi waiting for him. He had seen him on the terrace as the car came up the drive.

Ten minutes later Bashir arrived with a note from Ewing.

"Terribly sorry," Ewing wrote. "But I completely

forgot to tell you that for my sins I've got to dine with Luke West tonight. I've ordered dinner for you here. See you at breakfast. Yours, Ewing."

Arnold looked up. Bashir was watching him carefully.

"You want write answer?" Bashir asked.

"No, thanks."

"*Barrakelaufic, ya sidi,*" Bashir said. "Thank you, sir."

Bashir bowed limply and turned to go.

"Bashir . . ."

With a slack gesture of his hands Bashir turned back.

"Could you ask Riffi to come and see me?"

Bashir stared at Arnold with his heavily made-up eyes.

"Riffi not here," Bashir said.

"Not here? Where's he gone to?"

"Riffi go back to his village near Chauen. Maybe for two or three days."

Bashir spoke the words as if he had learned them by heart. Arnold was certain that he was lying.

"When did Riffi go?"

"This afternoon."

"At what time?"

"At four."

"But I saw him on the terrace less than a quarter of an hour ago."

Bashir shrugged his shoulders.

"Riffi go to Chauen," he repeated.

"Why did he go?"

"He go to see his family."

"Does Señor Baird know he's gone?"

For an instant Bashir's eyes flickered.

"Yes. He know," Bashir said. "Riffi come back in two or three days."

Then Arnold understood what had happened.

"Thank you, Bashir," he said.

Bashir no longer bothered to disguise his contempt. He smiled and made an elaborate bow.

"*Barrakelaufic, ya sidi,*" Bashir said, and left the room.

As he sat alone at dinner that night, with Ismail in his white gloves standing behind his chair, Arnold rehearsed the various maneuvers Ewing had engaged in since the moment he had sent Wayne to summon him to his table for a drink. He realized now that each move in their relationship—each episode at the villa, each story that Ewing had told him, each sentence even—had all been carefully planned. The climax of Ewing's tortuous plot had been reached in the Japanese room of the villa on the Marshan that afternoon. There was no doubt that the offer to give him the villa had been seriously intended as an effective bribe. It was the final twist of Ewing's intricately contrived scheme. The ground had been neatly cleared, the bait provided, the perfect bribe produced. But the plan had failed, so Ewing had done his best to recover from his failure by pretending it was all a joke. His sudden applause and loud laughter had been quite convincing. But even Ewing's expert performance could not erase the memories of various hints and allusions he had made previously.

The position was clear. From the moment Ewing had met Arnold in Wayne's bar he had determined in an almost insanely obsessive way to suborn Arnold into procuring a boy for him from his school. The elaborate and expensive meals, the visit to Conchita's bar, the two dancing boys, the expedition to the Caves of Hercules, the invitation to stay at the villa—all were part of an elaborate plot to weaken Arnold's resistance to Ewing's plan. Riffi had been used as a pawn in this scheme of things. But Ewing was only prepared to approve of Arnold's affair with Riffi if Arnold behaved according to plan. And Arnold hadn't. He had made it obvious that Ewing's plan revolted him.

So Arnold was now being punished. Riffi had been taken away from him.

❧ ❧ ❧ ❧ ❧ ❧

THE following morning Arnold found a note from Ewing on the breakfast table in the patio.

"I've had to go to Gibraltar on business," Ewing wrote. "Back tomorrow afternoon."

Arnold took a detective novel from the bookcase in the drawing room and sat down in a deck chair on the terrace and began to read. But he could not concentrate on the plot. Visions of Riffi's slight body moved across his mind like colored lantern slides. He could see the skin stretched taut across his bony chest and the gleam of his polished thighs. He could see the boy's white forehead and violet eyes beneath the wildly curling black hair. He saw the deep red of his lips and his pale tongue quivering between his even teeth when he laughed. And he was tortured by the fear that the boy had been taken away from him forever.

In the afternoon Arnold walked over the hillsides toward Cape Spartel, past avenues of eucalyptus trees, past yellow clumps of mimosa and banks of wild iris and narcissus, past tinkling flocks of goats and toward the headland. And as Arnold gazed down at the long foaming lines of the Atlantic breakers, he thought once again of Ewing's fantastic proposal, and immediately a glimpse of Melton Hall swung into his mind. He saw the grey school uniform; he saw a dozen rows of heads bowed wearily over the wooden desks. And suddenly the face of the shy boy who sat in the fifth row swung into his mind. Dan Gedge—one of Stobart's vicarious victims; the boy who had absconded and had been left for "punishment" in the gym. Would living with Ewing and the perversion it implied be any worse than the misery of Melton Hall for that boy? Was seduction any more harmful than constant ill-treatment? Then, suddenly, Arnold remembered Ewing lying on the beach. He saw the bulging limbs and hairy stomach, the grossness and virility. And he had a glimpse of that heavy body pressing down toward the scared boy's upturned face.

Arnold shuddered and walked quickly back to the villa.

As Arnold wandered uneasily through the empty rooms he began to be oppressed by the richness of their furnishings. The swags of the heavy velvet curtains, the damask of the sofas, the elaborate workmanship of the gilt sconces, the pale tints of the Aubusson carpet on the creaking parquet floor, the bulbous celadon lamps on bow-fronted Empire side tables, the dark-colored silk cushions in the narrow Moorish room with its intricately carved arches—all seemed to fill the villa with a luxurious scent that stifled him. He would have left the villa and spent the evening down in the town if he had not still clung to the frail hope that Riffi might yet return.

Toward sunset Arnold climbed up the stone staircase that led to the top of the villa's central tower. He pushed open a wooden trap door and stepped out onto the lead roof that was still warm from the sun. To the south he could see the snow gleaming like cream on the peaks of the Rîf mountains. Unless Bashir had been lying, little Riffi was at this moment in one of the Berber villages set between the folds of that mountain range.

Arnold turned away sadly, to watch the sun as it dipped below the horizon, leaving a deep-red glow above the shining green sea that was dappled with dark patches like a quilt. To the north, wisps of coral cloud floated slowly across the sky, turning to purple as the tattered strips trailed toward the east. From the tower, Arnold could hear the quick rhythmic tinkling of the goatbells as the flocks were driven back from grazing on the mountainside to the *fondouks* in the town. The firs at the end of the garden seemed very dark and as thick as a forest, though from below they seemed widely spaced, and above them thousands of midges floated up and down. To the west, now, the mountain crags were razor-sharp and jet-black against the orange glow of the background, and a sheen of bright smooth water stretched across the Atlantic like a lake surrounded by indigo banks. Dark purple clouds to the north were reflected in the tranquil sea. The hillside was now dotted with the tiny glows of the charcoal burners' fires, and the beam of the Cape Spartel lighthouse swerved across the dusk.

It was growing cold. Arnold left the roof and clambered down the twisting stone staircase, closing the trap door behind him.

That evening Arnold dined alone at the marble table in the candle-lit dining room, waited on in silence by Ismail with his leathery dark face and stiff cotton gloves. After dinner he went into the drawing room and drank two large brandies. Then he walked wearily along the corridor and across the patio to his bedroom.

❧ ❧ ❧ ❧ ❧ ❧

ARNOLD was walking restlessly along the terrace when Ewing returned late the following afternoon.

"Please do forgive me for leaving you all on your own," Ewing said blandly. "But I had the most boring currency problem to settle, and Gib was the only place to fix it. I do hope that Ismail gave you enough to eat and drink?"

"Yes, thanks."

"You don't seem wildly gay this afternoon."

"I'm not."

"Anything wrong?"

"You know what's wrong."

Ewing glanced at him in surprise. "Do I?" he asked.

"Yes."

Suddenly Ewing clapped his hands together. "Oh, of course I do!" he said triumphantly. "How stupid of me! You've been missing little Riffi. Isn't that it?"

"Where *is* Riffi?" Arnold asked.

"Didn't Bashir tell you? He went back to his village near Chauen to see his parents."

"He left rather suddenly, didn't he?"

Ewing smiled at Arnold as if he were a child to whom some obvious fact must be explained. "They get these sudden messages," Ewing said. "A woman from Chauen had come into Tangier that morning with a load of firewood and a message from Riffi's brother to say that their mother was ill and he must return immediately. So off he went."

"Can you find out the name of his village? I'd like to go and see him before I take the plane back to England."

Ewing chuckled. "You've really fallen for the little creature, haven't you?" he said. "Not that I blame you. I only wish I could work up some excitement for him myself. It would make my life so much simpler."

"I'd like to go to his village tomorrow," Arnold said.

Ewing smiled. "Don't be worried," he replied. "You don't need to move an inch. All is well. Just relax."

[1 5 2]

"I intend to see Riffi before I leave."

"And so you shall. Only give me a chance to explain. You see, by the time Riffi got back to his village he discovered that his mother had recovered. So he stayed there two nights and came straight back."

"How do you know?"

"How suspicious you've suddenly become!" Ewing laughed. "How do I know? Because I saw him down in town only an hour ago."

"Where is he now?"

"I don't know where he is at this moment. But I can tell you where he'll be this evening at eleven o'clock when we come back from dinner. Right here in this villa, waiting for you. So you needn't look so distraught, need you?"

"You're certain?"

"Absolutely certain. He's an intelligent boy. He wouldn't let me down. Besides, I think he's really become quite devoted to you."

"What makes you think that?"

"His eagerness to find out if you'd still be here."

Arnold was silent as waves of pain and happiness swept over him. He had only five complete days left to spend with Riffi, but at least he would see him again.

"Quite apart from Riffi I've got two special treats for you tonight," Ewing continued blandly. "We're going to Diego's place, which will fascinate you, and then I'm taking you to dine at the *Pavillon*."

"What's Diego's place?"

"Well, in the good old days here before the Moroccans got their independence, one could have described

Diego's place quite simply as a male bordello. But now that all brothels have been made illegal, it's slightly more complicated. You see, the boys can't live on the premises. They have to come in from outside. So Diego's little house is a sort of meeting place, a *maison de passe*."

"Why should I want to go there?"

"Because you'll be enthralled by it."

"I'd rather stay here and wait for Riffi."

"How unadventurous you are! Besides, as I told you, Riffi won't be here till after dinner. And Diego's place is quite an experience. All kinds of interesting things go on there."

"Such as?"

"Well, to start with, perhaps I should explain there's a secret about the house that very few people know. In the main room there are concealed holes in the mirror so that one can look in from the room next door and see everything that's going on without being seen oneself. It's a unique experience."

"I should have thought it was quite revolting. Just what *does* go on?"

Ewing smiled and spread out his fingers like a fan. "You'll just have to wait and see," he said coyly. "I can only promise you that you'll be quite fascinated."

"Can't I skip Diego's and meet you at the *Pavillon?*"

Ewing's face stiffened, and his fingers curled up into his palms.

"I'm doing my best to entertain you," Ewing said coldly. "You must admit I haven't done too badly so far. Surely the least you can do is to fall in with my plans?"

"All right," Arnold said. "Sorry to sound ungrateful. What time do we leave?"

"At seven," Ewing replied. "The performance is laid on for eight o'clock."

❧ ❧ ❧ ❧ ❧ ❧ ❧

It had been raining. The streets that led off the Zocco Chico reflected the lights of the cafés. Ewing led Arnold past the Ciné Américain and turned up a narrow winding passage between close-packed dingy houses with peeling façades. A Moor shuffled toward them along the gleaming cobbles, looking like a decrepit monk in the long cloak and hood of his *djellaba,* his feet splayed out as he pushed his toes into his slippers. He was followed by a prostitute clicking down the passage with brisk little steps on spiked high-heeled shoes, her antimonied eyes peering anxiously between the fold of her blue *haik* and her black veil.

At a dark bend ahead was a two-storied house with charred-looking walls. A single window fixed halfway up the house commanded a view down the passage. Outside the house Ewing hesitated and looked round quickly to make certain they had not been followed. As he turned, the door of the house was opened by a round-faced Spanish boy. Ewing walked quickly inside and beckoned to Arnold to follow.

Together they passed into a murky hall lit faintly by two red-shaded angle lamps and glazed with worn tiles to the height of three feet. The walls above were painted a dull ocher and decorated with advertisements for American cigarettes and Spanish beer. The plump Spanish boy gestured to them to be silent. Cautiously he pulled out a couple of the four wicker chairs that were grouped around a stained wooden table. A staircase and two doors led out of the little hall. On the landing above the staircase the red end of a cigarette butt glowed in the hand of the silent watcher by the window.

Presently, from the door on the left, they were joined by a slim Spaniard of about sixty who swayed delicately toward them. His face was powdered and rouged, and he reeked of lavender water.

"This is Diego," Ewing whispered.

Diego's thin lips stretched into a smile as he shook Arnold's hand limply. His shrewd black eyes examined Arnold's face as if it were a map to be glanced at quickly and memorized.

"Any friend of Señor Ewing is a friend of mine," he murmured. "I'm glad he has a companion to share his amusement. Come now, and I will show you the way."

Silently they followed Diego into a narrow windowless room. An advertisement for Fundador brandy hung on the scabrous green walls about a table and two chairs. A large faded print of the King's palace in Rabat covered the wall opposite.

Diego put his finger to his mouth.

"We no speak too much loud," he said.

Then he moved quietly across the room and took down the print and propped it against a chair. In the space of wall covered by the print were two eyepieces set a yard apart.

Diego turned to Arnold. "You stand here," he said.

"And you watch. You look into the other room. Come and see."

Arnold stood in front of the nearest eyepiece and looked through it. Immediately he recoiled. In the dimly lit whitewashed room next door a man was sitting in an armchair three yards away looking straight at him.

Diego tittered softly. "The man cannot see you," he whispered. "The other side of the wall it is a mirror. He can be all close to you and still he cannot see."

"Doesn't he know we're here?"

"Why should he know that you are here?" Diego replied. "Your friend has paid me good money. I know that he likes to watch people in this house when they do not know that they are being seen."

The man in the armchair was holding a short cigar between the bony fingers of his right hand. A gold watch-bracelet was clamped round his slender wrist. He wore a dark grey suit that seemed too big for him and a white silk shirt and a black satin tie. He was a tall thin man of about sixty with a long hollow-cheeked face the color of chalk. His left hand was thrust deep into the pocket of his trousers.

"Who is he?" Arnold asked quietly.

"The Arab boy who first bring him here call him 'Mister,'" Diego said. "We know no other name for him, so we call him 'Mister.'"

"He's a retired American film producer," Ewing said. "'Mister' retired because he was diseased. Two years ago they cut out half his insides. Since then he's preferred his sex by proxy. You'll see what I mean."

The round-faced Spanish boy slid into the room and whispered something to Diego.

"The first one has already arrived," Diego said. "Now I will leave you to watch. Do you want the boy to stay with you?"

"Not tonight," Ewing said.

"As you please."

Diego walked out of the room, and the Spanish boy followed, closing the door behind him.

"Why have you brought me here?" Arnold asked.

Ewing looked at him in silence, then smiled. "Because I think it's time you learned the facts of life," he said.

"What facts? The facts of male prostitution?"

"The odd experiences that money can buy. Look now. Look at the room next door and learn your lesson like a good boy."

Through the eyepiece Arnold saw Diego open the door in the next room and usher in a tall, heavily built Negro of about thirty, who was dressed in a loose yellow sweater and tight-fitting jeans.

"The first one," Diego said, and left the room.

The Negro stood in silence, his huge head and thick neck thrust forward and downward from his massive shoulders like a cornered bull, watching the man in the armchair.

"Strip," the man said.

For an instant the Negro hesitated. Then slowly he parted his protuberant lips in a smile so broad that Arnold could see his gums, bright pink against the blackness of his skin, as he raised his head arrogantly. Still smiling, the Negro peeled off the sweater from his gleaming hairless chest and pulled down the jeans from his heavy thighs and moved indolently toward the grey-haired man and stood before him, large and naked.

There was a knock at the door.

"Come in," the man said.

Diego put his head round the door. "Are you ready for the second one?" he asked the man called "Mister."

"Send him in," "Mister" said.

Diego went out. The Negro had turned away from the man. He was watching the door expectantly. He was no longer smiling. The door opened a little and a young, fair-skinned Berber boy in a tattered brown burnoose came nervously into the room. For one moment of stark horror Arnold thought that it was Riffi. But the boy was younger and thinner. He was frailer —scarcely more than a child—and his features were less sharply drawn. He glanced for a moment at the man in the armchair. Then he turned and stared at the Negro with wide eyes.

"Strip," "Mister" said.

The boy nodded his head. He moved away modestly toward the stained mattress in the far corner of the room. As he pulled the burnoose over his head Arnold saw that it was the only piece of clothing he had. Against the shining ebony of the Negro's skin the boy's body was as white as milk. His limbs were delicate. He looked very small and fragile.

Arnold moved his head away from the eyepiece and turned to Ewing. "I'm going," he said. "I'm not going to stay and watch this."

"You'll stay," Ewing said. "You'll stay and you'll

[1 5 9]

watch—because you know that if you leave now you'll always be tortured by the desire to know what happened."

"I'm going," Arnold repeated.

But as if his head were controlled by a separate being he found his eyes pressed against the peephole in the wall. His gaze was unwillingly fixed on the scene being enacted in the dimly lit room. In silence Arnold watched. It seemed an eternity of time before he could summon the strength to wrench his head away. Somehow he managed to force himself to walk out into the hallway. Somehow he stumbled down the steps and moved out into the dark street-passage. But by then it was too late. Though he stared down at the wet cobbled stones ahead of him, an image of what he had witnessed remained fixed in his mind, and his memory would never be able to reject it. As he shuddered in horror Arnold knew with the certainty of despair that what he had seen happening in that whitewashed, shabby room would poison his mind forever.

With dragging steps he walked along the slimy dark passageway. Vaguely he was aware that Ewing had followed him. He could feel the poison creeping through the recesses of his brain, tainting the past and the future. When Ewing caught hold of his arm, he tried to break away from him. But Ewing's grip was strong.

"Leave me alone," Arnold muttered.

"What are you so shocked about? Just tell me."

Arnold stared at Ewing with disgust. "What am I shocked about?" he said. "You can ask me that! You watched, didn't you?"

[1 6 0]

"I most certainly did."

"And you ask why I'm shocked?"

"I do."

"When that boy was a mere child?"

"He didn't have to come to Diego's place. He knew what was going to happen."

"He obviously came because he needed the money. He looked as if he were half-starved, the poor little wretch."

"That boy makes enough money in Diego's place to eat steaks every day of the week."

"I don't believe you."

"I know him, I tell you. His name's Allal. He's been on the game for the last two years."

"How could you stand by and watch, while that child . . ."

"I wish you'd stop calling him 'that child.' In fact, he's the same age as Riffi. If you want to know the truth, Riffi used to work in Diego's place. That's where his English friend that you asked me about first found him."

"You mean Riffi . . ."

"I mean Riffi did what that boy did."

"You're lying to me."

"Ask him, if you like."

"How long did he work there?"

"For a year with an interval of a month while Paul Ashton was in Tangier to keep him. He was working at Diego's when he caught my fancy, and I decided to take him on at my villa."

Arnold's eyes searched Ewing's fleshy face. "Was that

[1 6 1]

why you took me to Diego's place tonight?" he asked.

Ewing gazed back at him calmly. "I took you there to learn a lesson," Ewing said.

"What lesson?"

"The lesson of what money can buy."

"Meaning a boy like Riffi."

"A boy like Riffi, among other things."

"But to make me realize what Riffi could be made to suffer was the main point of your operation, wasn't it?"

"The point was to make you understand the importance of having money if you want to protect Riffi."

"But he's safe where he is. When I've gone back to England, he'll still be working at your villa, won't he?"

"I expect so."

"But you're not sure?"

"He'll go on working for me unless he misbehaves himself and gets the sack."

"Then what would happen?"

"He'd go back to Diego's, I suppose."

"You'd allow that?"

Ewing stopped walking and stood still. Arnold turned and faced him.

"Look," Ewing said. "I'd better tell you frankly, here and now, I don't feel myself responsible for Riffi in any way. *I've* never been besotted about him, remember."

"So because you've never wanted him, you'd let him go back to the hell of Diego's?"

"If he'd misbehaved badly, if he'd stolen money for instance, and I had to get rid of him, how could I prevent it if he wanted to resume his trade as a little whore?"

"You'd feel no obligation to help him?"

"Not if he'd stolen money, I wouldn't. But if I may say so, you're missing the whole point. I'm not saying that I intend to sack Riffi and send him back to Diego's. I'm merely saying that I don't want to be responsible for him, whereas you do. You *want* to look after him. All I'm pointing out to you is that to look after Riffi needs money as well as affection."

"And you've already pointed out that I can get that money by kidnapping a boy from Melton Hall. Isn't that correct?"

Ewing laughed. "Don't let's start that over again," he said. "I told you at the time that I'd only suggested it as a joke."

"Rather an elaborate joke, wasn't it?"

Ewing put his hand on Arnold's shoulder. "You score there," he said. "I admit it was rather elaborate. But perhaps that was because there was a tiny grain of truth behind it."

"More than a grain, I'd say."

They had been walking up the Rue des Siaghines and had come out beside the flower stalls of the Zocco Grande. Ewing hailed a taxi.

"My dear Arnold," Ewing said, "you must try not to get so cross with me. It makes me quite nervous. In fact, my nerves are positively jangling. I'm longing for a strong drink and lashings of wine at the *Pavillon*. So shall we make a pact? Shall we agree not to discuss either Riffi or Melton Hall until we've finished dinner?"

Two hours later they were sitting in the enclosed terrace of the *Pavillon* finishing the second bottle of Mouton Rothschild that Ewing had ordered.

While Ewing had made deliberately casual conversation about operas and ballets, Arnold had been sustained by the prospect of seeing Riffi at eleven. As Ewing talked of Vienna and Salzburg, Arnold was imagining his reunion with the boy for whom he now yearned desperately. When the pallid French waiter brought them coffee, Ewing ordered a bottle of liqueur brandy. Then he turned to Arnold and winked at him.

"We've finished our meal," Ewing said. "So the pact's over. I can mention Riffi's name. Aren't you excited to think he'll be waiting for you when we get back to the villa?"

"Very excited," Arnold replied.

"I envy you. Do you remember the lines? 'Christ, if my love were in my arms, and I in my bed again!' It's a long time since any love of mine was in my arms. You're very fortunate."

"When I've got to leave him in five days' time?"

"You can always come back again."

"If I can save up the money."

Ewing spread out his hands and examined his polished fingernails. "Finish your wine," he said. "Then let's consider those little grains of truth that you tell me lie behind my joke. Or shall we suppose for a moment that it wasn't a joke? Shall we pretend it was all true?"

[1 6 4]

"You *know* it was true."

"All right then. Have it your own way. It was true. But I'm still certain you didn't understand what I was getting at."

"I understood all right."

"You couldn't have done or you'd never have used the word 'kidnap' just now. The last thing I'm suggesting is that you should kidnap a boy."

"What are you suggesting then?"

"Listen, Arnold, I've tried to explain what I want to do. Perhaps I explained myself badly and you got the wrong idea. Let me try again, and see if I do better. It's quite simple really. I want to find a boy whom I can educate. That means the boy's got to be intelligent. By that I don't mean good at lessons. I mean quick to adapt himself, quick to learn."

"Quick to learn what?"

Ewing held up his plump hairy hands, palms outwards. "Now don't jump down my throat, before I've finished," he said. "Give me a chance to explain, will you?"

Arnold realized that he had only to endure the evening for another hour before he could be with Riffi. "I'm listening," he said.

"The second qualification is that the boy must hate his own home," Ewing continued, watching Arnold carefully. "Otherwise, however thrilling the life he leads with me abroad, the boy may suddenly long to get back to Mum and Dad. In fact, it's probably better that he doesn't even *have* a Mum and Dad. Or perhaps

[1 6 5]

they've separated and can't be bothered with him. The third qualification is that the boy must be utterly miserable at your school. Is that clear?"

Arnold sipped his brandy. "Clear enough," he said.

"Right. Now, all I want you to do is to select three or four boys of about thirteen or fourteen who have got those qualifications."

"And then?" Arnold asked. After all, he thought, there could be no harm in listening to Ewing's fantasy.

"I'd want to know everything you could tell me about the background and character of each one of them. And I'd want a photograph."

"And then?"

"I'd make my choice."

"Then what happens?"

"*You* come into the picture. You go to work. You talk to the boy. You tell him that you can help him escape or 'abscond' as you call it. You explain that you can get him to Tangier. And you tell him about me."

"What do I tell him about you?"

Ewing looked at Arnold steadily. "You tell him that I've got money and can look after him," he said.

"Do I tell him anything else?"

"No."

"Won't the truth come as rather a shock to him?"

"He won't know the 'truth' as you so tactfully put it. At least not until he's ready for it. You don't think I'd be such a fool as to risk scaring the boy?"

"So you'll take your time to seduce him."

Ewing's hand carved the air with an impatient gesture.

"Don't be stupid," he said. "I've told you I'm not interested in that side of things. Certainly not—unless the boy happened to want it."

Arnold finished his brandy. Ewing poured out another glass for them both.

"This is the advantage of ordering a whole bottle," Ewing murmured. "One doesn't need to interrupt one's conversation to catch the waiter's eye. I'm determined we shouldn't be interrupted. And I do hope that you're beginning to understand that at least I'm not proposing to kidnap a boy and pervert him. My scheme is on a very different plane."

"But I still can't see it working."

"Why not?"

"Let's suppose I've found three candidates for you," Arnold said. "Suppose you've selected one of them and I've approached the boy and discovered that he's longing to get away to Tangier, then what happens?"

"You plan for him to abscond when you've got a weekend free."

Ewing spoke without hesitation. His eyes were fixed calmly on Arnold's face. The wine Arnold had drunk in the discreetly smart restaurant together with Ewing's calm contemplation of a criminal act began to spread a veil of unreality across Arnold's mind.

"Why doesn't the boy abscond just before my next holiday?" Arnold asked.

"Because in order to avoid suspicion it's essential you don't leave England at the same time as the boy does."

"So when the boy absconds where does he go?"

"Is it possible for a boy to get away from your school at night?"

"Yes."

"Have you got a car?"

"Of sorts. Yes."

"Then you meet the boy somewhere outside the school grounds, and you drive him to Folkestone."

"Why to Folkestone?"

"Because that's where you'll hand him over to Tim."

"So Tim comes into the plan?"

"Yes. He's essential."

"Can you trust him?"

"I'm sure I can. If only because he's come to rely on the presents I send him. At the moment his coffee-bar isn't flourishing."

"So I hand the boy over to Tim. And then?"

"Your part in the operation is finished. You've got nothing more to do except to go back to Melton Hall and stay on there for at least another two months."

"Why two months?"

"To avoid any trace of suspicion. We don't want you followed to Tangier."

"What happens to the boy meanwhile?"

"Tim takes him across to France on one of those trippers' Channel boats where you don't need a passport. Those boats positively swarm with parents and their children, so they won't be noticed. Once in France, Tim knows the country well enough to get the boy down to the yacht in Marseilles. He'll probably take a *wagon-lit* so they can change into different clothes on the way."

"Why different clothes?"

"Because they don't want to arrive in Marseilles looking like a middle-aged Englishman and a thirteen-year-old English schoolboy. Once the boy's on the yacht it'll be all right. He'll be dressed as a cabin boy, and no one will notice him. On a fifty-ton motor yacht one *expects* to find a cabin boy."

"You realize that as soon as it's discovered that the boy hasn't gone back home—that he's really missing in fact—there'll be a tremendous hue-and-cry. Headlines in all the papers."

"Let's be quite clear about this. A boy absconds from Melton Hall on a Saturday evening. Now what do the school authorities do about it?

"They'd ring through to the local police and give a complete description of the boy for the police to circulate. As I told you, often a boy's picked up at the nearest bus stop by a patrol car. They'd also ring through to the police at the boy's home town. Sometimes a boy who absconds heads straight for his home. Even if he doesn't get on with his parents, he's probably got friends there."

"The boy's not found locally and he's not found at home. Now what happens?"

"If at the end of forty-eight hours there's been no news of him, the headmaster would ring Scotland Yard and enter a description of the boy in the *Police Gazette.*"

"By then I suppose there'd be some mention of it in the press?"

"Not necessarily. We've had seven boys abscond

from Melton Hall in the last three years, and there wasn't even a mention of it in the local papers. But the boys were always found within a week."

"So unless there's any suspicion of abduction—and there won't be, because you'll be safely back at the school—there's no chance of any story of international interest breaking for at least seven days. They certainly wouldn't bring in Interpol at that stage. And say they do, can Interpol question every cabin boy on every yacht? Besides, even by Tuesday morning Tim will have left Marseilles in the yacht and will be heading straight for Tangier."

Arnold sipped his brandy and stared at Ewing in dazed astonishment. "Are you really serious?" he asked.

"Can't you see that I've got it all planned? I've been thinking of little else for the last week. And you must admit that for a first draft my plan isn't too bad. You see, the perfect part of it is that there's no one for the police to suspect. Of the three of us involved, you're the only one who will be known to have had direct contact with the boy, and by Sunday morning you'll be back at the school and at work the same as ever. Supposing someone spots Tim crossing with a boy on the Channel boat, what proof have they got of his complicity? As soon as the yacht arrives in Tangier, Tim will fly back to London. So within a week of the boy's disappearance he'll be back at his coffee-bar in Folkestone —with no thirteen-year-old anywhere near him. And there'll certainly be no link whatsoever to connect *me* with the disappearance of a boy from an approved school."

"What's your yacht doing in Marseilles?"

"She's laid up there. But a month before the date that we fix for the boy's escape—and for various reasons I suggest it should be in May or June—I shall have the yacht put into commission and fully equipped so that she's ready to sail the instant that Tim arrives with the boy."

"What about the crew?"

"What about them? There's a fifty-year-old Spanish engineer who used to work on the smuggling ships and an old Moor who does the cooking. Neither of them reads a paper from one Christmas to the next."

"What about the skipper?"

"I don't have one. Tim's a trained navigator, and he knows the boat. He can easily take her from Marseilles to Tangier."

"And when Tim goes back to Folkestone?"

"I shall be the skipper, as I've always been. I was in small boats during the war, you know."

Arnold drank his brandy. "And got decorated, so I've been told," he said.

Ewing laughed. "What's that got to do with it?" he asked. "The point is that I can handle a yacht."

"Where would you take the boy?"

Ewing's right hand curved gently through the air. "Can't you guess?" he asked. "If you wanted to show a boy the most beautiful scenery in the world, the most perfect architecture and the loveliest sculpture, if you wanted to fill him with a passionate zeal to appreciate the finest civilization that mankind has ever known— where else could you take him but to Greece?"

[1 7 1]

Ewing leaned back in his chair and lit a cigarette. His small brown eyes were gleaming.

"We could spend the summer cruising round the Greek islands," Ewing said. "And when autumn came and it began to get cold we'd follow the sun. We'd head south for the Levant. In Turkey I could help him to learn about Byzantine art. In Syria I'd teach him about Roman civilization. In Egypt he'd be taught the customs and manners of the Pharaohs. In Alexandria perhaps he might have his first taste of the pleasures of a brothel. In the desert he'd witness the Bedouin's masochistic delight in self-denial and austerity. In Mogadishu he'd listen to the pulse and throb of the drums as they sounded the heartbeat of Africa. In Zanzibar he'd smell the cloves, he'd discover alluring intimations of the Orient in the twisting alleys."

Ewing's head was swaying slightly as he spoke, but his light voice with its slight American twang was clear. Each word was distinct. Ewing was not drunk from the wine.

"Somewhere along the line I'd have procured a passport for the boy, made out in a different name," Ewing explained. "After a while, we'd leave the yacht and travel slowly across India and fly from Calcutta to the shining temples of Katmandu."

Ewing raised his hands in apology and let them fall limply on to the table.

"But I'm getting carried away," he said. "I've forgotten to fill up your glass with this excellent brandy, and I've forgotten that you must be waiting to know precisely how your future is provided for in my plan."

"Only half a glass," Arnold murmured as Ewing tilted the bottle. "I don't want to get drunk tonight."

"I *want* to get drunk," Ewing said. "And I will do if I'm given half a chance—even if it's only from the delicious intoxication of my dreams. But let me bring your problems into the light. Let me 'put you in the picture'—as they used to say in the Services. Are you listening? You seem very far away."

"I'm listening," Arnold said.

But only part of him was listening. There was another portion of his being that had left the table and was now watching him as he sat with his receding pale hair and pink-skinned face gazing across the table at Ewing's heavy jowls and fleshy beaked nose.

"The instant you bring the boy to Tim in Folkestone," Ewing was saying, "Tim will give you a hundred pounds in cash and a check for three thousand dollars drawn out on my account here in Tangier. The title deeds to the villa on the Marshan will be deposited in your name at my bank. At the end of two more months at your approved school, you can hand in your resignation and fly straight to Tangier. Here you'll find both the Marshan villa, which will then belong to you, *and* your little Riffi—waiting for you. I'd advise you to let the lower flat in the villa, which is the larger one. You can live in the top flat on the rent you get from it."

The detached half of Arnold listened to Ewing's proposals with polite interest. The person concerned was the other half—the slender man with eager, protuberant blue eyes and a turned-up nose and a close-fitting tweed jacket, who was leaning across the table.

"You could always stop the check and cancel the deed of gift," he heard himself saying.

"I could," Ewing agreed. "But it's most unlikely that I would. On the contrary. If you examine the position you'll find that I risk far more from your betrayal than you do from mine. When I sail away with the boy you could always try to blackmail me."

"So could Tim."

"Certainly. But I know various facts about Tim's life which are enough to keep him quiet."

"Once you've left on the yacht, will you never come back to Tangier?"

"Not for three or four years. Not until the excitement of the missing schoolboy has been forgotten. Not until my young friend has grown very different in every way from the boy who absconded from Melton Hall. And there'll be no risk then. If I return to Tangier with an elegant young man of seventeen or eighteen who speaks fluent French and Spanish and who speaks English with just the faint trace of a foreign accent which I shall persuade him to cultivate, will anyone look back into the past and connect him with little Dickie Brown who absconded three or four years ago from an approved school? Of course they won't."

As Ewing spoke, Arnold made an effort to integrate his two selves who were now confusing his thoughts.

"Isn't there one factor you've left out of your plans?" Arnold asked after a pause.

"And what is that?"

"The boy you selected might loathe your guts."

Ewing stared back at him blandly. "He might," he said quietly. "That's one of the risks I've got to take. But I've discovered in this odd world that provided you never demand gratitude in any shape or form, people—especially young people—do respond to kindness. And I presume you won't have allowed me to select a monster. Obviously I need a boy who's capable of loyalty and affection. And just think what I shall have done to deserve it! I shall have taken him away from a school that he considers a prison. I shall have removed him from the sordid background of a family he dislikes and who don't care for him either. On the material side, I shall have given him decent clothes and good food and an exciting life on board an extremely comfortable yacht. On the spiritual side, I hope I shall have opened his mind to the beauties of music and literature and painting and sculpture. And perhaps I shall have made him aware of the wonders of ancient civilizations. At least you must admit that there's quite a good *chance* the boy will grow fond of me."

"But he still may not want to go to bed with you."

Ewing controlled a twitch of irritation. "I've already told you that sex isn't the important part," he said. "If I want sex I can get it here in Tangier—or in any of the ports we shall stop at on our cruise, come to that."

"Do you mean that you'll be capable of living day in day out, night after night, on a small yacht with an attractive adolescent without trying to seduce him?"

Ewing wrinkled his nose in distaste. "How I hate that word 'seduce,'" he said. "For all you know, the boy may be fully experienced in such matters. I admit that I shall certainly try to find out."

"But that might ruin everything."

"I doubt it. Not the way I shall play it. If I may say so, I've got considerably more experience than you have."

"What if the boy is disgusted and wants to go back to his home?"

"But then he *wouldn't* be going back to his home, would he? He'd be going back to Melton Hall. And I suppose if he wanted to leave me all that much, I'd let him go. That's a risk that you and I have got to take."

"So if you get drunk one night and make a pass at the boy and scare him stiff, then I shall go to prison."

"You don't suppose I'm giving you a villa worth ten thousand pounds for nothing, do you? The boy may get desperate to go back to England. That's the main risk—I'd say the only risk—you've got to take. But do you really think it's likely? Do you honestly suppose that I'd be so criminally stupid as to frighten the boy? I'm not an alcoholic, and I'm not a fool. Moreover, I'm lucky enough to have an *instinct* in these matters. You might almost call it second sight. And I've never been wrong yet."

"You should touch wood when you say that."

"Besides, I don't suppose that any of the boys at Melton Hall are completely innocent."

"Some of them are."

"Come off it. They may be innocent when they first

arrive. But after a week in a dormitory with the kind of little thugs that get sent to an approved school, I bet they've learned the form. They could probably teach you a thing or two."

Arnold was dimly aware that he was beginning to get drunk.

"You can argue all night," he said aggressively, "but I still think it's a hell of a risk, and I'm not prepared to take it. Not for a dozen villas on the Marshan. It's far too dangerous—quite apart from anything else."

"What do you mean by 'anything else'?"

Arnold gulped down his glass of brandy and poured himself out another.

"I mean I'm not keen about handing over a kid of thirteen to you as if he were a lump of meat."

"You have moral scruples, in fact?"

"Yes. I have."

"Then can we analyze those scruples? What will your part in this plan be? You'll be the instrument whereby an unhappy boy from a wretched home will be brought on a material plane to sunshine and fresh air and decent food and security, and brought on a higher plane to an understanding of art and of history, to an appreciation of culture and the works of genius. So you'll admit, thus far, that your action can only be described as positively good. But, alas, an action in this wicked world can seldom be wholly good—just as it can seldom be wholly bad. Our actions are almost always a choice between the lesser of two evils. And one must face the fact that inherent in your action there is an *element* of evil, which one could put briefly thus.

[1 7 7]

For the sake of money you are exposing a boy to the temptation—no more—of an affair with a middle-aged man."

Ewing held up his hands to silence Arnold as he began to speak.

"And just what do you think went on between Socrates and his young pupils?" Ewing asked. "Do you think their relationship was purely and solely spiritual? We know the Greek ideal of love between a man and a boy. We know that physical passion entered into it. And do you suppose that the lives of those pupils were blighted after they had been—as you would put it—'seduced'? Of course not. When they grew up they married and became respected citizens of the most sensible and brilliant civilization the world has ever known. And perhaps when they became middle-aged, some of them in their turn found themselves a charming boy to educate and to love."

Arnold glanced covertly at his watch. It was eleven o'clock. As Arnold's eyes slid back to Ewing, he was surprised to see him smiling with amusement.

"Eleven o'clock, isn't it?" Ewing inquired. "Precisely —which brings me to one other point—while we're on the subject of moral scruples. I said you would be performing this action 'for the sake of money.' But both of us know that that definition of your motives isn't quite true. 'For the sake of Riffi' would be more accurate, wouldn't it? You're really devoted to that boy, aren't you?"

"I suppose I am."

[1 7 8]

"So naturally you want to give him security and a decent background, so that he has no temptation to go back to Diego's place."

"I want to do all I can to help him."

"And isn't that yet another good element in your action? You know it is, Arnold. My dear man, I'm not asking you to make up your mind tonight or anything drastic. I only want to point out that if you *did* agree to my idea it would be entirely for Riffi's sake."

"If I did agree," Arnold said.

Ewing gazed at him blandly. "If you *did* agree," he repeated. "And speaking of Riffi, can I make a suggestion?"

"I'm listening."

"I think you ought to give him a little present."

"What would he like?"

"I should give him money. Then he can buy himself what he wants."

"Perhaps you're right."

Ewing beckoned to the waiter and asked for the bill.

"That brings me to another point," Ewing said, turning back to Arnold with a smile. "I realize you only expected to stay in Tangier for a week, so I suspect your money may be running short. Do please let me lend you a bit to tide you over the next few days."

"No, thanks," Arnold said quickly.

Instinct warned him not to accept a loan from Ewing, but he needed money urgently. That evening, when Arnold had taken his wallet out of the top drawer of the dressing table, he had found that half the banknotes in it were missing. He had determined to say nothing to Ewing about it in case Riffi were suspected.

"Why won't you let me lend you some dirhams—just the equivalent of twenty pounds or so?"

"For the simple reason that I shouldn't be able to pay you back till next quarter. I'm overdrawn at the bank as it is. I only get a thousand pounds a year, so there's not much left over at the end of each quarter, I can tell you."

"Be sensible. I'm in no hurry to be repaid. Let me lend you twenty pounds' worth of dirhams so you can make your young friend really happy during these next few days. As you know, Riffi isn't at all like the little tarts you see hanging round the Mar Chica. But all these boys out here do expect to be given presents from time to time. It's a convention with them. When, as I hope, Riffi goes to live with you on the Marshan, then it will all be different. You can give him so much a week pocket money to amuse himself with. And that will be that. But with things as they are, I honestly do think you ought to give him something. Obviously, I could give him a little present. But I don't want to pay him anything—apart from his wages. If I *did* it might be fatal. You see, it might give Riffi *quite* the wrong idea."

Arnold was silent. Ewing leaned forward and gently tucked some Moroccan banknotes into the top pocket of his jacket.

"No," Arnold protested.

"Please," Ewing said quietly, and turned away to the waiter who had brought the bill.

Arnold could feel himself blushing. For an instant, he hesitated. Then, while Ewing was paying the bill, he took the notes out of his front pocket and put them carefully into his shabby leather wallet.

Ewing glanced at the gold watch on his wrist. "It's well past eleven," he said. "Perhaps we ought to leave this delicious place and go home. I'm sure that Riffi will be waiting up for you."

Ewing drew back his chair. "Don't look so worried, Arnold," he said. "I'm not asking you to make any decision tonight. You've got five whole days to think it over."

As Mustapha sounded the horn outside the lodge, the dogs rushed up to the grille and began barking wildly. Arnold could feel his heart thudding against his chest. It seemed a long time before the old Moor in his army greatcoat shuffled out of the lodge to open the gate and the car rolled uneasily up the rutted drive to the illuminated façade of the villa.

Bashir, in a smart green tunic with white pantaloons, was waiting under the portico to greet them. Ewing spoke to him rapidly in Arabic. Bashir turned toward Arnold with a leer and slackly nodded his head. Ewing smiled.

"Your little friend's arrived already," he said, and crossed the garishly tiled hall and walked into the drawing room. Arnold followed him. For a moment he thought that the vast octagonal room was empty. Then he saw Riffi lying curled up asleep on a sofa by the chimney piece.

As they came in Riffi awoke and stared up at them in a dazed way. Immediately Arnold noticed that the boy looked tired and ill. The glow had gone from his face; there were dark smudges under his eyes. Then Arnold saw that Riffi was wearing a new and expensive-looking woolen sweater with blue and red stripes, and his heart lurched in suspicion. But at that instant Riffi emerged from his trance and recognized them. With a small cry Riffi rushed toward Arnold and flung his arms round him and clutched him tightly to his chest and kissed his face. Over the boy's shoulder Arnold could see that Ewing was standing at the drink tray with his back toward them.

"Don't mind me," Ewing said. "I'm collecting myself a nightcap. Then I'm tottering to bed."

While Ewing fixed his drink, Arnold kissed Riffi's forehead and ruffled his hair.

Ewing turned round, glass in hand. "Enjoy yourselves," he said. "Enjoy yourselves while you can. Good night."

Ewing walked out of the room, with quick, light steps.

❧ ❧ ❧ ❧ ❧ ❧

Two hours later Arnold lay comfortably in bed with Riffi asleep beside him, but he was worried. Riffi had obviously been delighted to see Arnold again. The boy had dragged him away from the drawing room to the privacy of his bedroom, and he had seemed in high spirits, splashing him with water while he cleaned his teeth and turning cartwheels around the room. Yet there had been a strained, nervous look in his eyes, and he had been oddly reticent when Arnold had asked him about his visit to Chauen.

"How was your mother?" Arnold asked.

"My mother better."

"Was your father in Chauen?"

"Near Chauen in our douar. Yes."

"Where did you get your new pullover?"

"Pullover?"

"Your new sweater."

"In Tetuan."

"Who gave you the money to buy that sweater?"

"My father he give me money."

"Were you happy to be back home?"

"My mother better, so I come back to you. And now I am tired. We talk tomorrow."

As soon as they had got into bed Riffi had wriggled away from him and curled up in the corner nearest the wall.

"Not tonight," Riffi had said. "Tonight sleep. You wait tomorrow."

The curtains were not fully drawn. Pale slivers of moonlight shone into the room. Arnold raised himself and looked down at Riffi as he slept. Riffi's thick curly hair fell over his forehead and touched his dark eyebrows. His face looked very white and drawn. He was sleeping restlessly, turning from side to side, heaving

[1 8 3]

with quick panting breaths as if he were having a nightmare. Suddenly Riffi's limbs jerked frantically.

"No," he cried out with a gasp. "No. Don't let him, Mister. Don't let him."

Then the boy began to scream. His whole body was trembling. His forehead was wet with sweat as Arnold woke him. For a moment Riffi stared up at Arnold in terror. Then he recognized him and smiled and put his arms round him.

"You've had a bad dream," Arnold said gently.

"Yis."

"But you'll be all right now."

"Yis," Riffi repeated.

Presently he went to sleep again.

When Arnold awoke, he could hear a faint rustling noise, as if someone were turning the page of a newspaper. Dawn was filtering through the slats of the Venetian blinds behind the half-drawn curtains. Without moving his head he was aware that he was alone in bed. Slowly his eyes followed the direction of the rustling sound and focused on the far end of the room where Riffi was standing naked, with his back turned. But Arnold could see him reflected in the tall looking glass behind the dressing table. Riffi was holding Arnold's wallet, and his lips were moving as he counted out the banknotes.

Arnold could not bear to be confronted with proof that Riffi was a thief. His reaction was immediate.

"Riffi!" he called out.

Riffi's arms jerked apart, then joined together rapidly as he stuffed back the notes into the wallet and threw it on the dressing table. When Riffi swung round to face Arnold his chest was heaving, but he tried to smile.

"I want to see if you rich," Riffi said, panting. "You no have too much money I tink."

"Come here," Arnold said.

Riffi hesitated, then moved a few paces toward him. "Why-for you angry?"

"Where have you been for the last two days?"

"I tell you. In douar. By Chauen."

"Where did you buy that sweater?"

"In Tetuan."

"Did you go alone to Tetuan?"

"Yis. I go alone."

"Did you meet an American, a tall thin man?"

"No. I meet my father and my mother."

"Who is 'Mister'?"

Riffi stared at him with wide violet eyes. "I not know 'Mister.' Why-for you ask these questions?"

"You talked about 'Mister' in your sleep last night."

"Yis. I sleep last night."

Riffi was trying to pretend he could not understand him. But Arnold was determined to persist.

"Before you came to this villa," Arnold said slowly, "you worked at Diego's place."

Riffi's eyes slid down to the floor and his hands twitched slightly.

"You have been to Diego's?" Riffi asked.

"You once worked there," Arnold said.

Riffi's narrow shoulders wriggled as he shook his head.

"Me no like Diego," he said. "He no my freng."

"But you worked for him."

"Me work for him? No. Work here."

"But you did once before work for him."

"Who tell you me work Diego? Señor Ewing?"

"Yes. Señor Ewing told me."

Riffi crossed the room quickly and sat down beside Arnold on the bed and put a hand on his shoulder.

"He no spik true," Riffi said urgently. "Me no work Diego. Me go there when no money for buy food. But go there no more. Work here now in villa. And you my freng."

Riffi gazed down at him anxiously. The dark smears were moist under his eyes.

"When did you last meet 'Mister'?"

"No meet 'Mister.' You my freng. You Riffi's one freng. And Riffi love you. But you no love Riffi. You ask Riffi questions. You no like Riffi. Riffi no your freng. No your freng."

Suddenly Riffi flung himself across the bed and covered his face with his hands. His whole body shook as he sobbed and gasped for breath. He was trembling violently. Arnold held him fast and tried to calm him. Gradually Riffi's breathing grew quieter, and the tears dried on his cheeks. Soon he went to sleep.

When Arnold awoke, Riffi was stroking his shoulder. Sleepily he peered into the boy's face. The smears beneath his eyes were fainter. The haunted look had gone. Riffi smiled at him happily. He took hold of Arnold's hand and drew it to him. Arnold touched the boy's warm skin. Slowly, he could feel his desire moving, creeping like a tide toward the shore. The silver breakers began to rise and fall relentlessly. They surged and fell rippling across the beach. But while the waves of passion hissed and swirled around him, lifting him high with their vast swell and dashing him into the white-flecked troughs, a picture which at first he could only see in blurred outline through the foam and spray, a picture that thrilled him more than the throbbing waves, formed and occupied his whole vision, filling him with an excitement so violent that it pierced him like a dagger thrust. The picture was still indistinct. But as the force of the waves increased until their pressure seemed unbearable, the picture became clearer, and suddenly in a fierce rush of ecstasy he recognized the scene. Then the waves dropped. The roar of the breakers grew faint, and Arnold lay staring at the ceiling of his room, shuddering and sick. For the scene he had recognized was set in a shabby room with damp streaks running down the whitewashed walls. The Negro's ebony chest glittered between his massive shoulders and bulging thighs. His gums were bright pink as he smiled triumphantly toward the chalk-white face of the motionless American.

Arnold had witnessed that instant before. But in the scene, this time, it was Riffi who had taken the place of the skinny Berber boy.

❧ ❧ ❧ ❧ ❧ ❧

WHEN Arnold went out onto the patio he found Ewing shaved and dressed and finishing breakfast.

"It's cold out," Ewing said. "But there's not a cloud in the sky, so I suggest we drive out to the Caves. Can you be ready—or should I say, have you the inclination to be ready—by noon? The time's now eleven o'clock."

"Fine," Arnold said.

"I presume your young friend will come too?"

"You presume right."

"Do you know I found it really touching the way he rushed across the room to greet you last night. I'm now convinced that he's devoted to you."

Two hours ago, Ewing's words would have delighted Arnold. Now, they filled him with guilt. For the love he offered Riffi in exchange for his devotion was tainted with a passion that disgusted him.

"You look rather ill," Ewing remarked. "I hope nothing we ate at the *Pavillon* disagreed with you?"

"I just drank too much. That's all."

"So did I. But a dip in the Atlantic will cure us both."

The sun was shining in a pale blue sky. The long breakers fell, slithering in a creamy foam over the flat sand. Ewing lay on his back, feet wide apart, naked and asleep. His hairy stomach heaved with his faint snores. Arnold turned to the corner of the cleft in the rocks where Riffi was lying on his side with his head pillowed on his arm, his chest rising and falling rhythmically as he slept. For a while Arnold's eyes roved slowly from the dusty clusters of curls on the boy's head, past the little crease of flesh at the boy's waist to the smooth, glistening stretch of his long thighs. Then Arnold walked over to Riffi and gently tapped his shoulder. As Riffi gazed up at him, Arnold put his finger to his lips and pointed to Ewing's hairy, scarred body, lying gross and asleep. Then he lifted Riffi to his feet and beckoned to him to follow.

Quickly Arnold walked away from the narrow gully and turned toward the path that led up the side of the cliff, looking back only once to make certain that Riffi was following.

"Where we go?" Riffi asked.

Arnold's finger was trembling as he pointed, and his voice was thick as he spoke.

"To your cave."

Later that afternoon as Arnold stepped down the stony path to the cleft between the rocks where Ewing lay inert, if not asleep, he realized that what he had always sought and now at last obtained from Riffi was not requited love but the fulfillment of a passion so violent and strange that a week ago he would have resisted it—even if he had been aware of its existence. He could pretend to himself that his wish to help Riffi sprang from affection. But he knew, now, that his desire to protect him was due to a fiercely intense passion to possess the boy completely, to keep him entirely to himself, to command all his affection, to satisfy all his desires, to dominate him utterly in every way.

The thought of leaving the boy in Tangier for three days, let alone three months, was now anguish to him. The future had always loomed grey ahead of him; now it seemed hideous and unbearable. He needed Riffi beside him as he needed the air he breathed. He felt he would stifle without his presence. Then for the first time he thought coldly and seriously about Ewing's plan. It seemed the only hope for him. And as he considered the plan, the name of one boy slipped into his mind—Dan Gedge, the boy who had absconded and had been mauled in the gym at Stobart's instigation. Dan whom he had visited in the sick bay, Dan with his pale, flat hair and thin, delicate face, Dan with his haunted blue eyes and nervous twitch. The boy fulfilled all Ewing's qualifications. He was intelligent, he had no affection for his parents, and he was wretchedly miserable at Melton Hall. The only person in the world that Dan loved was his "Auntie," as he called her. He had absconded to visit her in the hospital. And then she had died.

Dan Gedge. Arnold began to remember his case history. Father killed riding a motorcycle. Mother married again a year later. Wasn't her second husband a bricklayer? In any case he was ten years younger than she was. He was a drunkard, and he beat her. Dan was systematically ill-treated and neglected. For two years he had run wild with a gang of boys in the neighborhood. One evening they raided a tobacconist's shop. Dan was caught. In view of his home background he was committed to an approved school. It was all very simple. Dan Gedge. Highly strung and quick-witted. And, if you were drawn to delicate features, attractive. Dan. There was a photograph of him in Arnold's suitcase. He was standing in a group of three boys. Arnold had kept the photograph because the young freckled thug in the center was Charlie Mason, who had always attracted him—Charlie with his bristling red hair and green eyes and wide mouth, Charlie with his reckless impudence and raucous laugh. Charlie Mason was now almost sixteen and already molded. Charlie would never do for Ewing. But little Dan . . .

Ewing was still asleep. Though gross, his body was manifestly strong. But it was misshapen, and blunt and ugly. Arnold shuddered in disgust. He could never deliver Dan defenseless into those hairy arms.

❧ ❧ ❧ ❧ ❧ ❧

DURING the next three days, Ewing was friendly but aloof. He made no mention of the plan that had once seemed to be an obsession with him. He was casually pleasant to Arnold when they met, but he seemed absorbed in the social life of Tangier. He lunched out each day; he went to a cocktail party each evening. Arnold only saw him when he returned late for dinner.

"I'd take you with me gladly," Ewing explained. "But I know you're far happier left alone with Riffi. After all, you haven't very many days left."

There was no need to remind Arnold of that. He was now trying desperately to hold onto each moment of each hour. And Riffi was behaving even better than Arnold had hoped in his most optimistic imaginings. He was willing, and sometimes eager, to endure the fierceness of Arnold's passion. He basked and frolicked in the warmth of Arnold's guilt-ridden affection.

[191]

One morning Arnold slept late. When he awoke it was eleven o'clock. Riffi was standing beside his bed, dressed in his new sweater and jeans, with his hands behind his back.

"I have present for you," Riffi announced solemnly and handed Arnold a small flat parcel.

Arnold unwrapped the paper and saw an oblong little cardboard box with the name of a shop—Kitto—written across the lid. He opened it. Inside was a well-made thin gold chain.

"You wear round neck," Riffi said. "You remember Riffi."

Arnold was ecstatically grateful, and Riffi was proudly delighted with the success that his present had had.

When Arnold returned that evening from yet another day with Riffi at the Caves, he met Ewing crossing the tiled hall.

"I can see from your face that you've had another rapturous day," Ewing said. "For my sins I'm off to a cocktail party at the British Consulate. The one sacrifice I make to respectability is to keep in with the Consular authorities. One never knows when one may need their assistance."

"Will you be back for dinner?"

"Yes. Let's dine together at nine-thirty. What's that charming gold chain you're wearing?"

"Riffi gave it to me this morning as a surprise. Isn't it pretty?"

"Entrancing. I wonder where he got it."

"From a shop called 'Kitto' in the Rue des Siaghines. I saw the name on the box he brought it in."

"Yet more proof that he's in love with you. Kitto's is one of the most expensive jewelers in the town. He must have spent all the money you gave him to buy it. I'm beginning to envy you more and more. Why haven't I got a boyfriend who gives me gold necklaces? Why can't I stay here and drink with my beloved one instead of having to make polite conversation to the Consul-General? There's no justice! I shall think of you while I plough my way through the staider ranks of the British community. See you at nine-thirty."

The following morning the weather changed. Rain fell steadily from a leaden sky. As usual, Ewing was out to lunch. In the afternoon Riffi clamored to be taken to a cinema, so Arnold rang up a taxi and they drove down into town. The film had been made in Cairo for North African consumption. The banal plot served as a link between elaborate dances and protracted vocal performances. The film was loud and long and tedious. And Riffi enjoyed every minute of it.

Rain was still falling relentlessly when they hailed a taxi and drove back to the villa. As the taxi slithered up the drive between the avenue of dripping eucalyptus trees, Arnold saw that Ewing was standing under the portico. Arnold waved to him, but Ewing neither moved nor spoke. In silence Arnold paid off the taxi driver.

"What's wrong?" Arnold asked as the taxi drove away.

"We can talk in the drawing room," Ewing said. "Bring the boy with you."

They followed Ewing into the grey octagonal room.

[193]

"Sit down, please, both of you," Ewing said.

"What's all this about?" Arnold asked.

"Theft," Ewing replied. "Theft."

Ewing crossed to the side table and poured himself a drink.

"Help yourself," he said over his shoulder to Arnold.

"Thanks," Arnold said. "I think I will."

As he splashed the whisky into the heavy crystal glass, Arnold felt his heart pounding against his chest, for he had seen a look of fear slide over Riffi's face.

"I find all this extremely distasteful," Ewing said. "But I'm afraid it's got to be done."

Ewing stood facing them with his back to the log fire. For an instant his eyes flickered toward Riffi, then his gaze swerved back to Arnold.

"I must explain that for the past three weeks I've found that money has been missing from my room," Ewing said. "Loose change has been taken from my dressing table. Banknotes have been taken from my wallet. At first I thought that my suspicions must be mistaken. I seldom count my money, so I might easily have been wrong. But ten days ago I was certain. You see, I'd drawn two thousand dirhams to pay the wages. I'd spent nothing to speak of. But the following day there were only seventeen hundred dirhams left in my wallet."

Ewing's eyes slewed toward Riffi, who was sitting on the edge of a gilt chair.

"Do you understand what I'm saying, Riffi?" Ewing asked. "Or shall I repeat it in Arabic?"

[194]

"Yis," Riffi said in a husky voice. "I understand."

"Now the loss of the money as such didn't worry me," Ewing proceeded. "But what I found deeply disturbing was the thought that someone in my household must be stealing from me. I can't bear being suspicious of any of my servants. But I knew now for certain that someone working in this house was a thief. Do you understand me, Riffi?"

"Yis."

"I found my uncertainty intolerable. So the next time that I got cash from the bank, I drew the money in hundred-dirham notes, and I marked each note. I made a small cross in indelible ink in the top right-hand corner. The notes were old notes, and the cross didn't show. You wouldn't notice it unless you were looking for it."

Once again Ewing's gaze veered slowly toward Riffi.

"Do you understand me, Riffi?" Ewing asked softly. "I marked each note with a small black cross. Is that clear?"

"Yis," Riffi whispered.

"Seven of those marked notes were stolen," Ewing said, nodding his head. Slowly he took his black leather gold-edged wallet out of his pocket. He drew from it two banknotes and handed them to Arnold.

"If you look at the top right-hand corner of these two notes you'll see a small cross. Can you see it?"

"Certainly." Ewing took back the notes and held them up in his right hand and waved them toward Arnold.

"These two notes," Ewing said quietly, enunciating

each word with deliberate clarity, "These two notes were used to buy the gold chain that is hanging round your neck."

Arnold glared at him angrily. "How do you know?" he asked.

"Because I went down to Kitto's shop this afternoon, and the head assistant behind the counter remembers Riffi coming in to buy the gold chain. He remembers that he paid with two hundred-dirham notes. Your chain cost a hundred and twenty, so Riffi was given eighty dirhams in change."

Riffi was silent. He was gazing toward Arnold with imploring eyes.

"Did the assistant notice the little black cross on each note?"

"No."

"Then how in heaven's name can you be sure that it was Riffi who paid with those particular two notes? You can't possibly. It might have been Bashir who stole them for all you know. He changed the notes down in town, and someone used them to buy something at Kitto's. You can't accuse Riffi on that evidence."

"I can."

"Not possibly."

"I noticed your gold chain last night, didn't I?"

"You did."

"You told me that Riffi had given it to you that morning."

"Yes."

"On my way downtown last night it suddenly occurred to me that a gold chain was an unusually expensive present to give, so I decided to telephone Kitto's. They know me there, of course. I asked them if a young Berber boy had been into the shop that morning to buy a gold chain. They told me that was correct. The purchase had been made at nine-thirty that morning, shortly after they opened. I asked them how he'd paid for it. They told me he'd given them two hundred-dirham notes and they'd given him change. I asked them to keep those two notes."

Ewing held up his right hand. "And here they are."

"What about the money you lent me?" Arnold asked. "Weren't those notes marked?"

Ewing glanced at him coldly.

"You know as well as I do that the money I lent you was in denominations of ten-dirham notes," Ewing said.

Ewing walked quickly across the room and stood beside Riffi's chair.

"You stole that money, didn't you?" Ewing said.

"No. Me no steal. No thief. Other man steal your money. Not Riffi. Riffi no steal."

"Then turn out your pockets. And let's see that gaudy little leather wallet that Paul the Englishman gave you last year. The leather wallet that folds in two. Where you keep your money, Riffi."

"I keep no more. I lose it."

"No, you haven't."

"Yis. I have no more."

"You've got it all right. It's in the back pocket of your jeans. Give it to me. Give it to me, Riffi."

Riffi did not move. He stared up at Ewing with wide dilated eyes. Suddenly Ewing seized the boy's shoulder with his left hand almost pulling him to the ground. With his right hand he grabbed the yellow wallet from the hip pocket of the jeans. Carefully Ewing unfolded the wallet and examined the notes in it. Then he took out a hundred-dirham note and handed it to Arnold.

"Just look at the top right-hand corner," Ewing said triumphantly. "Just look at it."

As he handed the note to Arnold. Riffi began to sob hysterically. Suddenly he leaped up, rushed to the door and ran out of the room. Ewing looked toward Arnold and nodded his head. Neither of them spoke. They could hear the boy's footsteps scudding across the hall. They listened to the front door opening. They heard the boy running down the drive. Ewing crossed the room and rang the bell.

"What are you going to do?" Arnold asked.

"Send Bashir and Mustapha after him."

"Why?"

"Because I don't intend to let him get away with this. He's been dishonest and disloyal. He's caused a lot of trouble. He's not going to escape."

Bashir sidled into the room. Ewing spoke to him rapidly in Arabic. Bashir bowed his head and left the room swiftly.

"When they bring him back what will you do?"

"Hand him over to the police, I expect."

"Are you mad?"

"What's mad about that?"

"If you call in the police, the boy's certain to complain that . . ."

"To complain that one of us or both of us have assaulted him? Of course he will. But the Tangier police
aren't complete fools. They know that every Moroccan
houseboy who's had up by his master for stealing always maintains that he's been assaulted, so I don't
suppose they'll take much notice of Riffi."

Arnold crossed to the side table and poured out half
a glass of neat whisky.

"Why bring in the police?"

"Now that they all know down at Kitto's shop, I
can't see what else I can do. It would be difficult to
keep things quiet at this stage. I suppose I *could* hush
it up. But quite frankly, I don't feel inclined to."

"You want Riffi to go to prison, don't you?"

Ewing gazed at Arnold in surprise. "What nonsense!" Ewing said quietly. "Besides, I don't suppose
he *will* go to prison. They send young boys like Riffi
to join the gangs making the new roads down in the
south. And I may say that he'll be used there by night
as well as by day. As you know, the men out here go in
for that kind of thing—particularly when there aren't
any women about."

"And you'd let that happen to him?"

"I've told you time and again that I feel no responsibility for Riffi whatsoever. I've never been infatuated
with him. Nor he with me. I've never claimed I was in
love with him. He's never bought *me* a present with
the money he's stolen. He's got no claim on *my* affec-
tions whatever."

Arnold gulped down his whisky and poured himself
another glass.

"You can't hand him over to the police," Arnold said.

"What else can I do?"

"Send him back to his village."

"There's no work for him in his douar. They're starving as it is. So who's going to pay for his keep? His family can't. And I'm sure I'm not going to. If he goes back to his douar they'll throw him out at the end of a week. His only chance then will be to catch a lift to Marrakesh or Casablanca and try to earn a living by plying his trade on the streets. Whether he works down south in a road gang or whether he tries to sell his wares on the dockside of Casablanca—it's all the same in the end. So I might just as well prove to my household conclusively that theft doesn't pay and call in the police."

"How can you be so callous?"

Ewing shook his head wearily. "I'm not callous," he said. "I'm just not interested. How many times do I have to tell you? I don't care what happens to Riffi. He's betrayed my trust in him, and that's the end of it. If you want to take on the boy, then it's a completely different matter."

Arnold took a gulp of whisky. "If I took on the boy," he said slowly, "then what would happen?"

"If you decided that you wanted Riffi permanently, for good and all, then I'd suggest that he leaves Tangier tomorrow and goes to his douar. We could arrange for his family to be sent money each week for his keep. And there Riffi could stay perfectly happily and safely until such a time as you were in a position to welcome him to your villa on the Marshan."

Ewing stretched out his arms and let them fall to his side. The lid of his left eye was slowly quivering.

"But as you know," Ewing said, "that is a matter entirely for you to decide."

Bashir opened the door. His plump face was creased in a smile. Mustapha dragged Riffi into the room. The boy's face was bruised; blood was running from the corner of his mouth. He was sobbing with pain. Ewing spoke quickly in Arabic. Bashir bowed his head and left the room. Mustapha released his grip on Riffi, pushed him toward Ewing with a vicious jerk, and followed Bashir, closing the door behind him. Riffi looked desperately around him. Then he rushed over to Arnold and flopped down on his knees in front of him and clasped his legs with his skinny arms.

"No let them send for poleez," Riffi cried frantically. "No send for poleez. No poleez."

When Arnold did not answer, Riffi let go of his legs and groveled at his feet, beating his head wildly against the floor.

"No poleez," he moaned. "No poleez."

"Riffi," Arnold called out suddenly. "Riffi, listen to me. Listen to me."

The boy's moans ended in a gulp. Shakily, he raised his tear-stained bleeding face toward Arnold.

"It's all right, Riffi," Arnold said slowly in a voice of calm certainty. "There'll be no police. You've nothing to fear. I'll look after you. Don't cry. Everything's going to be all right. Get up now, and go to my room and wait for me there. I'll be with you soon. I won't be long."

Riffi dragged himself to his feet and took Arnold's hand and kissed it. Then he stumbled out of the room. In silence Arnold went to the drink tray and poured more whisky into his glass. Ewing was standing by the chimney piece watching him. His eyelid no longer fluttered, and his lips were stretched in a faint smile.

"So you've made up your mind at long last," Ewing said.

"Yes."

"I'm glad," Ewing murmured.

❧ ❧ ❧ ❧ ❧ ❧

THAT evening after dinner Arnold showed Ewing the photograph of the three boys in the playground of Melton Hall. Ewing took the photograph to the alabaster lamp behind the sofa and studied it carefully.

"What's the name of the tough little number in the middle?" Ewing asked.

"Charlie Mason."

"He's got rather a look of Riffi about him. But I expect you've noticed that already."

For the first time Arnold saw the resemblance. He could feel himself blushing. "You're right," he said. "But Charlie's nearly two years older."

"He's just your type. You must have fancied him."

"I did."

"But you did nothing about it?"

"Not a thing."

"From fear or from principle?"

"Both, I expect."

Ewing held the photograph closer to the light. "Who's the fat one with spectacles on the left?" he asked.

"Ronnie Mills. His father's in prison for g.b.h.— grievous bodily harm. His mother's a prostitute."

"Poor boy. He's desperately plain, isn't he? Is that the school uniform they're wearing?"

"Yes. I hate it. I'm sure it's wrong to make them all dress alike. But the whole policy seems to be to suppress their individuality as much as possible. Do you realize they're not even allowed to have photos of their families by their beds?"

"The whole system sounds quite inhuman."

"If only people knew. But no one seems to care."

Ewing's eyelid began to flutter slowly like a drowsy butterfly. "Who's the fair-haired little boy on the right?" Ewing asked.

"Dan Gedge."

"It's a sensitive face. Is the boy intelligent?"

"For his age—very."

"How old is he?"

"Fourteen."

"What was he sent in for?"

"Breaking into a tobacconist's shop with a gang of other boys."

"Does he get on well at the school?"

"No. He loathes the place. In fact, he's absconded once already."

"What about his parents?"

"His father's dead. His mother's married to a man ten years younger than she is. He's a bricklayer, but the man's generally unemployed. He's a drunk. He beats her up. It's a pretty typical case. Dan's had a fairly wretched life up to date."

"Why did Dan abscond?"

"Because he was unhappy. Because his aunt was ill in the hospital and he wanted to see her. But she's dead now. She was the only person Dan really loved— or so I gather from talking to him. You see . . ."

Ewing raised his white plump hands in the air to silence Arnold.

"Don't tell me now," he said. "For various reasons I'm tired tonight, and I can't take it in. Tell me all you know about the boy tomorrow when we're both rested. It's essential that I register each piece of information that you give me. I want to be fresh and alert so I can concentrate on every single word you say, because every tiny detail now becomes of overwhelming importance."

"You mean . . ."

"Yes," Ewing said softly. "Dan is the one. I knew it instinctively the instant I saw that photograph."

PART

3

RAIN dripped from the leaves of the chestnut tree onto the roof of the car. Arnold turned off the windshield wiper, switched off his side lights, buttoned up the collar of his coat, and settled down to wait. He was cold, and his stomach was queasy with fear. He looked at the wristwatch Ewing had given him four months ago as a parting present in Tangier. The time was half-past six. He had arranged to meet Dan Gedge in the disused trailer site at the end of Rooker's Lane at seven o'clock.

Uneasily, Arnold's mind rehearsed yet again the details of his plan. The boy had got permission from Stobart, his housemaster, to go to the village cinema. The performance on Saturday began at five and ended about eight. Arnold, who was allowed one weekend in four away from the school, had left Melton Hall after the midday meal. He had told the staff that he was going up to London for the day and would return early on Sunday morning. If Dan turned up at the meeting place at seven, they would reach Folkestone at about nine o'clock. Tim was waiting for them at his flat. In a parcel in the back of Arnold's car were a pair of old flannel trousers and a brown sports jacket, so that Dan could change out of his grey school uniform on the way to Folkestone. The plan had been carefully worked out. Unless Stobart had changed his mind and had canceled his permission for Dan to go to the cinema, Arnold was certain that Dan would appear on time.

From his very first meeting with Dan after his return from Tangier, Arnold had been amazed how quickly Dan had fallen in with Ewing's elaborately devised scheme and how eager he had been to accept the risks involved.

Their first meetings had taken place in the school buildings, sometimes in the damp-smelling corridor—a darkly glazed avenue of gloom, the lower half lined with brown tiles, the upper half with green tiles a size smaller. Sometimes they had met in the school room at the end of class. They had talked in abrupt spurts of conversation, nervously gazing at the arithmetical sums still scrawled on the blackboard, or they had spoken briefly together as they stood in front of the school notice board or outside the grim dining room. Arnold's first object had been to win the boy's confidence. It had been surprisingly easy, for there was no need to hurry. Ewing did not want the boy to be persuaded to abscond until the first week in May. Arnold began slowly. First, he had persuaded the boy to talk about his home town and his friends there. Later, he had drawn him out to speak of his life at home before his father had died. Dan had even confided in him the details of the gang's raid on the tobacconist's shop. Whenever Dan had the chance, Arnold noticed that he would come up and talk to him. And gradually Arnold began to form an odd impression. He began to feel that at the end of each meeting the boy was disappointed and that somehow he had failed him.

One morning Dan ran up to Arnold as he was crossing the asphalt playground. There was a desperate look in his blue eyes, and the corner of his mouth was twitching. But when Arnold stopped, the boy seemed to have nothing urgent to say.

"Good morning, sir," Dan mumbled.

"Good morning. Anything wrong?"

"No. Nothing."

"Then what are you looking so worried about?"

"Nothing."

"Go on. Tell me," Arnold persisted.

"There's nothing to tell."

"Have it your own way!" Arnold said gently and moved away.

"Sir."

The voice was so anxious that Arnold turned.

"Can't I come to your place one Saturday? Then we could talk really properly."

Arnold hesitated. Other masters invited boys to tea in their rooms in the grounds. Arnold had never done so because he was afraid of the temptation.

"Yes," Arnold said. "Come round next Saturday for tea."

Dan's face brightened. "Thank you, sir," he said. "Thanks a million."

Arnold had a semidetached, rent-free cottage halfway down the school's drive. He had done his best to make the angular sitting room look less bleak by covering the walls with brightly colored papers and building in bookcases. A new loaf of bread, a sponge cake and a honeycomb were on the table, and the kettle was simmering on the gas-ring when Dan knocked on the door and Arnold moved quickly to answer it. He hoped that Dan would not be seen by the P.T. instructor and his long-nosed wife who lived next door.

Dan sat down nervously by the gas fire, plucking at the knot of his blue school tie. His pale hair, plastered down with water, slanted damply across his forehead. His features looked very delicate against the coarse grey jacket and grey shirt of the school uniform. The heavy grey trousers were too big for him and hung in folds from his narrow waist. The right corner of his mouth slid upwards in the occasional spasm of a twitch. His light blue eyes were fixed on Arnold with an expression that seemed at once hopeful and yearning. He was too pale and fragile to arouse even a slight response in Arnold. The boy was far too nervous and too gentle. Arnold thought of Riffi's boisterous vitality and sighed.

When they had finished tea, Arnold knew that the moment he had been dreading for the last month had come. He must talk to Dan about Tangier. He must tell him about Ewing.

"You're not happy at Melton Hall, are you?" Arnold began quietly.

"No. I'm not."

"What is it you don't like about the place?"

"Everything, sir. From the moment I get up to the moment I go to bed again. The lot. The only thing I don't mind is Math and English, because when you're there I know I'm all right."

"Do they give you a rough time?"

"Yes."

"Have you told Captain Stobart?"

Dan's eyes flickered toward the gas fire. "No, sir," he said.

"Why not?"

Dan put his hand to the corner of his mouth to conceal his twitch. "I'm not going to tell tales," Dan said. "Besides, they'd only make it worse for me if I did."

"Is there anything I can do to help?"

Dan shook his head. "Thanks just the same."

Suddenly Dan leaned forward. "If I tell you something, sir, do you promise you won't tell anyone else?" Dan asked.

"Yes."

"Promise? Not even Captain Stobart?"

"Yes."

"Well, it's like this. I'd run off again tomorrow if I had the chance and if I knew they wouldn't catch me again. I'd give anything to get away. And I'd do anything. I'd lie and I'd steal. I would. But what's the use? They'd catch up with me in the end, and I'd get hell again when they brought me back."

Arnold stared at the boy's haunted eyes. "Dan," he said gently, "do you think I can trust you?"

The eager response in the boy's face gave Arnold his reply even before Dan spoke.

"You can trust me for anything, sir," Dan said. "You don't have to ask me that. I'd do everything I could for you."

"It's not so much for *me*." Arnold said.

"What is it then?"

The room was growing dark. Arnold switched on the lights and drew the curtains. When he turned he saw that Dan had stood up and moved toward him.

"You don't have to go," Arnold said.

"No, I don't. I don't have to be back for an hour yet."

"Then sit down."

Dan hesitated. For an instant his eyes slid toward the settee. Then he moved back to his chair.

"All right," Dan said in a whisper. "All right."

"Dan, you've got to listen to me carefully," Arnold said. "It's not going to be easy to explain."

"I'm listening."

Arnold took a long breath as if he were going to dive under water. Now the moment had come, he was horribly afraid. Yet, after all, the plan he had to outline and the facts he had to tell were so improbable that even if Dan betrayed him and repeated what he had been told no one would believe his story.

Slowly and carefully Arnold explained to Dan that he had a friend in Tangier, a fifty-year-old Anglo-American, who wanted to adopt a young boy. He described Ewing's villa and the cruise that had been planned on the yacht. Cautiously Arnold suggested that Ewing might in time grow fond of the boy and that the boy might feel some affection for him. Arnold's explanation was weakened by evasive pauses and understatement. But Dan listened intently, his pale blue eyes fixed on Arnold's face.

When Arnold had finished, Dan leaned forward, his scarred hands clutching his knees. "And do you think this man might take me?" Dan asked.

"I know it. I know he would."

"But why *me?*"

"He saw a photo of you."

The worried expression left Dan's face. He brushed back his pale hair with a quick gesture and smiled. "You've got a photo of me?" Dan asked excitedly.

"Yes."

"You had it with you in that place you said? In Tangier?"

"Yes."

"So you *do* think of me sometimes?"

Arnold felt it would be unkind to tell Dan that he had kept the photograph because he was attracted to Charlie Mason.

"Of course I think about you," Arnold said in a flat voice. "It's always worried me that you're so unhappy here. If you weren't unhappy I'd never have told you about Tangier. But you must promise you'll keep all I've said to yourself."

"I promise. They can beat me silly, and I'd never tell them."

[2 1 3]

"And I want you to think over all I've said."

"I've thought it over. And the answer's 'yes.' "

"I'm not going to let you make up your mind so quickly. You've got to think it out from every angle."

"What is there to think out? I can't stick it here, and I've got the chance of a new start over there. No matter what happens, it can't be any worse, can it? I won't get beaten, will I ?"

"No, Dan. You won't get beaten."

"Then what have I got to lose?"

"You might not like the man."

"He's a friend of yours, isn't he?"

An image of Riffi groveling on the floor swung into Arnold's mind. He swallowed.

"Yes," Arnold said.

"Then if he's a friend of yours he won't treat me bad."

"That's not the point."

"What is it that's worrying you then?"

Arnold turned away from the anxious blue eyes. "If you didn't like him, you wouldn't be happy living with him on a yacht."

"But I wouldn't get knocked about, would I?"

"No."

"Then what's there to worry about?"

Arnold looked at his watch. "It's getting late," he said. "We'll have to talk about it another time."

"When?"

"What about next Saturday?"

"Not before then? Can't I come and see you before then?"

"We don't want anyone getting suspicious, do we?"

"But I could get out at night when they were all asleep. I know a way down into the grounds."

Arnold shook his head. "No. It's too dangerous. Besides . . . I want you to have at least a week to think it all over. Now you'd better cut along and get back to your house."

Dan seized Arnold's hands and clasped them. "Thanks," he said. "Thanks for everything. I've got something to look forward to now."

Arnold withdrew his hands and moved away to the door. "If anyone sees you coming out of here—if anyone asks you why you've been here," he said, "just tell them that I asked you in for a cup of tea and we talked about your home."

"You can trust me," Dan replied, and walked out quickly leaving Arnold alone with his guilt.

Throughout that week, whenever Arnold thought of Dan's pale face and tremulous mouth he felt sick. From timidity he had given the boy no warning of Ewing's intentions.

When Dan appeared the following Saturday for tea, Arnold was determined to force himself to give an explicit warning. But it was essential that he should not shock Dan or frighten him, so he began cautiously.

"I don't suppose you're completely green," Arnold said, loathing the forced note of joviality in his voice. "I mean, I expect the boys play around in your dormitory quite a bit."

"Sometimes."

"I suppose you know all about that kind of thing?"

"When I first came here I didn't. I do now."

Arnold made his voice sound casual. "You know that men go in for it as well."

"Course they do. I know that."

"The idea of it doesn't shock you?"

"Why should it? That's what goes on, doesn't it?"

Arnold could feel himself blushing.

"If men do it with boys they can go to prison for it. I mean, it's against the law."

"So are lots of things. That doesn't mean they're wrong, does it?"

Arnold's hands were trembling. He put them in his pockets. "Last time we met, I told you about this friend of mine in Tangier," he said.

Dan leaned forward eagerly. His words came in a rush.

"I've thought it all out. Carefully, like you said I was to. Really I have. And my answer's 'yes.' Yes, every time."

Arnold spoke slowly and hesitantly. "Supposing this man in Tangier—supposing he wanted that kind of thing—would you mind?"

Dan glanced up at him quickly, then looked away. "That wouldn't bother me."

"You mean it wouldn't be the first time?"

Dan's hands were writhing nervously on his knees. "Let's just say that it wouldn't bother me and leave it at that," Dan said.

When Arnold had cleared away the tea things and Dan had helped him to wash up, Arnold began to talk about Ewing. But though he tried to present an attractive portrait of him, stressing his war record and his courage, his intelligence and generosity, unpleasant aspects of the truth filtered into his description. He found it impossible to avoid warning Dan that Ewing was physically unattractive and morally callous, and as he spoke Arnold began to be afraid that by allowing the truth to creep in he had spoiled his chance of persuading Dan to accept Ewing's scheme. But he need not have worried. Dan seemed oddly uninterested in Ewing. Indeed he was only half listening to what Arnold said.

"I don't care what he's like," Dan said when Arnold had finished. "So long as he doesn't knock me about."

"He won't hurt you," Arnold had answered, "I can promise you that."

"Then I'll go to join him," Dan had replied.

Arnold was now waiting in his car beneath the dripping branches at the corner of the lane for Dan to meet him.

✿ ✿ ✿ ✿ ✿ ✿

THE car door opened and Dan got in quickly. His school coat was sodden with rain. Strands of pale hair lay across his forehead. "Dead on time," Dan said, with a tremor in his voice.

When Arnold had considered Ewing's scheme, his mind had always refused to accept the possibility that it would in fact succeed, sliding away from the plan in reality, gaining comfort from the improbability of its success. But now the instant Arnold dreaded had come. The boy was sitting in the car beside him. When Arnold pulled the switch and the engine started, he would put into action a chain of events which would take Dan from Melton Hall to a cabin on Ewing's yacht. Eventually that yacht would sail across the Aegean with its two ill-assorted passengers. And Ewing . . .

"Listen to me, Dan," Arnold said urgently. "Are you sure you want to go through with this? There's still time to change your mind. We can still turn back. I can easily get you back to the school before eight. Are you certain you want to go to live with this man?"

"If you knew what I'd been through in that place, you wouldn't ask."

"All right, Dan, but just supposing . . ."

"Can't we start, sir?" Dan interrupted anxiously. "I'll feel better once we're on our way."

Arnold hesitated.

"Please, sir. Please let's go. Anyone might find us here. I'm scared. I'll be all right as soon as we're away."

Arnold started the engine and let in the clutch. The car slithered through the rain and darkness.

"Listen, Dan," Arnold said. "You can still change your mind. Supposing I could get you sent away from Melton Hall—I don't promise, but I could try—or say I could get you sent home."

"Home!" Dan said with a hoarse laugh. "Home! You didn't read the court case, did you? No. That first time when you came to see me in the sick ward I knew that you hadn't. You asked what the lines were on my arms, remember? And I said I'd been in an accident, remember? Well, it wasn't an accident. It was from when they got torn when he'd hang me up by my wrists from the bar he'd fixed on the side of the wall. My Dad I had to call him—the man she married after my real Dad died. He was kinky that way. Or at least that's what my Auntie said. If he got sore at me he'd hang me up there by my wrists, and each time he'd pass by he'd give me a bash in the guts. I got real ill. That's how they got to know about it."

"Didn't your mother try to stop him?"

"When he'd got drink in him, she was as scared of him as I was. The only one that would stand up to him was my Auntie. Now she's dead. I never want to go home as long as I live."

"Perhaps I could get you transferred to another school?"

"I'm not worried, I promise I'm not. Besides, ever since you came to see me in the sick ward, I've always wanted to be with you."

Doubt like a cold mist began to seep into Arnold's mind.

"I've told you the plan, if we go through with it, haven't I, Dan? I'm going to drive you now to Folkestone, and we're meeting a friend of Ewing's there called Tim Deakin. He'll be taking you across to France and down to Marseilles, where the yacht's waiting already. I'm driving back to Melton Hall tonight."

Dan turned to him in the darkness. "You don't have to pretend any more," Dan said quietly. "I'm with you, and I'm glad of it."

"Pretend?"

"You don't think you really took me in with all that talk about a rich man in Tangier? Why should a rich man want to adopt *me* of all people and take me round the world, like you said? I knew it was really you from the start."

Arnold's voice trembled in dismay. "But it's not me, Dan."

"Course it is. Don't trouble yourself. I know what you want. And I don't mind. I told you, didn't I? As soon as you started off about this bloke in Tangier, I cottoned on. I guessed Captain Stobart must have said something to you. Or else you just put two and two together."

As Dan spoke, an image of Stobart lurched into Arnold's mind—Stobart sitting on his chair by the showers, red-faced and hearty, Stobart with his clipped black moustache and pig-eyes, Stobart with his raucous laugh and a ruler in his hand.

"What has Stobart got to do with it?" Arnold asked slowly.

"What are you pretending you don't know for? I don't mind, I keep telling you. I didn't have to go with you, did I? I wouldn't have come if I hadn't wanted to, would I? You made it clear what I was in for, didn't you?"

"Does Stobart know?"

"Not about us, he doesn't. Not likely! Do you think he'd have given me leave to go to the cinema if he'd known? He'd have half murdered me."

"Then what has he got to do with it?"

"Well, he started me off, didn't he?"

"Stobart?"

"You must have known it. What else made you pick on me so sudden? I've been going with him ever since that second time I ran away . . ."

Arnold listened in horror. And as the car slurred its way through the darkness Dan told his story in slow, halting phrases. The beginning of it was simple.

Dan had been so wretchedly unhappy at Melton Hall that he had decided to try to escape again. As before, he had waited until the boys in his dormitory on the first floor were asleep. He had then crept out to the lavatory. He had found a new escape route. In the corner of the two outside walls forming an angle of the building was a drain-pipe which ran down to the ground close to the tree-lined drive. It was raining. The pipe was slippery, but Dan reached the drive safely and made for the cover of the trees. But halfway along the avenue he saw Stobart walking back through the rain toward the school building, swinging a flashlight from side to side.

"I thought he hadn't seen me," Dan said. "So I crept down into the ditch. But he'd seen me right enough. He suddenly leaped forward and grabbed hold of me. He bent my arm behind my back and marched me down the drive again to the school and took me straight to his room. My clothes were all wet, so he lit the gas fire. Then he said, 'You're drenched to the skin, boy.' You know that voice of his. 'Take off your clothes and dry yourself by the fire.' "

As Dan spoke, Arnold could see the shiny yellow walls of Stobart's little room with a framed photograph of Baden-Powell on one side of the door and a group of the Royal Family on the other. He saw the litter of hockey sticks and cricket bats in the corner and the peeling covers of the detective novels in the bookcase.

"I took off my clothes as he said," Dan continued. "My teeth were chattering. I thought he might turn the other boys onto me, like he done before. But he went over to his cupboard and took out a bottle. I saw it was port.

"You're shivering, boy,' he said. 'Drink this.'

"So I did. And I must say though it burned my insides it made me feel better. Then he started asking me why I'd tried to run away again. So I told him it was because I wanted to see my Auntie who was still ill in the hospital—and besides I didn't like the place.

"So then he wanted to know *why* I didn't like it. Were the boys bullying me? I said, yes—some of them. Then he wanted to find out what they did to me. So I told him they'd kick me when I was undressing and they'd pull me down in the playground and mess up my books so I'd get into trouble.

"Well, then he asked me if they did anything to me after lights-out. I said no. One boy had tried but I wouldn't let him. Of course then he wanted to know the name of the boy, but I wouldn't say.

"Suddenly he said, 'I know the name of the boy. It was Charlie Mason, wasn't it?' Then I knew that Charlie must have told him, because otherwise he couldn't have known. All the same I said no, it wasn't Charlie.

" 'You're lying, boy," he said. 'I know it was Charlie.

And what did he do to you? Show me what he did. Take my hand and show me."

"I was frightened then. I must have shown it, because he moved away from me and poured out another glass of port for himself and another one for me, and he made me drink it right up. Then he went over to his cupboard again and took out his camera. As soon as I saw the camera I knew what I was in for. And I was right."

For the first time since Dan had begun to talk, Arnold spoke. "Why did the camera make you understand?" he asked.

"Because Charlie had told me," Dan replied. "The first time he'd made Charlie come to his room he'd taken his photograph before it started."

Suddenly Arnold had a glimpse of Charlie Mason standing in front of the gas fire—Charlie Mason with his bristling red hair and slanting green eyes and stocky build.

"Has he made other boys come to his room?"

"No. I don't think so. Charlie's the only one I know of. Charlie and me."

"Why didn't you complain?"

"Because it wasn't worth it. Because everything was different after that. I don't know if he spoke to the senior boys, but I wasn't bullied half so much. And every Saturday he'd let me go off to the pictures, and he'd give me three shillings a week pocket money. Besides, who was there to complain to—except Auntie? And she was real ill. Two months later she died. Then

[223]

I'd got no one till you came along. And when you suddenly picked on me, I thought you must know already. I thought that was why you wanted me to come to Tangier. I thought you were in the know—like Charlie Mason was."

"Does Charlie Mason know about Tangier?"

" 'Course not. I promised I'd never split, didn't I? He knew about me and Captain Stobart, that was all. Anyhow it's all over and done with now. I never wanted to do it, because I hated him. But you're my friend, so it's different. There's nothing to worry about. I'll go with you anywhere you like—anywhere you say in the world."

Dan's voice was husky with emotion. They had reached the outskirts of East Grinstead. It was no longer raining. Arnold stopped the car. Then he turned and looked at the boy's pale face and moist eyes. Not one tremor of desire could Arnold feel. Dan took his hand and held it. For a while there was silence. Gently, Arnold drew back his hand.

"Dan, there's been a terrible mistake," Arnold said quietly. "It's all my fault. When you hear what I've got to say you'll most likely want to go back. If you *do* go back I can promise you that Stobart won't trouble you any more. Now then, listen to me . . ."

Slowly and patiently Arnold explained that Ewing did exist, that he did own a yacht, that he did want a boy to take on a long cruise and to bring up to be his companion. Dan listened in silence, his mouth twitching. When Arnold had finished, Dan groped for the door handle and got out of the car.

"I'll be back in a minute," Dan muttered.

Arnold waited wretchedly, staring at the damp tarmac. He wished that he could feel even a flicker of emotion for Dan. He looked round. The boy was leaning against the wall of a darkened house; his shoulders were heaving. Wearily Arnold got out of the car and walked over to him. The boy was crying. Arnold put an arm on his shoulder, but Dan shook himself free.

"Don't mind me," he mumbled. "I'm just a fool."

"Shall I take you back to Melton Hall? Is that what you want?"

"What's there to go back for? I don't want to go back."

"Then tell me what you're upset about."

"I thought I'd got a friend at last. But now I'm alone again."

Arnold was disgusted at the spurt of irritation that he felt. He could not control his rage at his own guilt and his impotence to deal with a situation he had never foreseen. Concealing his anger he forced himself to console Dan as best he could. Foolish pledges poured from his lips. He would always be fond of Dan, he said. He would always try to help him. He would come to Tangier within two months. He ended by saying that if Dan ever needed him, then, wherever he was, he would always come to him.

"If I really need you, then you promise you'll come?" Dan asked through his tears.

"Yes, I promise."

"And you'll be living out there in this man's villa?"

"No."

"Why not, if he's a friend of yours?"

"I'll be living in a flat of my own."

"By yourself?"

"No," Arnold replied, driven to brutality by his irritation at the undisguised emotion on the boy's upturned tear-stained face. "Not by myself. I've got a young friend out there. He's a Moroccan boy of about your age. And he'll be living with me."

"I see," Dan said quietly.

"Now do you understand?"

"Yes. The lot."

"Do you want to go back?"

"No. Where I'm going to can't be any worse than what I've left behind," Dan said, as they walked back to the car.

❧ ❧ ❧ ❧ ❧ ❧

THE flat was on the third floor of a shabby Edwardian house in the center of the town. A printed card on the door spelled "Tim Deakin" in gothic type. Arnold rang the bell, and the door was opened instantly. Though Tim had put on weight, Arnold recognized the man who appeared in the doorway from the photographs Ewing had shown him. Tim was now immensely fat, and he carried his weight awkwardly as if pads of felt had been stitched inside his clothes.

"Good evening," Tim Deakin said. "Come right in, both of you."

Arnold followed Dan into a brightly lit, garish living room. Posters announcing bullfights and advertisements for the Riviera had been pasted onto the vivid green walls. Potato plants twined around a fretwork dado. A red satin sofa with pale blue cushions ran along the far end of the room.

"So you're Arnold Turner," Tim said cheerfully, shaking his hand firmly. "I've been wondering what you'd look like."

His pallid moonface turned toward Dan as he stretched out his large red hand once more. "And this I suppose is young Dan," he said.

Immediately Arnold suspected that Tim's heartiness had been assumed to disguise his uneasiness.

"I'm delighted to meet you both," Tim continued. "I've been waiting for this moment for quite a while now, and I've got everything laid on. I expect our young friend here is a bit peckish, so the first thing we'll do is to take him into the kitchen where there's a fair-sized spread. Then we can tuck him up in the spare room, such as it is, and you and me, Arnold, can have a drink and a natter before you drive back to the school. Does that suit you?"

"Fine," Arnold said.

"Then let's go in and eat," Tim said. "I've got some beer in the fridge, so we shan't be thirsty."

"I'm not hungry," Dan said suddenly.

Tim glanced at him in surprise. "You will be when you see the food," he said with a laugh. "Come along in."

An hour later Arnold and Tim were sitting on the red satin sofa drinking whisky. Dan had been put to bed in the narrow spare room.

"Nice-looking kid," Tim said. "But he's younger than I thought."

"He's fourteen," Arnold said quickly.

"You realize we're both taking a hell of a risk?"

"I know it."

"Don't worry, Arnold. Not to fuss. I tell you frankly I've been over the plan in my mind time and again. I simply can't *see* what can go wrong. You'll be back in the school tonight. No one's going to raise a stink about the boy's disappearance for at least a week. By then I'll be back here."

"Who's going to look after the coffee-bar while you're away?"

"My friend. He's on duty there tonight. I've told him I'm off to France for a week's holiday. He knows there's a little chicken in Paris that I fancy. He won't suspect a thing."

"How will you get Dan into France without a passport?"

"On the day trip to Boulogne. Then I'll take a *wagon-lit* straight through from Paris to Marseilles. From Marseilles it's all perfectly straightforward—so long as the kid doesn't give any trouble. Do you think he's a safe bet?"

"Yes. I do."

"You don't sound very sure about it."

"You can see that he's nervous," Arnold said, frowning at Tim's jovial expression. "You'll have to be very gentle with him. He could easily get scared. I'd like you to explain this to Ewing when you get there. Dan's unusually sensitive. He's got none of the tough assurance of other boys of his own age. He's led a pretty

[2 2 8]

wretched existence up to date. He needs kindness and affection above all things. He needs to be treated with consideration."

"I'll tell our friend that when I get there. And so far as I'm concerned, don't worry. He'll be all right with me, I promise you."

Tim got up and poured out two more drinks. "Speaking of promises," Tim said, fumbling in his breast pocket, "here's a sealed envelope I was asked to give you when you turned up this evening. I was told you'd know what it contained."

"Thanks," Arnold muttered, as he put the envelope into his pocket.

"Aren't you going to open it?"

"Not now."

"I see your point. At least one can trust our friend in money matters."

"Can we trust him with Dan? That's what's worrying me," Arnold said, fixing his protuberant blue eyes on Tim.

"Ewing's a lot older since the days I knew him," Tim replied. "He's learned a lesson or two. I'm sure he's changed."

"Whatever troubles you had with him, at least he was kind to you, wasn't he?"

"Yes," Tim answered after a pause. "He was kind all right. If he hadn't been, you don't suppose I'd let this kid in for it, do you?"

Arnold took a long drink of whisky. There was still a question that he felt bound to ask. "If he was kind to you," Arnold said quietly, "why did you leave him?"

Tim got up and stood with his back to the fireplace,

leaning on his left foot, his brown eyes searching Arnold's face.

"Why do you want to know?" he asked.

"Because I want to be sure that Dan's going to be all right."

"That boy will be all right. I know it. He'll be given the greatest chance any kid like him has ever had."

"But you still haven't answered my question," Arnold persisted. "Ewing gave *you* a great chance, but you still left him. Why?"

Tim ran his hand over his sagging chin and raised his head. "If you want to know, it was because I was a complete fool. I just got fed up and left."

"Why did you get fed up?"

"I was tired of being nagged at all the time. With our Dan it'll be different. He's still a kid. He's young enough to learn. But I was getting on for twenty when I got taken on. I couldn't learn all that easily, and he wouldn't just let me be. You'd think he wanted to make a fucking artist of me, the way he carried on."

"Was that the only reason you left him?"

"Well, as you can imagine, he wasn't exactly my cup of tea to be with night and day. But I'd have put up with all that if only I'd been certain of him. But the odd thing was that for all his presents and all his affection I still wasn't a hundred per cent sure of him."

"In what way?"

Tim shifted his weight to the other leg and took a gulp from his glass.

"It's hard to explain," Tim said. "Now it's all over I often wonder if it wasn't partly my imagination. But sometimes, when he thought I wasn't watching him, I'd turn and catch him glaring at me as if he were in a blind rage with me. And I'd have done nothing at all. Nothing. I'd just be sitting there. But he'd be glaring at me as if I'd done something wrong. It was real odd. Sometimes I used to think it was because he wanted to be alone and didn't want me in the room. But when I'd move to go, he'd call me back. I never did understand what all that was about."

"But he was never rough with you?"

"Heavens no! I'd like to have seen him try! No, he treated me all right on the whole, and I was a fool to leave him. If I'd known *then* all I know about life *now* I'd have stayed with him as long as he'd keep me."

Tim sighed and stretched out a large red hand for the whisky bottle. "What about one more for the road?" he asked with a grin.

"Not for me, thanks," Arnold said. "But can I ask you just one more question?"

"Fire away!"

"If Dan just doesn't want to know, if Dan doesn't want to have anything to do with it when Ewing makes his first approach, would there be trouble? I mean, might he try to use force?"

"Never," Tim said definitely. "For a start Ewing's far too proud. Secondly that's not his form at all. Stop fussing, Arnold. I can see that the kid's ready to learn. I reckon it'll work out all right. You're fussing because you've got a guilty conscience. But look at it this way. What alternative has the kid got? At least our friend will give him a good chance in life. If it makes you feel any better, I can tell you this. So long as the kid doesn't panic I'm perfectly happy about the job. Once he's settled down on board that yacht he'll have a wonderful time. I reckon we're doing him a favor."

Suddenly in his mind Arnold saw the tears sliding down Riffi's face as they had said good-bye. He could hear his hoarse voice saying the little speech he had obviously learned by heart. "I wait for you. I wait for my freng for alway."

Arnold could now be certain of seeing Riffi in the flat on the Marshan in three months' time.

"I only hope you're right," Arnold said to Tim, as he stood up. "I must be on my way now, but first I'll just look in and say good-bye to Dan if he's still awake."

"I'll come with you," Tim said and led the way along the short corridor.

Dan was lying on his back, wide awake, when they came into the narrow room.

"I've come to say good-bye," Arnold said briskly. "I've had a long talk with our friend Tim, and I'm dead certain you're going to be all right."

"I want to see you alone," Dan said.

Arnold turned to Tim. For an instant Tim hesitated, then he shrugged his shoulders and smiled.

"I'll wait for you next door," he said and lumbered out of the room.

Arnold forced his voice to sound calm as he smiled down at the boy's anxious face. "Well?" Arnold asked. "What's it about?"

"I'm frightened," Dan said.

Immediately Arnold's vision of his flat on the Marshan began to crumble. "You're frightened because you're tired," Arnold heard himself say. "Because all this is new to you."

"No. It's not that."

"What is it then?"

Dan's mouth began to twitch. "I don't like the way he looks at me."

"Who? Tim? He's all right. You don't have to worry about him, I promise you. You'll be perfectly safe, I swear it."

"He looks at me in the same way."

"What same way?"

"The same way as Captain Stobart did."

"That's pure imagination." Arnold could hear his voice trembling with vexation. "I was watching him while you were together. He was looking at you now and then, because he was interested to know what you were like. After all, he's got to take you all the way to Tangier. You're his responsibility from now on."

"I'm frightened of him."

"Listen, Dan, you do trust me, don't you?"

"You know I do, sir."

"Then you've got to trust my judgement. Tim's as safe a person to look after you as anyone could find."

Dan's hands writhed uneasily about the sheets.

"Can't you come with us?" Dan asked.

"You know I can't," Arnold said. "It would be far too dangerous. If I didn't go back to Melton Hall they'd suspect you were with me. It wouldn't take them long to track us down."

[233]

"Shan't I ever see you again, then?"

"As I told you, I'll be in Tangier in two months' time."

"But I'll be away by then."

Arnold began to lie again. "At least we can write to each other," he said.

"You won't forget your promise? You'll come if I really do need you?"

"I promise I will. If you find you can't go through with it I'll come and get you back."

"And I *can* write to you?"

"I've already said so."

"Can I write on the way out, I mean? If anything goes wrong?"

As Arnold hesitated he noticed a cardboard writing pad tucked into the bookcase by the bed. He opened it, took out an envelope and put a sheet of writing paper and a ten-shilling note inside it. Then he addressed the envelope to himself at his local bank, writing in small black letters and marking it, "to be called for."

"Listen, Dan," Arnold said very quietly, "I'm putting this envelope in your trousers pocket. Don't let anyone ever see it. If anything goes wrong, then write to me at this address."

"What's the ten-shilling note for?" Dan asked.

"Whatever country you're in, they'll change that note for you down in the port. Then you'll be able to buy the stamps to airmail your letter off to me. That way at least we'll be in touch."

"Thanks," Dan said.

[2 3 4]

"Don't be frightened. You'll be all right. You're going to have a wonderful time."

"Now I've got the envelope I feel better already."

Arnold stretched out his hand. Dan grasped it eagerly.

"I must be going," Arnold said. "Good-bye, Dan. All the best."

"Good-bye," Dan muttered. "Thanks for everything."

Tim was waiting for him in the living room. "What was all that in aid of?" he asked.

"Last-minute nerves," Arnold replied. "Nothing to worry about."

"One for the road?"

"No thanks. I must be getting back."

❧ ❧ ❧ ❧ ❧ ❧

WHEN Dan did not return from the cinema on Saturday evening the local police and the police in Guildford were notified that he had absconded. By the time Arnold returned to Melton Hall at two o'clock on Sunday morning, all patrol cars in the neighborhood had been given a description of Dan. On Tuesday morning, Blair, the headmaster, telephoned Scotland Yard, and a description of Dan was entered in the *Police Gazette*.

In the lunch break on Thursday morning Arnold drove to his bank. He had no reason to draw out money, for the hundred one-pound notes that he had found in the sealed envelope together with the check for three thousand dollars were hidden behind a drawer in his bedroom. But Arnold had calculated that if for any reason Dan had written to him from Marseilles the letter would have arrived that morning if not the previous day. The certainty that no letter had come would at least help to assuage his guilt.

Arnold felt his legs quivering as he walked up to the cashier's desk.

"Any letter for me?" he asked casually after he had drawn out five pounds.

"I'll go and see," the cashier said.

Let there be no letter, Arnold prayed to the God he tried to believe in. Please God, let there be no letter.

"Here you are," the cashier said, handing him the envelope addressed in small block letters.

"Thank you," Arnold said and walked quickly to the door. For an instant he had been afraid he was going to vomit.

In the main street outside, the sun was shining down on the dry pavement. Arnold forced himself to walk to the car-park behind the Odeon Cinema and get into his car before he opened the letter with shaking hands.

"Tuesday," the letter was headed in backward-sloping uneven letters.

"Were away in an hour and Tims working on the engines so I've got ashoar.

Last night he told me what I'd better expect when we get there and Im friten.

I can't go through with it honest I cant.
If you stick to your promise youve got to help me.
                                    Love
                                    Dan."

Arnold read the letter through several times, trying
each time to find a different meaning, as if by reading
the letter again and again he could change the words
or alter their sense. Then he leaned back in the car and
closed his eyes. The weight of guilt that had oppressed
him ever since the moment he had said good-bye to
Dan now bore down on him so heavily that he felt sick
and faint. Desperately he tried to discover some escape
from the implications of the letter and from the bleak
fact of his responsibility. What could Tim have said to
frighten Dan? Tim had assured Arnold that Ewing had
treated him with kindness. Was that a lie? Was Ewing's
talk of educating the boy to appreciate culture a bluff?
Had Ewing forced Tim to conspire with him in some
crime he had planned to satisfy desires he had concealed from Arnold? Did Ewing secretly delight in
cruelty?

Suddenly, as the questions rushed through his mind,
a picture lurched into his vision. Once again he stood
in the fetid hiding place and saw the gleaming ebony
of the Negro's thick limbs and the dark streaks of damp
running down whitewashed walls like stripes across a
pale body. For a long time Arnold sat motionless in
his car. Then he started the engine and drove back to
Melton Hall. As soon as he reached the school, he
walked along the glazed corridor to Blair's study.

When Arnold walked into the untidy room with its light green walls and light-colored wooden furniture, Blair raised his grey face from a Home Office form that he was filling in and smiled at him wearily.

"Morning, Arnold," Blair said. "What can I do for you?"

"There's something I should have told you before I came here," Arnold said.

Blair glanced up at him quickly. "Take a pew," he said, pointing to a leather armchair. "You look done in."

Arnold sat down. Blair took up a pencil and began to play with it.

"Now then, what is it?" he asked.

"Before I came here I had a breakdown," Arnold said.

"Had you been overdoing things or what?"

"I don't know," Arnold said. "I can only tell you that I began to get jittery. I couldn't sleep and I couldn't eat. At nights I'd just lie in bed sweating and trembling all over. It got so bad I went to the doctor. I was in the hospital for a month."

Blair ran his pencil through his grey hair.

"Why are you telling me this now?" he asked.

"Because I'm afraid it may be starting again."

"Have you seen the doctor?"

"No. What good can he do? The answer's so very simple. It was the same answer last time. Complete rest. So I've come to you to say this. I know I'm not due for my holidays for another month. And I know it'll be an awful nuisance having to switch things round. But I promise you this—I'm certain if I could get away for a week I'd be all right."

Blair scratched his head and sighed. "It's not satisfactory," he said. "In fact, it's extremely tiresome. I'll have to change the whole schedule, and that's the devil of a business. But I suppose there's nothing else for it. When do you want to leave?"

"Tonight," Arnold said. "After my classes."

"Where will you go to?"

"I haven't made up my mind yet. Somewhere quiet where I can be alone."

Blair stood up. "I'll see you a week from today," he said. "I'm sure your rest will do you good."

"Thanks," Arnold said, and left the room.

That evening Arnold took the train to London and went to the B.E.A. terminal in Cromwell Road. He managed to get a seat on the noon plane to Tangier the following day. He paid for his ticket with the money Ewing had given him.

As the plane droned steadily through the clear blue sky, Arnold tried to sort out the confused plans that tumbled through his mind. But each course of action he contemplated seemed inescapably disastrous. There was no way out of the maze he had been so cleverly persuaded to enter. Only one thing was clear. He must reach Dan. He must save the boy he had been prepared to sacrifice because of his fierce yearning to possess Riffi. He had calculated that he would now reach Tangier at about the same time as the yacht was due to arrive in the harbor. Ewing had planned to let the yacht ride at anchor for at least two days before he went on board in order to avoid giving the impression of a hurried departure. During that time Dan was to remain on board. Papers had been obtained which stated that he was a Spanish boy of fifteen who had been signed on in Barcelona. Arnold would arrive before the yacht had left. After he had rescued Dan, he would have to make fresh plans. Somehow he would break out of the trap, taking Riffi with him. Somehow. Perhaps the evening in Tangier would provide him with an answer.

❧ ❧ ❧ ❧ ❧ ❧

As Arnold clambered stiffly down the gangplank into the hot, dry air of the late afternoon, he saw Wayne sitting at a table outside the little airport café on the edge of the tarmac. Wayne stared at him with bleary eyes for an instant, then waved a hand in greeting.

"Hullo there!" he cried out shrilly, sidling toward the barrier. "Fancy seeing *you* of all people. You're not one *bit* like the passenger I was expecting. I was waiting here patiently for a very pretty dish in his early twenties who's supposed to be flying out from Madrid. But the wretched boy has probably settled for Rome after all. And here am I at this dreary airport at this ghastly hour, but at least you've turned up to keep me company on the drive back into town."

"Is Ewing in Tangier?" Arnold asked.

[2 4 0]

"Yes. Most certainly. And larger than life."

"Has his yacht arrived?"

Wayne fluttered his eyelids in surprise. "His yacht? He's not having his yacht come out, is he? I thought the old thing was so bored stiff with it he was leaving it laid up in Marseilles?"

"Have you got a car here?"

"But of course. Freda my Ford awaits your pleasure. Get past those tedious and quite repellent customs officials and I'll meet you in the car-park. Meanwhile I'll just have one more teenie-weenie double brandy to console myself for that wicked boy's treachery."

"Can you drive me to Ewing's villa on the mountain?"

"I'd be delighted to, my dear."

Ten minutes later Arnold was sitting beside Wayne, who was prattling brightly and reeking of brandy.

"Huge shoulders," Wayne sighed. "And legs of marble. A boxer's waist. Divine green eyes. Wholly glabrous. Do you blame me for saving up to pay for his passage?"

"I suppose you haven't seen Tim Deakin around?" Arnold asked.

"My dear, I haven't seen that *numero* since the Battle of Gettysburg."

Arnold tried to make his voice sound casual as he put his next question.

"How's Riffi?"

"Now there's another wicked creature!" Wayne exclaimed, swerving to avoid a flock of goats. "What a naughty *numero* that one is! I hope you didn't come all the way out here to see *that* fickle lady? But of course you didn't. Ewing must have written and told you."

Arnold could feel his heart pounding fiercely. "I haven't heard from Ewing for some time," he said.

"What a lazy type that one is!" Wayne tittered. "At least he should have written to tell you the sad news."

"What sad news?"

"Well, 'sad' from *your* point of view, I mean—'sad' if you've still got a crush on that little Berber piece of nonsense."

"What happened?"

"Paul Ashton came back, that's what happened. You know whom I mean! The old 'county' queen who was so mad about Riffi last year. And what's more, Master Paul came back a free man. His madly rich, desperately drab, and horribly respectable wife fell off her mount—or whatever you call the animals—out in the hunting field and broke her fat neck. So Paul Ashton's inherited a fortune. *So,* my dear, hardly was the old hag interred in her family vault than our enriched and radiant Master Paul popped into a plane and arrived in our wicked city of vice positively panting for his little Riffi. And despite Ewing's threats and despite all my wily devices he tracked Riffi down to his douar above Chauen and whisked him off in a new Bentley convertible and a cloud of dust. That was a month ago. They were last heard of in Monte Carlo. I may tell you that Ewing was livid. You'd have thought he fancied the boy himself the way he carried on."

[242]

"Did Riffi want to go off with him?"

"Want! My dear, are you mad? As soon as Riffi saw that car I'm told there was no holding him. And when they passed through here on their way to Cannes, you should have seen Master Riffi flashing his gold bangles."

"And that was a month ago?"

"At least."

"And Ewing knew about it."

"I'll say he knew! He did everything short of lassoing the boy to get him back. I'm told he's still trying. Some hope! But that's our dear Ewing all over. When he's *got* a boy, he's bored rigid with him. It isn't until the boy leaves that he admits he's been fond of him. It was exactly the same story with Master Tim Deakin. Ewing wouldn't admit he was dotty about *that* number until Tim had left for good. Our dear Ewing's trouble is that he resents every single one of them."

Arnold stared blankly at the blocks of white concrete apartment houses looming through the dusty haze and framed between the eucalyptus trees. The shock of losing Riffi had paralyzed his senses like the injection of a powerful drug. He felt no pain. There had been a quick stab of anguish, and that was all. The long agony would come later. Meanwhile he must continue to breathe and sit upright in the car and react to Wayne's remarks.

"Resents them?" Arnold asked, vaguely remembering Wayne's last sentence.

"Of course. In fact, he positively loathes each one of them."

[243]

"Why?"

"Because Ewing resents being attracted to his boyfriends. Because he passionately resents the fact that he's a queer. You see, at heart Ewing's deeply conventional. And he's a cracking snob. Essentially what he'd like would be to be married to a countess and live in a large house in Kent where he'd entertain royalty. Instead of that he's a hallmarked old queer living with a lot of riffraff in a notorious homosexual's paradise. And he just hates it. But he won't admit it. Not even to himself. So when he falls for a young man like Tim he subconsciously resents it. Tangerine Ewing may love the boy, but Kentish Ewing detests him. It's quite simple, isn't it?"

Wayne glanced at Arnold. "Are you feeling ill?" he asked.

"No."

"You look a trifle pale if I may say so, my dear."

"I'm all right."

"Would you like to stop for a moment?"

"No. I'm fine."

"Oh dear! Now I've forgotten what I was saying!"

"You were talking about Ewing."

"So I was! Poor Ewing! But you know, my dear, essentially they're all the same. You've just got to have had the experience of knowing two or three of these upper-middle-class queens to understand the lot. You've only got to look into their past to unearth precisely the same story. It's not at all the same tale with people like you and me—who've risen, as one might say, from the ranks. *We* may have seen something in

[2 4 4]

the woodshed at the end of the garden that's scared us. But *their* life is one long woodshed from the day they're born."

With a quick movement of his right hand Wayne took a loose cigarette from his pocket and lit it with his gold lighter.

"At first it's Nanny Norah," Wayne said. "Nanny Norah with her do's and don'ts and her nursery school of morality. She's not *fatal,* Nanny Norah isn't, because she's a kindly old soul with her roots fair and square in the ground. She's an old oak, and she's determined that all her charges shall grow up just like her—stalwart and solid and unyielding. No willow bending to the wind is Nanny. Dear me no! Bluff and tough, broad and trustworthy, for Queen and Country, for Duty and Debrett."

Wayne sounded his horn impatiently at an old Moor in a tattered *djellaba* riding a donkey in the middle of the road.

"But when Master Johnny gets too much of a handful," Wayne continued, "Nanny Norah's pensioned off. Then comes the real terror. There's the sound of a stridently genteel voice in the hall, and it's Gertrude the Governess who's arrived with her worn leather trunk and her spanking new handbag to stay in the Manor or the Square in Belgravia. Gertrude, the purveyor of conventionality, the supporter of arch-snobbery, the douser of originality, the detector of the slightest moral deviation, the destroyer of any individual personality. Gertrude, with her remorselessly puritanical watery eyes and her rigidly disapproving long nose. Gertrude, the scourge of indolence, the slayer of impropriety. Gertrude, the spinsterish ogre who's going to peer over Johnny's shoulder for the rest of his life. Gertrude the Governess has arrived, and she's there for good."

Wayne paused and sighed.

"My dear Arnold," he said. "Gertrude is indestructible. The lady herself may be eventually removed to mold another little Johnny in her own dismally strait-laced image, but her influence persists. Our Johnny who underwent her treatment for three years will never be the same again. Talk of brainwashing! The Fascists and the Commies have got a completely new technique to learn from our Gertrude. Because Gertrude has wrecked our poor Johnny. The boarding school they send him to when he's removed from her clutches merely stamps a smart seal on his Gertrude-caused doom. Dear Johnny's had it—and for life.

"He revolts, of course. They all do—generally in precisely the same fashion. They fling aside their stiff shirts and hats. They waltz into jeans and T-shirts. For two or three uneasy years at Oxford or Cambridge they flaunt their uninhibited bright shirts and ideas. And to look at them you might suppose that they were unenslaved individuals—like you and me, dear. But you'd be desperately wrong. They may have turned their backs on Gertrude, but she's still there. Gertrude is lurking. Gertrude is ever vigilant. And in the end her influence triumphs. So the T-shirts are sent to the wash and given to the discarded boyfriend. The jeans are used for occasional weekends at Newmarket. The bright colors of the clothes fade to grey. And five years later you can see our dear Johnny with the meticulously worn hallmarks of his class—the Jermyn Street white shirt, the Savile Row drab suit, the Sulka dark tie, the Lobb shoes, the Brigg umbrella— and an invisible sheath over his whole personality. And Gertrude is with him again.

"Show me a pallid-faced, well-trimmed, stiff-backed, hard-collared, drably dressed, oppressed-looking young man at a cocktail party, and I'll suspect he's a queer. Examine the man standing next to him with a floppy green shirt and peacock-blue trousers and you'll probably discover he's a happily married stockbroker with seven children.

"And why does Johnny look so oppressed? Because Gertrude is eternally peering over his shoulder. Of course, the dear man still has occasional spasms of revolt. Aged forty he may cast a glance at that curly-haired young waiter at his club. But he looks away jolly quick. A sharp rap from Gertrude has brought him back under control. So he orders a glass of port and then another and presently some brandy. And then he takes the taxi back to his bachelor flat in Westminster. And Gertrude has triumphed again. Sometimes, of course, they get their revenge for the misery that Gertrude's caused them by taking it out on other people. Ewing got his revenge when he strangled all those men with his bare hands during the year he was fighting with the partisans. You know how often he looks at his hands. I reckon it's because he likes to remind himself that he did it."

They had reached the upper level of the mountain road, and the air was heavy with a tang of spices as they drove through the eucalyptus forest. Arnold knew every bend of the road. Each dip and twist brought back memories of Riffi.

"If Ewing could have got rid of Gertrude," Wayne was saying, "he wouldn't have resented Tim."

It was getting dark. Wayne switched on his headlights.

"Poor Ewing!" he sighed. "I'm afraid Gertrude nags at him quite desperately. He's positively waterlogged with guilt. That's why we get all that carrying-on about educating the boy he happens to have fallen for. It's only to assuage his guilt. He feels that if he can teach them about El Greco then it's somehow all right. The next thing we shall hear is that he's picked up a boy from Diego's bordello and is teaching him to read Euripides in the original. It wouldn't surprise me one bit."

As they turned the corner Arnold saw the crenelated central tower of the Villa Gault and the long grey wall that surrounded the property. Wayne had stopped the car outside the wrought-iron gate and sounded the horn. Two dogs rushed at the grille and began barking wildly. With a spasm of pain Arnold remembered the first evening he had been taken to the villa.

"Do you mind if I drop you here?" Wayne asked. "To tell you the truth there's been a slight *froideur* between Ewing and me. The silly old thing seems to think that Paul Ashton bribed me to give away the location of Riffi's douar. It's perfectly untrue, of course.

[2 4 8]

But I don't think I'll come in. You don't mind, do you?"

Arnold had been searching for an excuse to get rid of Wayne.

"Of course I don't mind," he said. "Thanks for the lift."

"Perhaps I'll see you tonight in my louch establishment?"

"I expect so," Arnold muttered.

"Cheerie-bye!" Wayne said and drove quickly away.

The bearded Moor shuffled out of the lodge and pulled open the gate. The evening was warm. Arnold took off his coat. Carrying his small bag with one hand and his coat with the other, he walked up the rutted drive between the eucalyptus trees. The front door was shut. He pressed the bell. He could feel his heart pounding against his chest. The door opened. Bashir peered out at him in the dusk, and blinked his long lashes in surprise.

"*Msalkhair,*" Bashir simpered.

"Good evening," Arnold answered. "Is Señor Ewing in?"

"Yis," Bashir said. "Follow me."

Arnold followed Bashir as he swayed across the tiled hall toward the drawing room.

Ewing was sitting on the yellow sofa reading a magazine by the light of the tall celadon lamp. He was wearing dark Shantung-silk trousers and a bush shirt which was undone so that Arnold could see the hairs on his chest and stomach. For a while he stared at Arnold in silence. Arnold could feel his legs quivering.

"Why have you come here?" Ewing asked, without moving.

"I want to see Dan."

"He's not here. The yacht's not arrived yet. Why do you want to see him?"

"Because I think he may want to go back to England."

Ewing got up and crossed to the chimney piece. "What makes you think so?" he asked.

"I had a letter from him."

"A letter? From where?"

"Marseilles. Just before the yacht sailed."

"What did the boy say?"

"He was frightened. He didn't want to go through with it."

"You took the noon plane from London?"

"Yes."

"Do they know at Melton Hall that you've flown to Tangier?"

"No."

"What excuse did you make for leaving the place?"

"I got a week's holiday."

"Have you got the boy's letter?"

"Yes."

"Can I see it?"

Arnold took the envelope out of his breast pocket and handed it to Ewing.

"At least you had the sense to give him the address of your bank so he didn't write to the school," Ewing said.

"Read the letter."

Ewing took out the sheet of white paper and read the eight lines on it. Then he crossed to the drink tray and poured himself a whisky.

"The boy talks about sticking to a promise," Ewing said. "What was your promise?"

"That I'd come to his help if he needed me."

"So you fancy the boy yourself?"

"No."

"Then why make such a promise?"

"Because I was sorry for him."

Ewing turned angrily. "Sorry for him! You sentimental idiot! If you were really sorry for him you wouldn't have risked his one chance of happiness by coming out here, you sloppy fool. You've fallen for the boy and you want him for yourself. Why not admit it?"

"I've told you that he doesn't attract me."

"Do you expect me to believe that?"

"I don't care if you believe it or not."

Ewing examined Arnold's face as if he were studying a complicated chart. "Then why *did* you come out here?" he asked.

"I've told you. I've come out to help the boy."

"To help him! What in the world do you think *you* can do to help him?"

"If he wants to go, I can take him back to England."

Ewing's hands sliced the air in a vicious gesture of impatience. "Are you completely mad? Do you honestly suppose for one moment that at *this* stage the boy will want to go back?"

"You read his letter."

"Did you take that seriously? A young boy's slight fit of nerves before a long journey?"

"He was frightened when he wrote that letter."

"Nonsense. He had a moment of doubt, that's all."

"Dan said Tim had told him just what he'd 'better expect' when he got to Tangier. Can you explain that phrase? What did Tim tell him he was to expect?"

"I simply can't imagine."

"But whatever it was made the boy frightened, didn't it?"

"How can I possibly know what Tim said?"

"Isn't it conceivable that you can guess?"

Ewing flung back his arms and held them outstretched behind him. "You're beginning to make me angry," he said. "So I suggest you're silent for a moment and listen to me. I'm now going to tell you precisely what you're going to do. You're going to take the next plane back to England. *If* anyone finds out you've been to Tangier and suspects you flew here to find Dan Gedge, you can tell them you did indeed believe that Dan might have gone to Tangier because you'd told him about your holiday and Dan had developed an obsession to visit the place. So you flew to Tangier on your own initiative but discovered no trace of the boy. So you came back. Finish."

"I'm staying here till Dan arrives."

"If you go back now, our deal is still on. In two months' time you'll have that villa on the Marshan and you'll have Riffi, who's safely in his douar waiting for you."

[252]

"Wayne gave me a lift from the airport," Arnold said.

"So what?"

"He told me about Paul Ashton."

In the silence that followed, Arnold heard the ring of the front door bell.

"What did Wayne tell you about him?"

"That he'd gone off with Riffi."

"You don't seriously believe that?"

"Yes. I do."

"Wayne was being his usual malicious self," Ewing was saying, when the door opened and Tim Deakin walked slowly into the room. His heavy arms bulged out of a white singlet that seemed too small for him. His head turned uneasily from Ewing to Arnold. Then he addressed Ewing.

"Hullo!" Tim said quietly. "What's *that one* doing here?"

Ewing handed Dan's letter to Tim. "Read that," he said. "Read it and you'll see his excuse for coming out and risking our whole plan. I'm still trying to find out the real reason he came."

Tim read the letter quickly. "The little bastard!" he muttered. "The little bastard!"

"Is the boy all right?" Ewing asked. "Have you got him safe on board?"

"I've got him here. But the kid's not well."

"You've not . . ."

"Don't be a bloody fool, Ewing," Tim broke in roughly. "Do you think I'm mad? Of course not. No.

[2 5 3]

The boy's ill. That's all there is to it. He's outside now —fast asleep in the back of the car."

"What car?" Ewing asked.

"I hired a car down in the port."

"Why did you bring him here?"

"Because the kid's sick, I keep telling you. He needs a doctor."

"What's wrong with him?"

"Vomiting and headache and fever."

"It may be something that he ate. Or it may be pure nerves. I'll get hold of Dr. Valdez to look at him. But not here. On board. I don't want the boy in this house. I don't want the servants to see him here. I'll phone Valdez now and arrange for us to meet him at that café on the quayside."

As Ewing crossed to the telephone Arnold rushed to the door.

"Stop him," Ewing said to Tim over his shoulder.

Tim caught Arnold's arm as he passed and dragged him round. Then he hit him hard in the face. Arnold staggered back for three steps and fell on the floor. Tim grabbed hold of his shoulders and hauled him to the sofa.

"Sit down there and be quiet," Tim said. "You've caused enough trouble already."

Blood was pouring from the corner of Arnold's mouth. He leaned back his head and tried to stanch it with his handkerchief. He felt sick and dizzy. From far away he could hear Ewing talking in Spanish on the telephone. Tim was speaking to him.

"God! You were an idiot to come out here," Tim
was saying. He could hear more clearly now.

Ewing put down the receiver. "Valdez can meet us
in an hour's time," he announced. "We'll take him on
board as far as Ceuta."

Tim pointed to Arnold. "What about goldilocks?"
he asked.

"Arnold's going straight back to England," Ewing
said.

Tim crossed to the side table and poured out a whisky
and drank it neat.

"He'd better go quick," Tim mumbled. "Because if
he doesn't, both of us have had it."

"No, Tim," Ewing said quietly. "Not both of us.
And I want Arnold to hear this because it affects him
closely. Suppose the worst happens. Suppose Arnold
was followed out to Tangier. Suppose the police break
into the grounds and find the boy asleep in the back
of that car, then let's remember this. There's a prima
facie case against Arnold—because he knew the boy
and helped him to escape. And I'm afraid there's a case
against you, Tim—because Arnold and the boy can
give corroborative evidence against you. But neither of
you will be extradited if you stay here."

"Do you expect me to live in this bloody country for
the rest of my life?"

"No, Tim. I don't. If you go back and get caught
and don't involve me in any way, I'll give you two
hundred pounds for every month you get."

"It'll be more than that I can promise you. But what

about Arnold and the boy? If they're caught you can bet they'll shriek your name to high heaven."

Ewing spoke quickly in a voice pitched a tone higher than usual. His left eyelid was quivering.

"Arnold could give me away. I hope he'll be sensible enough not to risk it. But should he decide to name me as the author of this plan, then two things will occur. First, I'll have two of the boys from Diego's place denounce him to the police for acts punishable with seven years in a Moorish prison. Secondly, you, Tim, will tell the police that Arnold bribed you to take Dan across to Tangier. You'll tell them that the boy's ill and you've now realized that he's a runaway from an approved school."

"But Dan is bound to tell them all about you."

"How can he? He's never even met me. And if Arnold decides to be difficult, the boy will *never* meet me."

"He still *knows* about you."

"Certainly. But our case will be that Arnold told the boy this rigmarole about my wanting to adopt him in order to persuade Dan to run away with him. And remember this. Arnold will have been exposed as a pederast by the evidence of two Berber boys. His evidence won't count for much after that."

"Let's hope not," Tim said sulkily.

Ewing turned to Arnold who was still holding a handkerchief to the corner of his mouth. It had worried him to see the blood falling onto the yellow damask of the sofa.

"So you see, Arnold, there's little you can do to

harm me," Ewing said. "And quite a lot I can do to harm you. On the other hand, I can still help you considerably."

Arnold did not reply. He was still dazed; he was afraid he was going to be sick. He looked vaguely round the room for an empty bowl. Ewing glanced toward Tim. "Go and see if the boy's all right," he ordered.

"Don't fuss," Tim said as he moved toward the door.

Ewing waited until Tim had left the room before he spoke.

"Look, Arnold," he began gently, "I'm sorry Tim hurt you. But I'll make up for it. My original offer's still valid. The deeds of the Marshan villa are in your name at the bank. If you go back on the early morning plane and keep your mouth shut, I'll give you an extra five thousand dollars. What do you say to that?"

Arnold was silent. He was wondering if he could crawl as far as the flower bowl on the corner table to be sick. Ewing raised his hand to the corner of his left eye to control the tremor. For a while there was silence.

"I can give you the money now if you like," Ewing said in a sudden rush of words. "And you can bank it yourself."

He took three quick paces toward Arnold.

"Arnold, you've got to trust me," he said, forcing his lips into a smile. "Don't you see that if I sail off with the boy it means that I'm in your hands. You've only got to go to the police and say that you know that Dan's on my yacht and I'll be caught. So I must have *some* form of security. I'll give you five thousand dollars now. I've got the cash ready to take off in the yacht. I can give it to you right here and now. All I ask is that you sign a receipt for it."

"I don't want your money."

"Then what *do* you want? Riffi? I promised you he'd be here in two months' time, and he will be. I can get him away from Paul Ashton. Don't you worry! Is it Riffi you want? Is that it?"

Arnold was silent.

"Is that what you want?" Ewing repeated. He was staring down at Arnold, his lips still parted in a grimace, when the door opened and Tim came back into the room.

"The boy's gone," Tim said.

"Gone?"

"He's not in the back of the car."

"Hamido shut the gates after you, didn't he?"

"Yes."

"If he's still in the grounds, why aren't the dogs barking?"

"All three of the dogs were running in front of the car when we arrived and making the hell of a row, so I told Hamido to lock them up and keep them locked up. We don't want the boy scared to death."

"Did Hamido see the boy at the back of the car?"

"No. I'd put a rug over him."

"That's one good thing. I don't want the servants brought into this. Now follow me."

Tim glanced toward Arnold. "What about him?" he asked.

"He can't move far if he tries," Ewing said as he walked quickly out of the room.

At the door Tim turned. "You'd better *not* try," he said, and followed Ewing across the hall.

Arnold heard the front door close behind them. Then he slowly raised himself to his feet and staggered across to the flower bowl and was sick. As he raised his head, he made his decision. On a lacquer table beyond the flower bowl was the telephone—with a telephone directory beside it. Step by step Arnold moved across the room and sat down by the table and opened the directory. He turned to the letter B. But the British Consulate General did not seem to be listed. Feverishly he turned over the pages and at last found it under the main heading CONSULADOS—Consulado de Gran Bretaña. He dialed the number. A man's voice answered.

"British Consulate speaking." The voice spoke with a foreign accent.

"Is the British Consul there?"

"One moment please."

There was a pause, and the line went dead. Arnold was afraid that he had been cut off. His throat was dry and his head throbbed painfully. At any moment Ewing and Tim might come back.

"Hullo?" a voice said suddenly in his ear.

"Are you the British Consul?"

"Speaking."

Arnold took a long breath and tried to make his voice sound calm. "My name's Turner," he said. "I'm a master at Melton Hall approved school. A boy ran away from the school last week. I'm speaking from the Villa Gault. It's on the mountain road toward Cape Spartel. The boy who ran away is here on the grounds. You must come here quickly."

For a moment there was silence. Then the voice said, "You're speaking from the Villa Gault beyond Park Donabo?"

"Yes."

"Is that Ewing Baird's villa? The one with the big iron gates?"

"Yes."

"And the runaway from your school is up there?"

"He's somewhere on the grounds."

"Does Baird know about this?"

"Yes. He does."

There was a brief pause. Then the voice said, "What did you say your name was?"

"Turner. Arnold Turner."

"When did you arrive in Tangier?"

"By this afternoon's plane."

"And you're telephoning me *from* Villa Gault?"

"Yes. But you must come quick. They're trying to get the boy away on the yacht. You'd better bring a police car with you, and a doctor if you can. The boy's ill."

"Will you be there when I arrive?"

"Yes."

"With the boy?"

"I hope so. But hurry."

"Wait where you are," the voice said. There was a click as the receiver was put down.

Suddenly Arnold heard a noise at the far end of the room. He moved quickly away from the telephone and stumbled toward the sofa. Then he looked up. The curtains at the end of the room were half drawn and the French windows were ajar. A boy was standing outside them in the faint moonlight, peering into the lamplit room. The boy was wearing a white singlet and tight black jeans. For one instant Arnold thought that it was Riffi. Then Dan rushed across the room toward Arnold and flung his arms round him.

"I woke up and it was dark, all dark," Dan said, stammering in excitement. "So I walked toward the light. And then I saw you. But what have they done to you? Oh, I've missed you so much. You'll never know how much I've missed you."

Even with the boy pressed sobbing against him, Arnold could feel no flicker of emotion. He was only conscious of a dull despair. His mind was torpid. With a fierce effort he made himself work out that Ewing and Tim were still on the grounds outside searching for Dan and it was possible that they might return at any moment. Arnold detached himself gently from Dan. He crossed the room and opened the door leading into the corridor. The patio was empty. He turned round to Dan.

"They'll be back any moment," Arnold said. "They mustn't find you here. Don't speak. Just follow me."

Dan did not move. Suddenly Arnold lost control. "Don't stand there gaping like an idiot," he hissed. "Follow me quick, I tell you."

Dan flinched as if he had been struck, but he fol-

[2 6 1]

lowed Arnold out of the room. Arnold closed the door behind them and led the way across the patio to the heavy nail-studded door which opened on to the staircase leading to the top of the central tower. In silence Dan followed him up the flights of stone steps and waited without speaking while Arnold pushed open the wooden trap door. Quietly, Dan clambered out after him onto the warm roof which glistened in the moonlight. Arnold closed the trap door before he spoke.

"I'm sorry I snapped your head off," he said quietly, trying to smile.

"Doesn't matter," Dan muttered. "Forget it."

"Are you all right?"

"Not too bad. I was sick, that was all. I think it was something I ate on board. I feel better now."

"Sorry I was in such a hurry to get you up here. But at least we're safe. They'll never look for us here, and we can see the lights of the car arriving."

"What car?"

Arnold looked up at the stars and prayed to the God in whose existence he tried to believe for strength to control his leaping nerves so that he could at least give to the boy some gleam of affection, some crumb of sympathy.

"Dan, I'm afraid you've got to go back to England," he said gently.

"No."

"You must."

"Not now that I'm with you."

"You won't go back to Melton Hall. I can promise

you that. And I can promise you that there'll be no Captain Stobart to be afraid of again."

"I'm not going back."

"There's no alternative now."

"Can't we go someplace where they could never find us?"

"We'd need money to buy food, for one thing."

"I could find work. I could work in a café, washing up or something. And you could be teaching in some school."

"You must go back, Dan. Wherever we went now, they'd catch up with us in the end."

Dan turned away from him. "You don't want me to be with you, do you?" he said in a stifled voice. "You don't need me like I need you. You're just trying to get rid of me."

"No, Dan. I'm going back to England too."

Dan's head swung round in surprise. "You mean we'll still be together?"

"No."

"Why not?"

"Because I'll be arrested and sentenced."

"Why? Whatever for?"

"For helping you to escape."

"But I'll say you didn't. I'll say you'd got nothing to do with it."

"They know I'm here."

"I'll say you flew out here to bring me back. That's the truth, isn't it?"

"You can tell them the truth, Dan. It won't make any difference."

"Do you mean they can send you to prison just for taking me to Folkestone?"

"I expect so."

"The car you said you're waiting for? Is that the one that's going to take you off?"

"It's the car that's coming from the Consulate. I phoned them just now and told them we were both here."

"And they'll take us back to England?"

"Yes."

"But you'll go to prison, and they won't let me see you. I'll have no one to go to at the next place where they send me. I'll be all alone. And they'll have it in for me because I got away—you know they will."

Suddenly Dan seized his hand. "Don't make me go back right away," he pleaded. "Don't make me go back just yet. Even if they catch up with us in the end, let's have a few months together."

Arnold raised his head to the sky. The stars seemed very close. "It would only be worse in the long run," Arnold said. "Please believe me. I'm not just thinking of myself."

"Do you know that you're the only person who gives a curse for me in the whole world?"

"I can say the same back to you, Dan."

"Is that right? Am I the only person?"

Arnold stared at the speckled blue vault above him and lowered his head.

"Yes," Arnold said. "The only person."

"How long will you get?"

"I don't know, Dan. Not long with any luck."

"I'll wait for you—even if it's for a whole year. I'll get a calendar and strike off the days."

Arnold walked across to the balustrade where the corner of the tower cast a shadow across the moonlight. He looked down. The lights along the drive had been switched on. The beams of two flashlights were flickering at the lower end of the garden. Beyond the wall to the east he could see a long stretch of the mountain road. But there was no car approaching. Dan came up to him and touched his arm.

"If I tell you something, do you promise you won't be angry with me?" Dan asked quietly.

"Yes. I promise."

"Well, it's this. You know the letter I wrote you from Marseilles. Well, it was true what I said. I was scared, honest I was. Tim had had a bagful to drink, and he told me just what kind of things went on in Tangier."

"Why should I be angry with you? Of course you were scared."

"But that wasn't the reason."

"The reason for what?"

"That wasn't the reason I wrote you. I was frightened all right, but I'd still have gone through with it—even after I knew the lot. I didn't write just because I was frightened. I wrote because I knew it was the only way I could get you to come out here to be with me."

In the distance Arnold could hear the waves shuffling on the beach. A meteor streaked across the sky and vanished below the horizon.

"Now I've got you into all this mess," Dan said.

"And it's all my fault. If I'd not written that letter you'd never have come out, and there'd have been no trouble. You'll never forgive me, will you?"

A wisp of cloud was trailing like a ragged scarf across the moon.

"Don't worry, Dan," Arnold heard his voice saying from far away. "I forgive you."

Suddenly the headlights of two cars were shining along the flat stretch of the mountain road.

"That may be them," Arnold said.

"Promise you'll let me be with you when you come out," Dan cried out suddenly. "Promise you won't forget me."

In the moonlight Arnold could see each feature of Dan's pale, uptilted head. Carefully he observed the flat hair and anxious eyes, the delicate nostrils and twitching mouth. But as he stared down at the boy he could feel not one twinge of passion. His whole body felt numb and empty of all desire. He was only aware of an overwhelming tiredness that seemed to press down on every limb.

"Promise?" Dan asked. "Promise?"

As he listened to the boy's insistent voice, sadness began to seep into Arnold's mind like a grey fog drifting into a room that has grown cold, covering each familiar object with veils of gauze, darkening the carpet, blurring the outlines of the chairs, concealing the pictures, filling the empty grate, until all the room becomes shrouded with grey. Both past and present were now wrapped in a cold greyness. But through the

[2 6 6]

murk of fog he could still see the boy's face distraught with anxiety. Then, with a stab of pain, Arnold realized that he could not avoid the truth of the plain statement written across those worried eyes. For the first time in his life another person needed him. There could be no possible escape from that stark need.

"Promise?" the voice pleaded.

"Yes," Arnold said, and the words fell like leaden weights across his heart. "I promise."

The headlights of the two cars turned toward the gates at the end of the drive and stopped still.

"This is it," Arnold said. "We must go down. But let's say good-bye up here, shall we?"

Awkwardly he stretched out an arm and patted Dan's shoulder. The corner of the boy's mouth was still jerking frantically. Arnold's eyes slid away in pity.

"Good-bye, Dan," Arnold said. "The best of luck till we meet again."

Even as he spoke, Arnold thought back to his farewell with Riffi in their bedroom in the villa below. With a pang he remembered the future that he then seemed to have in front of him. But even as he recollected Riffi's passion, he felt ashamed of his disloyalty. He searched his mind for some words of comfort for Dan.

"We'll get through somehow," he said, cursing the triteness of his words. "Things are never so bad as one expects."

He was afraid that the boy would break down. He dreaded a hysterical scene. He glanced at him warily.

But Dan met his glance calmly. He took Arnold's hand in a firm grip and stared up at him for a moment in silence. His eyes were serene; his mouth was motionless.

"Don't worry," Dan said. "I'm all right now. Even when you're not there, I shan't feel alone any more."

The iron gates swung open. The headlights of two cars moved slowly up the drive, and the gates closed behind them.

PART

4

"WAYNE, do you see any reason why I shouldn't have another drink?" Ewing asked.

"No reason at all," Wayne replied, swaying toward him swiftly and picking up his glass. "It would be a pleasure to get you one, Master Ewing."

"You're not very full tonight."

Wayne blinked his eyes apologetically.

"It's always quiet in the full heat of summer. You know *that*, Ewing. All the gay birds have flown."

As Wayne swept away to fix his drink, Ewing looked around the half empty bar with disapproval. There was not one interesting or attractive face to be seen. Not a single one.

A minute later Wayne returned with his gin and Dubonnet and sat down at his table.

"You seem a bit *distrait* tonight," Wayne said.

"I was just thinking," Ewing replied. "But it was a very banal thought."

"Tell."

"Has it ever occurred to you how satisfactory it would be if one could be *certain* one could attain complete oblivion?"

"Constantly," Wayne replied. "But I'm always scared stiff it wouldn't be *complete*. Think if one swallowed a bottle of luminal and went into a perpetual nightmare. You know those horrid dreams one gets after too much lobster. Just imagine enduring them for eternity! It's unthinkable. If only one could escape from life for a short stretch of time! If only one could stuff one's old carcass with mothballs and hang it on a peg and just *leave* it there for a season!"

"But one *can't*," Ewing interrupted impatiently. "One's just got to keep dragging the wretched thing around. And *now* what am I to do with mine? Just tell me that. Where shall I take it to this evening? Where?"

"Not to the dance at the British Consulate," Wayne said with a titter.

"No. Not to the Consulate. In fact, probably never again to the Consulate."

"But why should *you* care?"

"I *don't* care. In fact, I'm delighted," Ewing said. "When you think that I might have been extradited you'll admit that to be banned from that boring establishment is no great hardship. Of course I don't care. I was merely asking you what I could do to amuse myself tonight."

"Why don't you ring Lavinia and ask her out to dine at the *Pavillon?* Shall I get her for you on the phone?"

"No, don't. I can't face being told the full pedigree of her latest lover."

"What about Luke West? I'm told he's redecorated his whole living room. Pure Victorian, he's gone. You can hardly see a chair for the antimacassars, and you can scarcely plough your way through the potted ferns. Shall I get Luke for you? Shall I?"

But Ewing was no longer listening. His eyes were fixed intently on the end barstool that had just been occupied.

"*Now* what is it?" Wayne asked.

With an effort Ewing turned his gaze away from the far end of the bar. Slowly he spread out his hands on the table and examined them. Then he looked up at Wayne. His left eyelid had begun to quiver slightly like a leaf in a gentle breeze as he put the question, but the expression of his face remained unchanged.

"Who's the new customer?" Ewing asked indolently.